Murder in
the Lady Chapel

A Hannah Weybridge Thriller

Anne Coates

Published by Urban Fox Books 2023

Copyright © Anne Coates 2023

Cover design & text preparation by Wildcat Design
wildcat1@ntlworld.com

ISBN paperback: 978-1-7395648-0-3
ISBN ebook: 978-1-7395648-1-0

For my gorgeous Elizabeth Rose

ONE

Thursday 24 November 1994

THE BRIEF WALK from the vicarage – his paces measured in a prayer – had chilled the Reverend Peter Savage. He shivered as he unlocked the side door, which led to the vestry, the sacristy and then the nave. He did this at the same time most days to prepare for Morning Prayer. Rarely did anyone join him except the odd homeless person or someone who needed some respite. But St John's was open – that was the main thing, according to the archdeacon. He locked the door behind him, left his coat, scarf and gloves in the sacristy and walked through the narrow and awkwardly appointed corridor to the nave, the central part of the church, his highly polished shoes creating an eerie echo.

At the back of the church, he unlocked the inner doors and opened the large oak front doors, which protested noisily as he pulled and hooked up the chain. They needed some oil and attention. *Just like me,* he thought with a barely suppressed sigh, remembering his bones creaking as he got out of bed that morning.

He filled the stoup with water, which he blessed, then dipped in his finger and made the sign of the cross. A sacred daily ritual – it always comforted him – but today, since the moment he woke in the early hours, he was filled with a feeling of unease, a sense of foreboding that he couldn't define or shake off. He walked down the central aisle allowing the serenity of the holy place given to his care to fill him with peace, as it never failed to do. Bowing to the altar as he passed, he turned left to the Lady Chapel. He stopped in front of the statue of the Holy Mother and lit a candle and then walked over to light the altar candles. A glance at his watch told him he had a few minutes to wait just in case anyone joined him; then he'd start. Each day he prayed for the sick, the disenchanted, the grieving and the lost. He sat in quiet meditation, reflection on the day ahead. He wondered how many of his parishioners prayed for him. Some were probably praying for him to move on. *God willing,* he thought, *God willing.*

AT FIRST HE DIDN'T NOTICE the figure sitting in the shadows. The sudden revelation that he wasn't alone startled him. Had someone walked in while his back was turned? He'd heard nothing. "Good morning." His voice sounded croaky, unused. He breathed in deeply. There was an indefinable odour... He walked over to hand the man a service book, which fell to the floor, its sound a muffled echo.

The priest knelt before the person and touched his hand. Barely warm. He felt for a pulse and as he did so the man's hand gripped his with surprising strength. "Stay with me, Father." His voice was barely above a whisper.

Peter sat in the chair next to the man he recognised as one of the choristers. "I need to phone for an ambulance for you, Daniel."

"Too late."

"Can I call someone for you?" Peter now prayed fervently that no one else would turn up for Morning Prayer. An audience was the last thing he needed.

"Rosa needs to know."

"Rosa?"

The man closed his eyes. Peter thought he heard, "Pray with me, Father."

Peter felt in his pocket for his holy oil and as he made the sign of the cross on Daniel's forehead he said, "Daniel, I anoint you in the name of God, the Father, the Son and the Holy Spirit. Receive Christ's forgiveness, His healing and His love. May the Father of our Lord Jesus Christ grant you the riches of grace, His wholeness and His peace."

Daniel's face broke into a smile. "Thank you."

The priest began: "Our Father who art in heaven," and heard a whispered "hallowed be Thy name." They got to the end of the Lord's Prayer. Daniel was still clinging on to life. "The Lord is my shepherd..." He began to recite the twenty-third psalm as Daniel's grip slackened. Peter kept the hand in his. There was a longer pause between each strangled breath. The intervening silences seemed to echo in the building. Throughout his ministry, Peter had sat with many dying people, usually with their relatives present. Mainly they had been ill for a long time or had suffered a terrible accident, or were old and at the end of their time. A shudder. Each death was different. Some died peacefully with little more than a sigh. Others struggled and fought the inevitable.

"Into Your hands, Lord, we commit Daniel for he is Yours in death as in life. Fulfil in him the purpose of Your love, gather him to Yourself in gentleness and peace, that rejoicing in the light of Your presence he may enjoy that rest You have prepared through Christ our Lord. Amen."

Peter felt the spirit leaving the body. He remained very still. Every sense alert to the mystery. Minutes passed. Once more the vicar gave thanks that no one had joined him for Morning Prayers. He leaned forward, closed Daniel's eyes and mouthed a blessing, overwhelmed by a deep sadness for the loss of life even if he had gone to a better place. He sat beside Daniel for a few minutes longer then, sighing deeply, made his way into the sacristy and phoned the emergency services.

WHILE HE WAS WAITING, he sat beside Daniel, a recent addition to the choir, wondering why no one had made sure everyone had left the church after choir practice the previous evening.

He assumed Daniel had had a heart attack. He hadn't known he was ill. But then he knew very little about the man. Some of his parishioners contacted him if they had a cold. Others were more stoic, waiting until some serious illness had been diagnosed before asking, sometimes in trepidation, for his prayers at their bedside. Then he noticed the dark stain on Daniel's shirt, just visible from where his jacket was unbuttoned. He stared. Alarms rang in his mind. It was cold and he hadn't turned on the heating. It hadn't seemed worth it just for himself. Idly he wondered if that was why people didn't attend early morning services in winter. Too bloody cold. He shook himself into action and went back into the sacristy to phone the archdeacon.

"Good Lord!" The Venerable Andrew Fanshawe's voice rose an octave or two. "That's all we need for Advent."

"Well it was hardly…"

3

"No need to discuss this on the phone, Peter. Call an extraordinary meeting of the PCC for this evening and I'll meet you beforehand to discuss what you have found out about this poor soul. Shall we say six o'clock?"

The vicar agreed as the archdeacon terminated the call. He phoned the two churchwardens whose reactions echoed the archdeacon's. He left it to them to organise the meeting of the Parochial Church Council. There were two choir members among them so perhaps they could throw some light on the situation.

He would leave contacting their musical director until after he had spoken to the police. He looked at his watch. They were taking their time. Maybe a suspicious death in a church didn't warrant a speedy response. He returned to the Lady Chapel, knelt at the altar rail and prayed. The scent of flowers seemed more powerful now and he looked across at the display by the altar. The cold seemed to keep them fresher but their scent was definitely becoming overpowering.

"Excuse me, Reverend."

He glanced up to see a young woman officer in uniform. Behind her another officer was talking quietly into his radio.

"I'm Sergeant Jones and this is my colleague PC Quin." Her smile was a little condescending, he thought, as he braced himself to answer questions to which he knew no answers.

TWO

HANNAH WEYBRIDGE was sitting at her desk in the study, an electric fan heater boosting the temperature in what was the coldest room in the house. She was staring out of the window at the bleak winter garden, which did nothing to improve her mood. How she had got it so wrong? She had prided herself on how she could read characters but recently it seemed her skill was out of kilter. She hoped it didn't apply to everyone. But there were some people who had slipped through her filters. For a long time she had felt a vague sense that someone was manipulating her. She was aware she was often followed but she had no idea who was behind it all. Until now. The more she thought about it the more it made sense. And the bigger the feeling of foreboding engulfed her.

She rang Rory.

"Do you have time for lunch soon? Away from the office."

The assistant editor at *The News* – he'd had a recent promotion – chuckled. "Always the same Hannah. Never a good morning or how are you?"

"Why waste time?" She laughed. "I'm sorry. I'd like to take you out to lunch – or dinner if it's more convenient?"

"Mm, tough decision. If you want to meet in town better be in the evening and it just happens that I'm free after six this evening as I have a meeting in Soho. If that's not too soon?"

Hannah hardly hesitated. "No perfect. I'll book a table at Joe Allen's for 7pm." She rang off and her next call was to arrange for a babysitter.

PETER SAVAGE SAT in his study musing over the demise of Daniel Lyons. His death, the police agreed, looked suspicious but they would need to await the results of the post mortem. The priest's thoughts wandered. Who was Rosa? Something was niggling at the back of his mind but Rosa rang no bells and none, it seemed, with the musical director Craig Fletcher, who seemed to know next to nothing about Daniel. Nor did he know how he'd managed to be left in the church when everyone else had left.

"We're all adults, vicar. I don't count them in and out like kids on a school trip."

"Well perhaps you should," Peter said, probably louder than he intended.

Craig looked affronted. "What have the police said?"

"Nothing much." He paused. "Do you know anyone called Rosa?"

"Rosa? No, why?"

"Daniel said to tell her."

"Well, all I have is an address for him and I gave that to the police when they rang me."

The priest sighed heavily. "I'm sorry, Craig, I should have asked how you're bearing up."

Craig's face reflected his sadness. "I'm shocked and dismayed, of course. And I keep asking myself why? Why did he come here in the first place?" He paused. "He had a good voice but he never joined in socially. Always left really quickly after rehearsals. Although he did linger after Mass. He never seemed to talk to anyone in particular. I wonder why."

"Perhaps we'll never know." But there was still that something niggling at the back of his mind. If only he could reach that memory perhaps he'd be on the way to knowing the answer.

RORY WAS ALREADY at the restaurant when she arrived. He waved and put down the newspaper he had been reading as he stood to greet her.

After a brief hug and a kiss on the cheek, she sat opposite him and smiled at the waiter as he approached. "Gin and tonic, please. Do you want a top-up?" She pointed to Rory's glass but he shook his head.

"So what can I do for you?" he asked after Hannah's drink had arrived.

"Am I that transparent?"

Rory smiled. They had got to know each other well since Hannah had started freelancing for *The News*. She knew he respected her and admired her for the scoops she'd managed to pull off, after initially dismissing her as a women's magazine journalist as though that were an insult. He'd once confessed in an inebriated moment to being a little in awe of her. "I never underestimate you." It was a policy others would do well to follow. So many saw her as someone who could be played. Some came to regret that decision.

Hannah knew she needed to play the long game here. "Shall we order?"

They both studied the menu and were ready when the waiter arrived. He returned quickly with a bottle of wine, which he poured for both of them. For a moment Hannah was back to the summer of the previous year when DI Tom Jordan had invited her to lunch here. She hadn't known whether to trust him. Then she'd fallen in love with him before…

"Hannah?" She refocused on Rory, whose face bore a look of concern.

Hannah twirled the stem of the glass between her fingers then looked straight at Rory, his face serious. "I'm beginning to feel like I'm about to be interrogated by the Stasi."

Hannah's raised eyebrow said it all. "Do you remember my first exposé for *The News*?" When she had first met Tom.

Rory didn't answer immediately as though trying to gauge the temperature.

"The article exposing the sex clinic run by Lacon and the murders of prostitutes?" It still hurt that she had been unable to protect Caroline, the young sex worker who had turned up at her house, beaten and abused, begging for her protection.

"Of course I do." She couldn't read Rory's expression. Was he humouring her?

"Who spiked it?" Hannah's story had never seen the light of day. She had been paid a large sum of money but she hadn't read the small print on the contract until it was too late and she realised she'd signed away all her rights, as the company lawyer delighted in telling her. So the story was never published.

Rory stared in disbelief. "Why are you raking over old coals?"

Hannah had been furious at the time. And impotent. Rory had never mentioned it again until he had shown her the article he'd seen about Gerry Lacon who had been deported over some other charge. He was arrested as soon as he arrived in South Africa and had supposedly committed suicide in prison. He had obviously been eliminated by the old regime clearing the decks for the incoming president, Nelson Mandela.

"Why do you ask?"

Hannah appeared to be concentrating on her food. When she looked up the pain in her eyes was evident. "I need to know."

"Why? You were paid. The story was spiked. End of. Several of the perpetrators died from one thing or another…"

"Exactly. There was a retribution of a kind."

"Well I wouldn't go as far as saying that…"

"What happened afterwards was a clean-up operation. It was well organised and forensic."

"So maybe justice was done. I don't see …"

"I need to know, Rory. Who spiked it?"

"The editor's decision is final," he said, quoting the journalists' mantra.

"I don't think it was George's decision." Georgina Henderson was the editor. No one called her George to her face except the proprietor, Lord Gyles.

"Oh?" They had both finished their starters and the waiter had arrived to clear their plates.

Hannah recalled the emotion, the fury and frustration she'd felt when she'd spoken to Larry Jefferson, the lawyer at *The News* who had explained she had signed away all rights – for which, he stressed, she had been paid a princely sum. She had been silenced and she was fully aware that her subsequent role at *The News* was a sop to keep her quiet and, presumably, control her activities. Her role at the newspaper had moved on since then – to an extent.

"So who do you think it was then?" Rory smiled as he took a sip of wine. She knew he needed to hear her say the name aloud.

"Lord Gyles."

He didn't miss a beat. "Very possibly. He's a very hands-on proprietor."

Their main course arrived. Hannah gave him a moment to collect his thoughts. She had calculated – correctly – that this was the last thing he had expected her to discuss over dinner.

"*Bon appétit.*" She smiled, knowing he would now be wondering what else was coming before they got to dessert.

He raised his glass. "So what's brought all this up?"

Hannah sipped the wine. "I feel as though I'm being manipulated all the time."

"Well you're doing well out of it. The book has been on the bestseller lists for weeks. That must make you feel good even if Lord G did arrange for you to write it."

Joan Ballantyne: A Life had been published after the actress had been murdered on stage at The Old Vic. Once again Hannah had been instrumental in solving the case, which had also included the death of Sam Smith and the attempted murder of Joan's son, Leo Hawkins, who had followed his mother's profession and was something of a television heartthrob.

"Yes, that was a surprise really. I never thought it would sell so well but I suppose all the hype about her death and the attempted murder of a television star added to the intrigue."

"It certainly didn't do any harm. And the paperback will be out in a few months."

Hannah had only half eaten her chicken but pushed the plate to one side. "And what about Albert Croxton?"

"What about him?" Rory looked totally relaxed and not perturbed by Hannah's questioning.

Albert Croxton was the wild card in the story. His name had been linked to Joan Ballantyne years ago and his previous criminal connections had, it seemed, given him access to what had been going on. She was eternally grateful to him for rescuing Elizabeth and Edith Holland from their kidnappers. But she had a dread that this might be used against her.

"What about him, Hannah?"

"There's something about them."

"Them?" Rory had finished his steak and his attention was totally focussed on his companion.

"Lord Gyles and Albert Croxton. There's a connection."

Rory made a face. Hannah wasn't sure if it was an expression of disbelief or consideration of an unpalatable fact.

"Of course there's a connection." Hannah looked pleased but was disconcerted that Rory had known something she didn't.

"They're related."

The waiter appeared again. "Have you finished? Was everything to your satisfaction?" He looked at Hannah's half-eaten meal.

Hannah nodded. "Yes, thank you. I wasn't very hungry." She smiled. "Shall we have some more wine?"

Rory admired her aplomb. "Why not?"

When the waiter had withdrawn, Hannah asked, "So how are they related?" She tried to sound cool. But she had guessed it! That evening at the book launch at The Old Vic when she'd seen them together – she'd known there was something between them.

"They're cousins twice removed or some such thing. Their mothers were cousins so they share a set of grandparents. The two families went very different ways."

Did they indeed, thought Hannah, *I wouldn't be too sure of that.*

THEY WERE WELL INTO the second bottle of wine when she asked, "Did they ever find whoever was supposed to be the mole?" Both Georgina and Lord Gyles were convinced that someone in the organisation had been leaking information to other news outlets. They had provided her with a state-of-the-art mobile phone and set it up to prevent calls being intercepted, although she had been aware that maybe they were monitoring some of her calls.

Rory nearly spat out his wine. "You never give up, do you?"

She stared at him. "Have you forgotten what I went through with Elizabeth and Edith?" She still felt nauseous when she thought how near she'd come to losing her precious daughter – and Edith, the photographer, who had become a friend and ally.

"Of course not. But there were no repercussions and…"

"No repercussions? I suppose the firebombing of a club in Soho doesn't count? Or Sam Smith's death and Leo Hawkins' assault?"

"Hannah, calm down." He spoke quietly but he kicked her under the table and nodded his head slightly to the left where diners at the next table were obviously absorbing her every word.

She smiled and raised her glass to him mouthing "sorry".

The waiter brought the bill to Rory, causing Hannah to raise her eyebrows. "My shout," she said, glancing at the bill and placing her credit card on it before handing it back to the waiter.

She finished her wine.

The waiter seemed to be taking a long time with the transaction, but when he returned, he handed her the receipt to sign and her card with another piece of paper folded behind it. "Thank you." She tipped in cash and made a show of packing up her bag, managing to unfold the piece of paper: *Be careful when you leave. Someone has been asking questions about you.*

IT WAS SNOWING OUTSIDE. "How are you getting back?" Rory asked.

"Cab, if I can find one. Would you mind waiting with me?"

Rory didn't comment on her pallor or the tone of her voice. "Of course not. Shall we walk towards Charing Cross station? Bound to be some taxis there."

They made their way down Southampton Street and on to The Strand. Hannah couldn't shrug off the feeling that someone was following them. Who had been asking questions about her in the restaurant? And why?

In spite of the weather there were lots of people on the streets, making it easy for anyone to tail them without being seen. Maybe she was being paranoid. Perhaps the waiter had been asked to give her that note in order to spook her? That was a possibility but why would anyone want to do that?

"Sorry I was a bore this evening."

Rory linked arms with her. "Don't be silly. Of course you weren't. Infuriating, tenacious, stubborn but never boring."

Hannah smiled up at him. "Well, Mister Assistant Editor, I'll take that as a compliment."

He didn't have a chance to reply as someone brushed past them, and would have pushed Hannah off balance, had she not been supported by Rory who shouted out, as did several other people. Hannah was still clutching her bag to her side. When she looked down, the leather strap had been slashed.

"Do you think he was after my bag, or my life?" The joke sounded thin even to her own ears.

"You all right, love?" A woman was moving closer towards her. There was a look about her Hannah recognised but couldn't place. She wanted to scream.

Then suddenly she was gone and a police officer, who seemed to have appeared out of nowhere, was asking questions. She gave her name and address and showed him the cut strap on her bag.

"Everything's fine," she said. "But we do need a taxi…"

Miraculously one appeared and pulled over when the officer raised his arm. Hannah thanked the officer; Rory followed her inside and gave her address.

For one awful moment, she thought he'd got the wrong idea about their evening. "Then can you take me on to Hackney?"

"Right, guv." The driver smiled. "I live near there so this'll be my last fare."

Hannah relaxed back into the seat.

"Thank you."

Rory looked concerned. "Hannah, you're shaking."

The incident had propelled her back to the concourse at Heathrow Airport with DS Mike Benton, as he had been then. They had spotted Edward Peters, Lucy's son, who had murdered several Australian men in the UK who had been trying to find their English families, and was trying to flee the country. However just as they approached him, he moved forward and stabbed Hannah…

"Hannah, why are you asking about Lord G?" Rory's voice brought her back to the present. "Is there something else I should know?"

Hannah was silent for so long it seemed as though she wasn't going to answer. "So many things are beginning to add up. I probably sound like some mad conspiracy theorist but there always seems to be an undercurrent of people pulling strings. Cover-ups. I wondered if Elizabeth's kidnapping, and more importantly her rescue, was a way to make me more compliant, grateful."

Rory was silent for a moment. "Well from where I was standing, I don't think so. I remember Lord G was incandescent. He pulled out all the stops, had a reward for information organised…" He shook his head. "I hated having to write that lead story but was delighted to rewrite it with the happy conclusion."

It had been another major scoop for the newspaper but at what cost to Hannah?

"I know but there's something niggling at the back of my

mind. Like I should be aware of but … It's like when you wake from a dream that has disturbed you but you can't quite remember the details."

"So what are you going to do? You don't need me to remind you to be careful and cover your steps. Especially after this evening."

"I don't know really. Perhaps nothing. I'll keep my eyes and ears open – you never know what will surface."

"True and shit rises." He stared out of the window. "Will you be coming back to *The News*?"

Hannah laughed. "I'm out of contract. I'd have thought you'd know that."

"Of course I do. But I also know that the editor is keen to have you back on board if only on a consultancy basis." He grinned at her. "She probably doesn't want you going to another news outlet with anything. We all know your investigations, however innocuous at the beginning, have a habit of turning into major front-page stories. I'm sure other editors have been sniffing around."

"That would be telling."

"Well we'd miss you."

There was something in his manner that made Hannah's skin prickle. He acted casual but how much did he really know? And would he be reporting back to Georgina Henderson?

But she too knew now how to play the long game. "Well I have my invitation to the Christmas party."

Rory laughed. "I hope you accepted."

"Three-line whip from Halstone Press. I also have a book publicity tour coming up next year for the paperback. Couldn't get out of it."

"Should keep you out of mischief."

"Don't bank on it."

They had arrived outside her house. Rory got out with her and saw her to the door. "Thank you for the meal. It was lovely to see you away from the office." He gave her a brotherly hug and kissed her cheek. He waited for her to unlock the door and returned to the taxi, which swiftly moved off as she closed the door.

"DID YOU HAVE a good evening?" Alesha looked up from the book she was reading. "Gosh, Hannah, you look like you've seen a ghost. Are you okay?"

Hannah smiled. "Oh, I just had a bit of bad news. It's nothing I can't cope with. Everything okay here?"

"Not a peep from Elizabeth. I'll phone Dad." The call was answered immediately and all she said was, "Ready, Dad," and hung up.

"How's the studying going?" Hannah paid her and sat on the other sofa. She had become fond of Alesha, who was studying for her A levels, and her family.

Alesha glowed. "Really well. Mocks in January…"

They heard her father arrive outside. He always came to the door. Alesha collected her things. "See you soon."

The doorbell rang and from force of habit Hannah checked the video before she saw Alesha out.

"Good evening, Hannah. How are you?"

"Very well, thank you, Sanjay. I hope you are well too."

After a few more social pleasantries, father and daughter left and Hannah locked up before going to the kitchen for a glass of water. The attempted handbag snatch – she had to convince herself that that was all it was – had affected her more than she'd care to admit. She checked the back door. Locked. Everything was as it should be.

Removing her make-up in the bathroom, she stared at her reflection in the mirror. She looked awful. Drinking so much wine hadn't helped. At least she'd had her suspicions confirmed about Albert Croxton and Lord Gyles. Her thoughts turned to the note the waiter had passed to her. Was the attempted handbag snatch connected? Or was she seeing links where none existed? Should she mention her worries to the police?

Before going to bed she crept into Elizabeth's room. Her child's gentle breathing reassured her but it took a long time for her to relax in bed. Her sleep was disturbed with nightmare images of dead bodies calling to her.

THREE

PETER SAVAGE FINISHED his prayers. He was exhausted but didn't feel sleepy. He went downstairs and poured himself a medicinal brandy. He stood in the dark, looking out of the window at his church across the road. Daniel Lyons' body had been removed after what seemed a cursory police search of the Lady Chapel and church, plus advice to make the building more secure. He pulled his dressing gown more tightly around his chilled body, remembering his interview with the archdeacon.

"Whatever happens, Peter, whatever happened to Daniel Lyons must not under any circumstances reflect badly on the Church."

The Church in particular or St John's specifically?" He had been unable to keep the sarcasm from his voice and noticed Andrew Fanshawe's monobrow rise slightly.

"Both. Now we must work out how to proceed at the PCC and see how we can minimise any scurrilous gossip."

The vicar sipped his tea and mentally prayed for God's forbearance for his unchristian thoughts towards this man.

"Of course."

HALF AN HOUR later they were sitting in the vestry facing the hastily summoned members of the church council. Not everyone could attend at such short notice. Apologies were read out by the secretary. Before Peter Savage had handed over the chair to the archdeacon, he introduced DI Mike Benton who had been invited to attend, and asked everyone in the room to introduce themselves. He nodded to the woman sitting to his left.

"Belinda Horton, PCC secretary."

"Ruth Robertson."

"Marjorie Fielding."

"Graham Buxford."

"Alison Gregory."

"David Smythe."

"Leah Braithwaite."

"Steve Barclay, treasurer."

"Petra Gainsford, churchwarden."

"Trevor Compton, churchwarden."

"Andrew Fanshawe, archdeacon."

DI Benton was making notes and smiled at each person as they gave their name.

Before the archdeacon could take the chair, Graham Buxford raised his hand. "Sorry, vicar, but given the number of absences this evening, are we actually quorate?"

Peter Savage glared at him. Why was he always so confrontational? Before he could answer, the archdeacon replied, his monobrow making him appear more angry than ever.

"May I reassure you?" Peter's heart sank further. An irritated archdeacon was all they needed. "As we shall not be voting on anything, whether we are quorate or not is immaterial. I trust that suffices."

His tone was glacial; Graham looked as though he'd like to say more but desisted. The Venerable Andrew Fanshawe groaned on about the legal responsibilities of the PCC, the need for confidentiality and the specific role of the council at this time. Then he turned to his right. "Inspector."

"Thank you." DI Benton observed the assembled company for a moment. "I am grateful to the archdeacon and vicar for inviting me this evening. I'm sure many of you must be deeply shocked at the loss of life of one of your choir members and I offer you my sincere condolences. A sudden death is often difficult to get your head around.

"At the moment we are awaiting the results of the post mortem so are treating this as a suspicious death. I understand that this meeting is confidential but some of you may not wish to air your views publically even in this forum." He paused and looked around the room. He smiled at those who met his gaze. Not all did. "Because of this I would like you all to take one of my business cards and feel free to contact me totally confidentially." He passed around his cards. "You may also remember or think of something that is pertinent after this meeting."

While he was speaking, the vicar scrutinised each face. Leah

Braithwaite looked shocked but she smiled reassuringly at him, as did the churchwardens.

"Does anyone have any thoughts?" The archdeacon looked bored. "Perhaps we could start with the members of the choir?"

The two choristers present, David and Alison, looked startled to be singled out so abruptly.

"He hasn't been in the choir long and he kept himself to himself." David appeared uncomfortable. "He didn't seem to want friendship, he just came to sing. And he is, was, a gifted tenor."

"Thank you, David," said Peter. "Alison?"

The woman, in her mid-thirties and wearing a dark business suit over a cream shirt, blushed crimson and ran her fingers under her collar. "I went out for a drink with him after one rehearsal." David smirked and said something under his breath. Alison looked as though she would have liked to kick him. "He asked a lot of questions actually – about people in the choir."

"Well he went to the right place for answers, didn't he, Miss News of the World?"

"David." Peter glared at him. "If you haven't anything relevant to offer, please keep your thoughts to yourself."

David glared at him but said no more, perhaps in deference to the archdeacon's presence. The man in question smiled at Alison. "What sort of questions?"

"Oh the usual, you know. How long someone had been in the choir. What did they do for a living? Married or single? That sort of thing. Innocuous really."

"Quite." The archdeacon exuded disinterest. "And what did he reveal about himself?"

Alison clearly hated being the centre of attention. "Nothing much. Said he lived in digs as he was only in the area for a job he was doing and when that finished he'd return home."

"And where was that?"

"He didn't say."

"And the job?"

Alison studied her fingernails. "Insurance, I think." She looked up. "There was one thing. He always had a briefcase with him. Leather and quite battered. When he opened it once, I glimpsed inside and it seemed to be filled with documents and there was an inner locked compartment." There was an audible sigh and an undercurrent of comments. "Perhaps the contents would tell you more about him."

DI Benton was staring at her. No briefcase had been found with the body. He glanced at the vicar, who shook his head slightly.

"Quite. Thank you, Miss Gregory." This was going nowhere. The archdeacon raised his hands. "Do either of you know how he came to be left alone in the church after your rehearsal?"

They both shook their heads.

"Who is responsible for checking the church before locking up?"

David shrugged. "Craig, I suppose."

"That's Craig Fletcher, our director of music, Archdeacon. Inspector Benton and I spoke to him this afternoon. Sadly, there was no protocol. We have agreed one now." The vicar looked distinctly embarrassed.

"Shutting the stable door…" Graham's voice was loud enough for everyone to hear.

"Thank you, Mr Buxton. I assume you have never raised any security concerns before?" The archdeacon's smile was full of menace that Graham ignored.

"Nothing to do with me." His hostile tone was a red flag to the archdeacon.

"May I remind you, Graham – and all of you – that the PCC has a joint and legal responsibility for the church and what happens within it?" For once the vicar was grateful for the arch-deacon's pomposity.

"RIGHT, LADIES AND GENTLEMEN. Thank you for your time and patience. Needless to reiterate but anything said at this meeting should remain confidential." His glance went around the room. "I would advise you not to speculate on Daniel Lyons' demise in the absence of facts. If you hear anything you think is pertinent, please contact DI Benton."

Peter felt slighted as though he could be under suspicion. "Or me, of course."

"Of course." The reply didn't sound like a resounding

endorsement. "Let us stand and ask for God's blessing upon us and pray for our departed brother."

There was a shuffling of feet and a scrape of chairs as the members stood, heads bowed. "The Lord be with you."

"And also with you," came the rejoinder.

The Venerable Andrew Fanshawe prayed for Daniel Lyons' soul and a speedy resolution to all enquiries. In conclusion, the archdeacon made the sign of the cross and said, "In the name of the Father, and of the Son and of the Holy Spirit. We say together the grace of the Lord Jesus Christ, and the love of God, and the fellowship of the Holy Spirit be with us all. Amen."

The members of the PCC donned their coats and made their way out in twos and threes, their goodnights muted. The archdeacon shook each one's hand. Peter wanted to kick him. As if a handshake would make anything better.

Once outside the church, the archdeacon made a hasty departure after thanking the inspector, who remained with the vicar as he locked up.

"I'll get someone round to give you some security guidance," he said as they walked across the gravel in the churchyard.

"Thank you."

"I take it you didn't see the briefcase when you were with him in the Lady Chapel?"

"No I didn't, but I wasn't looking for one. Your officers would have found it if it was there."

"Of course. Well it implies someone else was with him, I suppose. Unless he didn't bring it with him this week."

Peter felt diminished, lacking. He wanted to say so much: to apologise for his PCC for his own lack of foresight, for the archdeacon. But the thoughts whirling in his head would not form into sentences. Instead he just said, "Sorry, the meeting must have been a boring waste of time for you."

Mike Benton smiled. "Nothing's ever a complete waste of time." They shook hands and the inspector went over to his car and drove off. Peter Savage had thought about inviting him into the vicarage for a drink but it probably wasn't the done thing. Shame, as he seemed a genuinely nice guy.

THE VICAR SHOOK AWAY his heavy thoughts and went back upstairs to his bedroom. In bed he reached for his bible on the bedside table and opened a page at random as he often did when troubled. He closed his eyes and ran his finger down the page. Opening them he saw he'd landed on Mark Chapter 4 Verse 22, and read:

"All that is now hidden will some day come to light. If you have ears, listen! And be sure to put into practice what you hear."

He read it several times. He fervently hoped that what was hidden about Daniel Lyons would come to light sooner rather than later. He didn't need the archdeacon on his case throughout Advent.

FOUR

ON FRIDAY MORNING Hannah felt at a bit of a loose end, experiencing a restlessness unfamiliar to her. She had taken Elizabeth to nursery, which was now under new management and had stringent security protocols in place. Hannah had been unsure about sending Elizabeth back there after they had so miserably failed in following her security instructions and had allowed an unknown person to collect her child. But she couldn't wrap her in cotton wool and keep her hidden in a tower, however much she'd like to. Elizabeth loved being with the other children and it was Fran Croxton along with Janet who helped convince her.

Fran was also a single parent now, having separated from her waste-of-space husband, and they were slowly becoming friends. Janet had been the intermediary, as she'd known Fran at school although they hadn't been friends then. Strange how life was so full of coincidences. And Fran was the niece of Albert Croxton who had used his contacts and influence to find Elizabeth and Edith when they had been abducted.

Rory's revelation that Albert Croxton was related to Lord Gyles had confirmed her suspicions about the two men. The power and influence they enjoyed alarmed her, although she had cause to be grateful for both. That was what worried her – the thought that she was somehow in their debt, a debt that one day they would call in. She had to find a way to make herself less vulnerable. Maybe she could discuss it with Claudia. Whatever her new job involved, she seemed to have her finger on the pulse.

Her friend Joe sprang to mind. As an MP he might also know of ways and means she could use to protect herself. She hadn't seen Joe, or his partner Phil, for a while now. She should arrange a dinner. She missed Joe more than she cared to admit and those thoughts directed her to James, another friend she needed to touch base with, although his hospital commitments meant his free time was limited. Idly she wondered if his enigmatic neighbour Mark, the army officer engaged in Bosnia, would be back over the festivities.

While he was on her mind, she sent off an email to Joe. She needed to get a grip on her life. But for the present she had an interview coming up on a radio programme about her Joan Ballantyne book, which she had to prepare for. If you could actually prepare when you didn't know what the questions would be. But otherwise she had little to do. She played with the idea of writing another book. A novel this time? She had wondered about fictionalising her prostitutes' story in some way. It could be a way of bringing some closure for her. Her previous forays into the world of short stories hadn't brought any success. But she was differently placed now. She had her name on a book, albeit non-fiction.

There was another niggle. At the back of her mind was the note given to her at the restaurant and the handbag-slashing incident the previous evening. It seemed a huge jump of credibility to assume a connection between the two events but…

The doorbell cut through her thoughts, and looking at the video screen she was surprised to see a priest. As she watched, he greeted someone who was passing in the street then turned back to the door with a worried look on his face.

Hannah deliberated about opening the door. Her last run-in with a man of the cloth, Edward Peters, the son Lucy hadn't known had survived, had left her in hospital with a stab wound in her abdomen. But there were other priests she'd had dealings with who had been kind and supportive… She took a deep breath, went downstairs and opened the door.

"Hello. How may I help you?"

The man before her looked even more haggard face to face, as if his sleep or lack of it had been worse than her own. His tentative smile was not reassuring.

"Are you collecting for something?" That was the only reason she could think a priest would be knocking on her door.

"No, not at all." His laugh was hoarse. "If only I were." Hannah's face must have revealed her total incomprehension. "I'm sorry to trouble you, Ms Weybridge, but I would very much like to speak with you."

"And you couldn't telephone beforehand?" Her irritability levels were rising.

He looked abashed but his eyes begged her forbearance.

"I apologise, I didn't mean that to sound quite so rude. But you have the advantage of me – knowing my name. And if you know anything about me you'd…"

"I'm Peter Savage, I am – I was – a friend of Patrick Ryan from St John's Waterloo." He seemed to think that was introduction enough. "I saw you at his memorial service at Southwark Cathedral."

Hannah stared at him. There had been so many clergy there and most of them stuck together in an amorphous group clad in black. *For God's sake*, she wanted to shout at him, then thought that was probably totally inappropriate.

His expression crumpled – there was no other word for it. "I need your help."

HANNAH INVITED HIM IN. She was intrigued that he made the sign of the cross before entering and mumbled something that sounded like a prayer. He was tall and slim with dark hair that was sprinkled with grey. In fact, grey was a good description of him – he looked ill. As she made coffee she wondered how quickly she could politely get rid of him. When she returned to the sitting room, he was standing looking at Edith's photos of Elizabeth. He turned with a smile, which transformed his features. "Lovely photos. Your daughter, I presume?"

"Yes." Hannah didn't elaborate. "What do you want to talk to me about?"

Her brusque tone did nothing to encourage the priest whose attention seemed concentrated on his shoes, which were black and looked recently polished. "A man died in my church – St John's just up the road – yesterday."

Hannah could feel her spirits sinking. Death haunted her. The Grim Reaper was taunting her yet again. She was a magnet for people who … She tried to assume what she hoped looked like a compassionate expression. "I'm sorry to hear that."

The priest now looked at her directly. "It looks like a suspicious death and the police agree though they have little to go on. The man was a chorister and somehow was locked in the church after choir practice. No one remembers seeing him go into the church – the choir meets in the vestry – and no one seems to know much about him. Which is odd as the choir is a sociable group and I'd have thought … well I wouldn't think he would be so anonymous. But everyone says he kept himself to himself and had only joined a month or so ago. He didn't attend St John's previously." He paused to sip his coffee.

Hannah was feeling tetchy. She had enough self-awareness to acknowledge she had nothing else important claiming her attention and time but she really didn't need to hear this. No, she didn't want to hear it.

"So where do I fit in?" Anyone with a lesser sense of determination would have been put off by her clipped tone.

"I was rather hoping you'd be able to discover some more about him." The vicar smiled tremulously. "You seem to have the knack of ferreting out information and finding links …"

Hannah interrupted him. "How do you know where I live?"

He smiled. "Leah Braithwaite is a member of my congregation."

"And?"

"A while ago she came to see me to discuss the situation with her brother. She mentioned how helpful her neighbour, a journalist, had been. It didn't take an Einstein to work out…"

"Quite but I still don't see…"

"Leah is a member of our PCC – church council – she knew how worried I was and suggested I contact you."

"But why? I'm sure the police will sort everything for you."

Peter Savage mumbled something that sounded like "God help me –" then looked directly at her and said, "I think someone may be trying to frame me for Daniel Lyons' death."

Hannah stared at him. "Why on earth would anyone want to do that?"

"To discredit me." He sat back on the sofa as though wishing it would engulf him and make him disappear. "I have been the vicar here for nearly two years. Some of the congregation still refer to me as the 'new vicar'." A deep sigh escaped him.

"And?" she prompted.

"When there's a change of incumbent there's often a group of people who feel someone else should have been appointed."

"Isn't that the case in most professions?"

The vicar gave her a wry look. "Perhaps. But the Church of England is a law unto itself and its methods of appointment aren't always transparent. I wasn't the obvious candidate."

"Still this seems a bizarre and extreme way to discredit you."

"Maybe, and maybe I'm wrong. I hope so. But I would like you to see if you could find out anything about Daniel. I can employ you on behalf of the church." He looked as though he'd been caught out in a lie.

Hannah was drumming her fingers on the arm of the sofa. The last thing she needed was local complications. But she was intrigued in spite of her misgivings. It wouldn't hurt to do this for him. "Who's in charge of the police investigation?"

"An Inspector Mike Benton." Hannah nodded. "Do you know him?"

"I do." She smiled at his amazed expression but gave no further explanation. "So tell me what you know about this chorister."

There were not many facts the priest could offer other than his address. He seemed hazy on what he did for a living – something in insurance?

"He mentioned someone called Rosa. He said, 'Tell Rosa. Rosa needs to know.' At least that's what I think he said."

"Have you any idea who this Rosa is?"

"None at all. We don't keep records – like next of kin – of our choristers apparently. We have a church electoral roll that has details but he didn't register. You don't have to."

He finished his coffee. "Closing the stable door and all that but I have asked the musical director to get details of all our choristers. He's taken umbrage that both the police and I asked why he had not checked everyone had left the building after choir practice. Of course, the other dilemma is how the perpetrator managed to do this and leave the church."

"How strong is your security?"

The priest looked sheepish. "Not as strong as yours, I fear." He gave her a wry look. "We have no CCTV. The vestry door just has a Yale lock, which you can open from the inside without a key. It is possible that someone came in while the church was open and hid when it was locked up after evening prayer at six."

"So the death may not be connected to the church at all?"

"No, I suppose not." He didn't sound convinced.

"Could it have been suicide?" Hannah suggested quietly. She had been loath to ask that question given that most people had assumed that Joan Ballantyne's death on stage might have been suicide, although there had been no evidence to suggest it.

The priest stared at her. "Do you know that never crossed my mind? The police didn't ask that either." He paused. "But I suppose if you wish to end your life a church is as good a place as any to do so." He looked immeasurably sad. "There is one strange thing."

"Yes?"

"At our meeting yesterday evening, one of the choir members mentioned that he always carried a large leather briefcase with him. "It wasn't there when I found him."

The vicar stood up. "I've taken up enough of your time. Thank you for listening." His expression darkened. "Please help us. Me." He handed her a card with his contact details on.

"I'll see what I can do. No promises."

As he was leaving he surprised her by asking, "Have you had your daughter christened?"

"No. I'm not a churchgoer."

"Most parents aren't but they like the ceremony and a chance to celebrate with family and friends. Belts and braces." His smile was genuine. "Think about it."

FIVE

HER PHONE RANG almost as soon as the vicar left. She was still using her mobile phone from *The News* and wondered if it was time to stop having all her calls diverted to it now.

"Hi Hannah, I'm in your neck of the woods and wondered if you'd like to meet for lunch at that pub on the corner near you?"

"The Uplands? Love to. What time?"

How fortuitous, she thought, that Mike Benton should contact her when she could do with picking his brains. She hadn't seen him since the book launch so it would be good to catch up. As she prepared to leave, it occurred to her to wonder how much of a coincidence Mike's invitation was. Perhaps he was on a fishing expedition too?

WHEN HANNAH HAD first moved into the area a few years previously, the pub had been called The Upland Tavern. From what she'd seen on the one occasion she'd popped in, it attracted older men who often sat in groups playing dominos or on their own doing crosswords or reading newspapers. Then the pub changed hands and became The Uplands, a more upmarket establishment, which served food and also had some outdoor seating. Hannah had been there once or twice pre-Elizabeth but, as she entered now, she noticed from the highchairs serried along the wall that they were hoping to encourage families.

DI Mike Benton was already sitting at a table when she arrived, a half of lager and glass of wine in front of him. He appeared every inch the inspector now, and Hannah felt a rush of warmth towards him for the times he'd saved her skin. He stood and hugged her. He seemed genuinely pleased to see her so perhaps it was just a social catchup. "You're looking well – being a famous bestselling author suits you." She gave him her arch look and he grinned. "I took the liberty of assuming you'd like a glass of wine. And I ordered a couple of ploughman's."

"Both are great, thanks." She sat opposite him. "So how are Phoebe and the children?"

He grinned. "All well. Phoebe loved being at your book launch – she dines out on it." His own happiness at being reunited with his wife glowed. "Tim has made the school football team so I get to stand out in the cold on the sidelines most Saturday mornings."

Hannah laughed. "I remember my father saying he was glad I was a girl so he wouldn't have to do that."

"Maybe not these days. Just think, Elizabeth might want to play for the school under-sevens …"

A barman came across with their platters.

Hannah heard her stomach rumble. "I didn't realise how hungry I was until you rang."

"Me too. You're doing me a favour, as I hate eating a sandwich in the car. Especially in this weather."

Hannah's mind went back to the last time they'd shared sandwiches for lunch. Mike had arrived with an obnoxious sergeant when Edith had been reported missing. It seemed a lifetime ago yet foreshadowed one of the worst, no *the* worst, experience of her life: the abduction of Elizabeth from the nursery.

They concentrated on the food for a few minutes. Hannah broke the silence. "I had a strange experience last night." She hadn't known whether to tell Mike but it seemed like an opportune moment.

"Go on."

"I had dinner with Rory from *The News* and when I paid the bill the waiter passed me a slip of paper telling me to be careful as someone was asking questions about me."

Mike took a gulp of his beer. "Nothing else?"

"No, but when we left to get a taxi someone nearly knocked me over and when I looked my bag strap had been slashed."

Mike's face had drained of colour. Hannah realised that he too had immediately thought of Edward Peters' attack on her at Heathrow. "But you're okay?"

"Yes it was all over very quickly. I didn't see the person so nothing to go on. A policeman flagged us down a taxi. I couldn't help wondering if that incident was linked to the note."

"Do you still have it?"

"Yes." Hannah took it out from her bag and handed it to Mike.

He read the note and shook his head. "I'll keep hold of this. No need to tell you to be extra careful."

"No." She took a sip of wine. She felt a huge sense of relief having shared that with the detective but now she needed to change the subject.

"A little bird tells me you're investigating a suspicious death at the church up the road."

"How the hell…?" He looked at her and laughed. "Don't tell me you go to that church?"

Hannah glared at him. "Would that be so improbable?" Then she relented and smiled at his discomfort. "No, I've never even been inside the place. What's it like?"

Mike paused as though searching for the right description. "The building is beautiful and there's a quality of … I don't know maybe you'd call it serenity even though someone has just died there."

Maybe because someone had just died there, Hannah thought. "However?" she prompted.

"However there's something strange going on and I don't think people are being honest with me." He looked genuinely perplexed.

"Perish the thought, inspector."

"Well you'd think church people would tell the truth, wouldn't you?"

Hannah sipped her drink and waited. Lies by omission?

"And I don't think you're being entirely up front with me." Mike's face bore a look of amusement. Tolerance. "Would you like a coffee?"

"Yes please." She finished her wine and Mike went up to the bar to order their coffees. Hannah's eyes scanned the room. There weren't many other people in the bar but some looked like they'd been there since opening time and wouldn't be leaving soon. She noticed a man sitting on his own nursing a half-drunk pint and presumably doing a crossword. He looked up and for a moment she caught his gaze. She felt a chill run down her spine. Ridiculous to think he was trying to intimidate her. And anyway she had great protection in Mike.

"Nice place this," he said as he returned.

Hannah ignored that. "Do you know that man sitting in the corner with the tartan scarf and a sour expression?"

Mike glanced over. "Think I need the loo. Excuse me." To get to the Gents he had to walk past the man in question. Hannah feigned searching for something in her bag but actually kept her eyes on the man until her line of vision was broken by a group of women who sat at a table between them.

Mike returned.

"Well?"

"Well what? I just went to the loo. Is there something you need to tell me?"

Was there? she wondered. "Actually I was going to tell you that I had a visit from the vicar this morning."

"Really, and how did that come about?"

"My neighbour, Leah Braithwaite, goes to the church. She's a member of their church council or something. Anyway, he was worried and apparently she suggested he contact me."

"Apparently?"

"Well I'm not sure she would have suggested something like that without running it past me."

"True." Mike looked thoughtful. He remembered seeing Leah at the meeting. She had looked shocked but supportive of Peter Savage. "How is the indomitable Mrs Braithwaite?"

"Well she's not baking as many cakes." Mike obviously hadn't a clue as to what she was talking about. "She often used to invite me over for coffee and cake. She is the only friend I've made amongst my neighbours and she has been very kind to me. And then of course her brother contacted her and – well you know all about that. After her visit to Australia she set up a charity helping people who had been part of the Child Migration Scheme trace lost relatives. She's a different woman now."

"And?"

"And so much happier. I'm just being selfish thinking about missing her cakes."

"They have some here if you fancy one with your coffee?"

"Stop being so solicitous, Mike. Let's talk about the vicar."

"What did you make of him?"

"Not much to be honest. He seemed a bit... oh I don't know. He wouldn't inspire me with confidence in the afterlife."

Mike chuckled. "Poor bloke does seem a bit out of his depth." The coffees arrived and he stirred his as though lost in thought.

"It's strange though."

"What is?"

"That the vicar should turn up on your doorstep like that."

Hannah paused. "I don't think there's anything sinister in it. He hasn't been here long and he feels that he hasn't been totally accepted yet." She didn't think that was a breach of confidence.

"Stranger things. Did he say much about the dead man?"

"No, and no one, he said, knew much about him. Apparently, his briefcase should have been with him. Perhaps he left it at home?"

"Nice try, Hannah." Then he relented. "Actually we haven't found the briefcase. Let me know if you do." There was an understanding between them now; they had relied on each other before and it had paid off. Maybe it would this time.

"However, I think I'll go along to a service on Sunday. He mentioned having Elizabeth christened so that'll be my reason for being there."

Mike's phone rang. "Sorry, I have to take this." He moved away to the door and Hannah watched his expression but it gave nothing away. He came back after paying the bill at the bar. "Right, duty calls." He pushed his glasses up his nose. "Let me know if you need a godfather."

Hannah looked completely nonplussed.

"Unless you're looking for more famous godparents. For Elizabeth?"

Hannah grinned. "I said that would be my cover story, not that I was actually going through with it."

"Well the offer's there if a certain Leo Hawkins isn't available."

Hannah laughed. "Mike, you're incorrigible! Leo is in the US convalescing with his family. I don't think he'll be back any time soon."

"We'll see." He gave her a stern stare. "Take care of yourself." A brief hug and he was gone.

AT THE DOOR, Hannah tightened her coat belt. The cold air was bracing. It was too early to collect Elizabeth so she thought she'd call on Leah on the off chance she was at home.

The bell seemed to have the echo of an empty house but a moment or two later the door opened and Leah appeared, delighted to see her. "Come in, come in." She stood aside. "Let me take your coat." She fussed around Hannah. "Let's go through to the kitchen."

The room looked as it always had done. Warm and welcoming. A spicy smell lingered in the air.

Leah wiped her hands on the apron she was wearing. "I was just adding some brandy to my Christmas cake." She beamed at Hannah. "No prizes for guessing who's joining us this Christmas."

Hannah hugged her. "That's wonderful."

"A proper family Christmas." Then followed a moment of embarrassment. "What are your plans, Hannah? Are you visiting your parents this year?"

"No, they're coming here – easier for Father Christmas to deliver presents."

"Of course. And you have friends here. I hope you and your parents will join us for drinks on Monday 18th? I'd love you to meet my brother and his wife and you'll be able to catch up with Scott."

"Sounds perfect and I'm sure my parents would enjoy it."

"Coffee?"

"Yes please."

Hannah waited until they were sitting at the table with coffee and a slice of cherry cake before asking the question, which was the real reason for her visit. "Did you give my address to the vicar at St John's?"

For a moment Leah looked furious and Hannah wondered why. "No I did not. You know I wouldn't do that, Hannah."

"I do but I just wanted to check. He came to see me this morning." Leah nodded but didn't comment. "I take it you know about the man who died in church?"

"Yes we had an emergency meeting of the PCC –" she saw Hannah's expression – "Parochial Church Council. I'm a member. We met yesterday evening."

"I suppose that was confidential."

Leah gave her an odd look. "It was."

Hannah nodded. "Anyway, your vicar mentioned having Elizabeth christened. Not something I've given much thought to actually. However, I thought I'd go to a service and see how I feel about it." Hannah was mentally crossing her fingers.

"What a wonderful idea – the christening, I mean. I'm going on Sunday. Would you like to come along with me?"

It was the invitation Hannah had been hoping for. "If you wouldn't mind?"

"Of course not! I like to hobnob with local celebrities. It will do my credibility rating no harm."

"Oh please." Hannah cringed. It was the side of co-writing a bestseller and the fiasco surrounding the nursery that she really could do without. But being with Leah would make her presence in church a lot easier.

"So what time do we need to leave?"

"The service starts at ten but I have to be there a little earlier as I'm reading. So, shall we say, 9.40?"

"Perfect."

"And perhaps you and Elizabeth would like to join Brian and me for lunch afterwards?"

"That would be lovely, thank you."

Leah looked like the cat who had eaten the cream and Hannah felt a warm glow of appreciation. She left soon afterwards and went straight round to collect Elizabeth from the nursery. A cosy evening for two lay ahead.

WHAT HANNAH HADN'T ANTICIPATED after bathing Elizabeth and reading her favourite story, currently *Each Peach Pear Plum*, over and over until she fell asleep, was a phone call from Leo.

"Hello, how are you?" Just the sound of his voice made her stomach flip. Sporadically, he sent an email to keep in touch. But his voice… She reprimanded herself she couldn't, wouldn't, get involved with a man who was staying with his family in the US even if he and his wife were divorced. Maybe his near-death experience had reconciled them?

"I'm fine. More to the point, how are you?" She managed to keep her tone light.

"Getting there. Slowly. But it's been lovely to see so much of the girls."

And their mother? But it wasn't a question she had the right to ask.

"It must be. Hope their company has been healing. Especially after the loss of your mother." A pause.

"Yes it has been. But I'll be home soon. There are things I have to do in London. And I'm hoping we could meet up."

"I'd love to, Leo." She hoped she didn't sound too enthusiastic.

"I have to sort out my mother's affairs – the book included."

Her mood plummeted. Of course.

"I hear it's selling well – the book?" Leo, as Joan Ballantyne's heir, received her percentage of the royalties.

"Yes it seems to be. And the paperback comes out next year." She heard something, a voice, in the background. He chuckled.

"Anyway I'll be back in London next week so I'll ring you then, if that's okay?"

"Of course. It'll be good to see you."

Abruptly he ended the call. *Why ring*, she thought? He could have sent an email.

The conversation left her feeling restless and irritable. The phone rang again but this time the conversation wasn't stilted. Janet invited her and Elizabeth to lunch the next day.

"Sorry it's so last-minute but things have been hectic at work and I've been dying to have you round."

"Janet, we'd love to. What time?" It would be such a welcome distraction in her current frame of mind.

HANNAH DECIDED to go to bed early with a book. She felt curiously unsettled and the book failed to keep her attention. Scenes went round and round in her mind – Leah and her cakes, the vicar, Mike Benton, and all the conversations were curiously out of sync – until she wasn't sure if she was dreaming or awake. She must have fallen asleep eventually as she awoke at two in the morning with the bedside lamp still on and the book had fallen to the floor. So much for a good night's rest. Now she'd have trouble getting back to sleep. She turned off the light and in the darkness did the counting exercise. The next thing she heard was Elizabeth calling from her bedroom.

SIX

HANNAH HADN'T VISITED Janet's flat since her mother Sheila's departure to live with her sister in Essex. Janet opened the door and beamed at Elizabeth, who struggled to get out of her buggy and into the arms of her former nanny. "Jan-Jan!" She kissed her cheeks then turned to her mother with an expression of bliss that was reflected in Janet's face. The tiny shaft of jealousy she felt was blunted by the joy of knowing that her child was loved by other people. People who would always, she hoped, be there for her.

"Come in out of the cold." Janet took their coats and hung them next to hers in the hallway.

Hannah parked the buggy in the space which had once contained Sheila's wheelchair, and breathed in the air, which exuded happiness.

"Come and see what I've found for you to play with, Elizabeth."

They walked into the sitting room. The flat felt so different. There was a change of atmosphere as well. The place seemed joyful, as did Janet. Gone were all the framed photos of Janet and her sister. A lot of the furniture had been replaced and the walls had been given a fresh coat of paint. In pride of place on a dresser was one of the photos Edith had taken of Elizabeth and, they discovered, there was a low cupboard especially for Elizabeth that had toys and books just perfect for a soon-to-be two-year-old. Elizabeth was enchanted.

"I didn't want to invite you before all the decorating was finished. I wanted to welcome you to my home – not my mother's. Does that sound awful?"

"Sounds perfectly reasonable to me." Hannah handed her the azalea she'd brought and a bottle of wine.

Elizabeth, who travelled everywhere accompanied by her favourite baby doll, was setting out the tea set that had been in the cupboard. Janet smiled and knelt down by the child. "I used to play with that when I was a little girl."

Elizabeth responded with a hug then carried on chatting to her baby.

"Right, I'll pour us a glass of wine and check the lunch."

Hannah sat back in the armchair, remembering sitting in a very different environment with Janet's mother. It seemed like a lifetime ago yet it was only a few months. Janet had been furious with her mother for being dishonest with Hannah over the missing cousin she'd assumed was part of the Child Migration Scheme. So much water under the bridge. And Janet had returned to the police job she loved.

"Right, about fifteen minutes." Janet handed her a glass of wine and sat in the opposite chair. "So what's new in your world?"

"Nothing much." She took a sip of wine. "I've never asked you, but do you go to church?"

Janet gave her a strange look. "I used to now and again with my mother. More of a high days and holidays sort of thing. What makes you ask?"

"Had a visit from the vicar at St John's asking if I'd had Elizabeth christened."

"Oh? That's a bit random isn't it? I didn't think the church canvassed quite so aggressively to increase their congregations. They must be desperate."

"Thanks!" Hannah laughed. "He actually came about something else and mentioned it when he saw Elizabeth's photos. Just got me thinking, that's all."

"Nothing to do with the man who died in his church, I suppose?"

Hannah sipped her wine. "Oh, you know about that. Yes, that as well. I'm going to a service there with Leah tomorrow."

Janet didn't respond.

"I saw Mike Benton yesterday as well."

Janet had a soft spot for the inspector and smiled. "He's doing well for himself."

"Yes he's certainly grown in stature with his promotion." She had never shared with Janet the experience with Sergeant Benton when she'd discovered her friend murdered in St John's Waterloo. They had both changed since then. Now she considered Mike more of a friend, and she had precious few of those.

"And what about you? Are you doing well for yourself?"

Janet coloured slightly. "I'm doing okay." Hannah assumed there was something afoot but had to be satisfied with that reply.

OVER LUNCH ELIZABETH concentrated on her meal – all her special food from one of her favourite people reminding Hannah of how Mary and Celia Rayman liked to "spoil" her daughter – while the two women chatted until Janet laughed. "Look at her." Elizabeth could hardly keep her eyes open and looked about to end up face down in her ice cream.

Hannah carried her into the hall and placed her in her buggy.

"That was delicious, Janet. Thank you," she said on her return. "Everything always tastes so much nicer when you don't have to cook it yourself."

"And even if you do it's better than the canteen food."

"I can only imagine. So will you be able to see your mother for Christmas?"

Janet made a face. "Couldn't get out of it. We also have my sister's wedding so rather a surfeit of family obligations."

"I'd forgotten about that. Have you got your outfit?"

"Yes. I found something that fits the bill for sister of the bride." She chuckled. "Would you like to see it?"

"Yes please." Janet had never shown much interest in fashion so Hannah was intrigued to know what she had chosen for the occasion. Janet came back into the room wearing a fabulous wine-red fitted dress and jacket. The hem skimmed her knees and the skirt had a fluidity which matched the wearer's movements. Everything about the outfit complemented Janet's figure.

"Wow, you look stunning."

Janet laughed. "Well, at least my mother won't be able to say I didn't make an effort!" She gave another twirl then left to change back into her ordinary clothes.

Hannah smiled and wondered who had gone shopping with her. Not that it was any of her business. But it was someone who brought out the best in Janet.

"WHAT ABOUT YOU? What are your plans for Christmas?" They were back sitting in the armchairs finishing their wine.

"It will be lovely this year with Elizabeth old enough to open all her presents."

"It will. My parents are coming over and we're having Christmas dinner with Celia and Mary. It will be their first Christmas without Liz. And to be honest it will be good to be with them and take the pressure off of us. Mum of course will be delighted, hobnobbing with Lady Rayman. And Leah has invited us for drinks on the Monday before so we're going to be rather sociable." Her face clouded as she remembered that last year while they had been in France, Tom had been with them and Liz had still been alive.

"Anyway, going back to the vicar. If I do decide to have Elizabeth christened, would you consider being a godmother?"

Janet's face was a kaleidoscope of expressions. "Oh, Hannah, I would love to. I'd be so honoured." She sniffed. "Just one condition."

"Oh, what's that?"

"Make it soon so I can wear my sister of the bride outfit as a godmother dress. I'd like to get some wear out of it."

They both laughed. Then Janet became serious. "Did the vicar ask you to help find out about the dead man in the church?"

Hannah struggled over what she could reveal without breaking a confidence.

"Don't answer, I can see from your face he did." She finished her wine. "Just be careful." Then she sighed, as though knowing Hannah was already involved in some way. "Coffee?"

SEVEN

ENTERING ST JOHN'S CHURCH the next morning, Hannah felt as though she were accompanying royalty. Everyone greeted Leah, who seemed to be on first name terms with every single person and knew who was sad, ill, happy, and had a few words with each. She introduced Hannah to a few people as "my friend and neighbour" and Elizabeth, released from her buggy, was totally in her element, smiling and looking around in wonderment, attracting her fair share of attention.

Hannah could see what Mike meant about the church. There was a beautiful simplicity in the white walls and stained glass windows. Hannah glanced over to what she assumed was the Lady Chapel, but whatever had happened there had left no shadow. She recognised a few families from the nursery. Apparently church attendance was necessary for a place at the local C of E school.

Reverend Peter Savage was hurrying towards Leah and almost did a double take when he saw Hannah. She showed no signs of recognising him. Poker face.

"Father Peter –" Leah continued the subterfuge – "allow me to introduce you to Hannah, my friend and neighbour."

He clasped her hand. "Welcome, Hannah, and who is this gorgeous young lady?"

Elizabeth giggled. "Elbet."

"Elizabeth," Hannah said quickly.

He smiled and looked at his watch. "Right, I must away. I hope you can stay for coffee after the service, Hannah. Leah knows the ropes."

The woman in question guided her to a row about halfway down the aisle and to the left. Hannah wondered if she sat in the same place every week. Leah lowered her head in prayer. Hannah settled Elizabeth in the seat between them and smiled as her daughter began chatting to her baby doll.

The organ music began and everyone stood. Hannah was intrigued by the pomp and ceremony. A large silver cross, carried by a woman, led the procession. Hannah had no idea what roles these people played as the vicar and his team followed on after the choir while they all sang the first hymn.

The choristers were a mixed bag. Eight women and seven men, a range of ages though not many young people. The choir stalls were directly in front of Hannah's side of the church but she couldn't make out much as they were side-on to her.

"Welcome to our Advent service." Peter Savage's deep voice rang out. "Now I need someone to light the first candle in our Advent wreath. Do I have any volunteers?"

A laugh erupted when a little girl aged about eight strode up the aisle announcing, "Yes, me!"

The vicar smiled at her. "Thank you, Savannah." He stepped over to the wreath and lit a taper for her. Standing on tiptoes, she lit the first candle then beamed at the congregation. There was a ripple of applause. Elizabeth was clapping her hands enthusiastically as though everything was being performed for her benefit alone. Hannah was amazed at her daughter. She had hummed along to the hymn, attracting smiles from those nearby.

The service progressed and she was grateful to have Leah by her side guiding her, when to stand and sit and so on. Just as she began to relax during some prayers, her phone rang. Mortified, Hannah reached into her bag, disconnected the call and switched the phone off. She could feel the heat of her embarrassment on her face made immeasurably worse by her daughter saying for all to hear, "Naughty Mama," and wagging a finger at her. The priest continued as though nothing had happened and then Leah went to the lectern to read the lesson. She had a beautiful, well-modulated speaking voice, and when she finished Elizabeth showed her appreciation by clapping loudly.

If Hannah had wanted to be a discreet member of the congregation she'd well and truly blown it. Peter Savage walked over to the pulpit, climbing the steps slowly, to deliver his sermon. "May I speak in the name of the Father, and of the Son and of the Holy Spirit. Amen." He bowed his head for a moment.

"In today's Gospel reading we heard the words: be on your

guard so that your hearts are not weighed down with dissipation and drunkenness and the worries of this life and that the day does not catch you unexpectedly like a trap…" Peter Savage paused and smiled sadly. "'That the day does not catch you unexpectedly like a trap'." He cleared his throat. "On Thursday I was caught unexpectedly. Not, I hasten to add, because of dissipation and drunkenness." There were a few titters in the congregation. "But I was going through the motions, the routine of opening the church for Morning Prayers, thinking about why no one came and was it because the heating hadn't been on long enough?" He looked around as though waiting for confirmation of this thought. "And then I saw our brother Daniel Lyons sitting in the Lady Chapel. Alone. When I went over to him, he said he was dying and asked me to pray for him. He didn't want me to call an ambulance. He wanted my company. It was an honour and a privilege to sit with him. I did so for some time. We prayed together and I anointed him. I want to reassure you all –" he looked around the congregation – "that he was peaceful as he was dying." Silence echoed. The vicar looked so sad.

"Daniel's death is being treated as suspicious by the police. At the moment we don't know how or indeed why he died as he did. But God's judgement must fall on us all. All who did not take the time to get to know him. Or ignored him. He had been a member of our choir for a few months. And somehow he was left after choir rehearsal on Wednesday evening. Alone. Dying." The vicar paused as if for dramatic effect. "No one should be alone at such a time and I am glad I was able to be there with him. But I hardly knew him and that is my regret." He paused.

"It is incumbent upon us all – every single one of us – to be a brother, sister, friend when someone – anyone – needs us. We never know when that call will happen. May God open our hearts and minds to be ready and not find us lacking. May our heavenly Father guide us so that any day does not catch any of us unexpectedly like a trap. And may Daniel rest in peace and rise in glory." He made the sign of the cross. "If anyone would like to speak with me privately or share their thoughts, you know where I am.

"Let us pray…"

WHILE THE PRIEST had been talking, Hannah studied the reactions of the choristers. All looked serious as though shock had permeated their bones and was seeping from their pores. It was difficult to tell if they were sad. Only one wiped away a tear. A man. *Interesting*, thought Hannah, as she surreptitiously looked at the people around her. Nothing of note. Shock seemed to be the uppermost reaction. Maybe they thought he'd died of natural causes. Perhaps because they hadn't known him, his death didn't really affect them. Despite what the vicar had said. Mercifully, Elizabeth had been silent during the sermon and the following prayers.

They all stood for the creed. What really threw Hannah was the Peace. After the middle-aged woman standing alongside the vicar, who Hannah later learned was the curate, exhorted them to show each other a sign of Peace, everyone was hugging, kissing and shaking hands. Hannah looked longingly at the exit.

"Peace be with you, Leah." The vicar had walked down the aisle towards her neighbour and taken her hand before turning towards Hannah, his smile warm and welcoming. "Peace be with you, Hannah."

Seeing him in his milieu made Hannah reassess her first impression of him. He was more confident and in control in his church. More assertive. And maybe he had had time to discuss the ramifications of the chorister's death with the bishop or whomever a priest reported to. Archdeacon. The word came to her in a flash as she remembered her own encounters with the church hierarchy when Father Patrick at St John's Waterloo had disappeared soon after her best friend Liz had been murdered.

"And with you, little one." He ruffled Elizabeth's hair.

"Peace," she shouted at anyone and everyone.

Never work with animals and children. Hannah chuckled to herself. Elizabeth was supposed to be her cover. All she had done was draw attention to them both. Hannah avoided going up to the altar to take communion and it gave her a good chance to look at people as they returned to their seats. The congregation was diverse. Most of the West Indian women wore smart clothes and hats and the men – although these were fewer in number – wore suits, as did the older white population. Sunday best. But the younger members were far more informal in their attire. One youngish black woman caught her eye. Dressed casually in jeans and a bright yellow jumper, she beamed at everyone, looking totally relaxed, but there was something about her that Hannah couldn't fathom. A magnetic energy. An intelligence. An awareness.

During this time the choir sang 'People Look East' a Besançon carol medley according to the service sheet. Their voices were beautifully attuned but in Hannah's mind it sounded funereal. Perhaps they were singing for their dead choir member.

After the post communion prayer, the priest read the notices reminding them about the forthcoming Christmas services and ended on a plea for extra people to join the choir for the major services. There was a ripple of murmurs then the organ struck up the opening chords for the final hymn. The vicar and his acolytes followed the choir in a procession that stopped in the Lady Chapel, facing the statue of the Virgin Mary. They bowed their heads for a moment in silence, presumably for the dead chorister, then sang a series of Hail Marys, the words of which and the responses sung by the congregation were printed on the service sheet. It all sounded rather Catholic to Hannah. At the end, there was another moment of silence and the procession departed.

Elizabeth appeared fascinated. Hannah was terrified she would break the silence in the church. But no, the organ resumed playing and she breathed a deep sigh of relief.

"That wasn't so bad, was it?" Leah was smiling and, Hannah noticed, she wiped a tear from her eye. "Let's go and have a coffee."

They made their way to the back of the church and the area where tea and coffee was being served. To her relief and surprise, Hannah realised her ploy had worked. No one had the slightest interest in her, the mother. Elizabeth held centre stage. No one asked Hannah what she did, she was just Elizabeth's mother and Leah's neighbour – and, at that moment, very glad to be so.

However, one woman looked at her with an intensity that made her hackles rise. Her height added to her threatening demeanour. The penetrating stare from a face framed by fair hair cut in a sharp bob, did not bode well. But she said nothing.

"You have a lovely singing voice, Hannah. Maybe you should think about joining our choir for the Christmas services?"

Leah seemed determined to integrate Hannah, or maybe she was thinking of the dead chorister?

"Oh, I don't think that would be a good idea."

"No rush," she said. "Think about it. Now if you'll excuse me for a moment I must just have a quick word with Marjorie."

"We're always looking for extra singers at Christmas." Hannah turned to see the man who had played the organ so beautifully. "Craig Fletcher, musical director." He introduced himself, and shook her hand. "And I heard Leah say you are Hannah. It's not a big commitment to join us for a few services and, as long as you can read music, you'll be most welcome. No auditions necessary."

He smiled encouragingly at her. Earlier he had been wearing a black cassock and white surplice but those garments now removed revealed he was wearing a brown suit, yellow shirt and a green bow tie. His dark hair was brushed off his face and curled over his collar.

"Well, I'm not sure that I –" She looked across the room and saw the priest, who was looking directly at her, incline his head slightly. Had he put Craig up to this?

"You'll know most of the carols, I expect, and you can soon learn anything new."

Hannah smiled at him. She had been well and truly snookered. "When do you meet?"

"We rehearse on Wednesdays at 7.30 in the vestry but if you'd just like to join us for the carol service and Midnight Mass come along at 8.15." He smiled at her reticence. "We're a friendly bunch."

Not that friendly, she wanted to say. *One of your number was left alone in the church to die.* A cloud seemed to pass over his face as though in remembrance of his dead chorister. "There'll be a few other 'extras' joining us so you won't be the odd man, woman, out." He looked around as though seeking an escape, and found one.

"Excuse me, I must just speak to John over there. See you Wednesday, I hope." And with that he left Hannah to sip her coffee. Elizabeth had consumed a juice and biscuit and looked tired. "Why don't you pop into your buggy, darling?"

Elizabeth went willingly and snuggled up with her baby doll.

"I'm surprised to see you here."

Hannah spun round. It was the woman with the penetrating stare. "I'm sorry, do I know you?"

"You will do." She gave her a tight smile, which did little to assuage her disapproval. "Oh, you will do." And with that she left the church.

Hannah felt sick. How on earth had she upset that woman?

"Are you ready to leave, Hannah?" Leah was beside her. Hannah nodded.

"I see you met our very own Cruella."

"Who is she?" Hannah pushed the buggy outside. The coldness was nothing to the icy chill which had emanated from that woman.

"Ruth Robertson. I'll tell you about her later." Leah smiled and waved goodbye to everyone in a reversal of their arrival.

EIGHT

BRIAN HAD TEARS in his eyes. "Oh, I would love to have heard that." Leah was regaling him with Elizabeth's antics in church.

"The strange thing is," Hannah said after taking a sip of her gin and tonic, "Elizabeth seemed to be so at home there." Elizabeth was still sleeping peacefully in her buggy.

"I thought that too. There was something rather special in her appreciation of the service. Oh and, Brian, you'll never guess who put in an appearance today."

Her husband smiled indulgently. "Well as I won't guess, you'd better tell me."

"Ruthless Robertson." She looked across at Hannah. "Obviously, she's called Ruth but the nickname sums her up. She always manages to get her own way."

"Except, it seems, in the appointment of our vicar. Since he's been at St John's her attendance has been sporadic to say the least." Hannah wondered why Brian didn't accompany Leah to church but didn't feel it was appropriate to ask.

"Mm, well, she still does the flowers and she's not relinquished her place on the PCC. She was there on Thursday." Leah looked affronted.

Hannah was fascinated – so much intrigue within the church. "She tried to intimidate me. Said she was surprised to see me there. To my knowledge I have never even seen the woman before, let alone met and upset her."

"Really." Leah looked aghast then thoughtful. "I wonder why? Now I'm just going to finish a few things in the kitchen and we can eat."

OVER LUNCH Hannah mentioned her conversation with the musical director and the invitation to join the choir.

"Why not?" Brian was encouraging. "The Christmas services are lovely. They usually have a few extras joining the choir so you won't be the odd one out," he said, echoing Craig's words.

"But I won't know anyone."

Leah was looking at her strangely but said nothing.

"Then you could make some new friends," said Brian.

And, Hannah thought, *I might find out more about the dead chorister.*

AS THEY WAVED Hannah and Elizabeth goodbye and shut their front door, Brian and Leah turned to each other. Leah looked at her husband quizzically. "Do you think she bought it?"

"I think so. Now all we can do is wait and see."

IT WASN'T UNTIL she was back in her own home after what had been a delicious roast lunch with plenty of wine, that Hannah remembered her mobile phone had rung in church and she hadn't switched it back on. She'd deal with that after she'd given Elizabeth a bath.

Bath time was always special but that evening Elizabeth was in a reflective mood. That was if a soon-to-be two-year-old's moods could be described as reflective. She was singing to herself, imitating the sounds she'd heard in church. She didn't have the words but she had the melodies. Hannah was confounded.

"Did you like going to church today, Elizabeth?"

Her daughter paused. "Yes."

"Would you like to go again?"

But Elizabeth didn't answer; she had put her hands together as though praying. Hannah stared at her and felt distinctly uncomfortable. She had never been a religious person, only attending church on and off with her parents and grandparents as a child. She had never felt the need for a belief in a higher power. And what she had experienced over the last couple of years had revealed some of the pettiness and corruption of those involved in organised religion. And the sanctimonious twaddle – Father Patrick's situation came to mind. The cruelty, she added, thinking of Edward Peters who had been part of a notorious and abusive religious sect in Australia and had killed himself after wounding her at the airport. The physical wound had healed but the scar still ran deep.

ONCE ELIZABETH was in bed asleep, Hannah checked her phone. There was no message. Tomorrow she'd see about having her phones reinstated. Surely she didn't need to have her calls diverted now? Strange that *The News* hadn't asked for the phone to be returned to them. Maybe they were still keeping tabs on her. Not a reassuring thought.

Hannah settled on the sofa to watch an episode of *The Vicar of Dibley,* a new series starring Dawn French that she'd recorded. She wondered what Leah thought of women priests, and the vicar of St John's. Then she remembered there was a female curate there. She hadn't really taken much notice of her. She'd ask Leah about her, she thought, as Alice the verger said something that made her laugh out loud. Dawn French's character would even tempt her into attending church regularly.

SHE FELT RELAXED as she went to bed and thought about the day. Maybe church had some benefits. Then she giggled. More likely all the wine she'd drunk with Leah and Brian afterwards at lunch. Her thoughts turned to how she could discover more about Daniel Lyons, before she fell into a deep and untroubled sleep.

NINE

A BLEAK MONDAY morning. Cold and grey. Hannah rather
envied her daughter being at nursery where everything was bright,
colourful and warm. They had celebrated Diwali at the beginning
of the month. Alesha, her regular babysitter whose family had
more or less adopted her, asked around her extended family and
had found her a beautiful red child's outfit for Elizabeth which
had tiny mirrors sewn on. Her daughter had adored it and was
loath to return it after the celebrations. Now the nursery staff
was gearing up to Christmas. There was a definite sense of
excitement in the air.

She should think about some Christmas decorations for the
house. Elizabeth would love that and she wanted her home to be
as festive and as welcoming as possible for her parents. She was
hoping they would relax and enjoy the festivities. She was sure
her mother would delight in the fact that they would be having
Christmas dinner with Lady Celia Rayman. It would be their first
Christmas without Liz, and Hannah knew they were relying on
Elizabeth's company to help them get through it. A party at Leah
and Brian's would also be a welcome diversion.

HANNAH HAD POPPED INTO a coffee shop on Lordship
Lane. While she was there she went into the ladies' loo, which
was fortunately empty as she rummaged in the bag she'd brought
with her. The short blonde wig suited her, she thought, and was
different enough from her own hair to create a disguise. She
swapped her scarf with the other one she'd placed in her bag
earlier and put on some dark-rimmed glasses. That would have
to do, she thought, leaving the café without a second glance from
staff or other customers, and walking to the bus stop on East
Dulwich Road to catch a bus into Peckham. She'd worked out
her route early that morning when she had decided to visit the
dead man's home. She didn't think the police would have missed

anything but it would be good to place him in his context. However, she didn't want to draw attention to her real self and had decided to introduce herself as a concerned friend after he hadn't turned up for their usual meeting.

The house was a small two-up two-down on a side road and from the outside looked well cared for, as did all the other houses in the street. Obviously part of the regeneration scheme the council had instigated with grants for homeowners.

She rang the bell. She had her lapel camera and a recorder ready.

No answer. She rang again. Nothing. There was little point in standing there if no one was at home but as she turned to go, a woman walked up the path.

"Can I help you?"

Hannah took in the smart leather coat and silk scarf. As she came nearer Hannah could see that the woman was older than she might appear at first glance and she didn't look as though she'd suffer fools gladly.

"I'm looking for Daniel Lyons. He does live here, doesn't he? This is the address he gave me."

The woman gave her a shrewd look. "And who might you be?"

Hannah smiled and tried a coy look. "A friend."

"Really. And do you have a name?"

"Of course." Hannah smiled in what she hoped was a disarming way. "Jill. Jill Bradshaw."

"Well, Miss Bradshaw. Daniel did live here but not anymore."

"Oh how strange. I'll wait for him to contact me then." She took a deep breath, thinking on her feet. "I'm sorry this is all so difficult. We have an arrangement. We meet up once a fortnight." The woman had already opened her door and placed her shopping bags inside. She looked as though she might just close the door on Hannah. "He didn't turn up for our last appointment and, as I hadn't heard from him, I got worried. I thought he might be ill or something."

"It's the or something. Would you like to come in for a moment? It's too cold to talk on the doorstep."

FROM THE HALL, the woman led her into a small but well-appointed kitchen where she placed her bags on the table.

51

Everywhere was spotlessly clean. The walls were bright yellow with blue cupboards, which seemed strangely at odds with the woman who owned them. She filled a kettle and turned to Hannah. "You haven't asked who I am." Hannah could have kicked herself. She knew who she was. What an elementary mistake.

"I'm so sorry, I assumed you are Daniel's landlady, Mrs Felton. He mentioned you."

"That's right, Melanie Felton." The kettle boiled. "Tea?"

"Do you have any coffee, I don't drink tea?"

Mrs Felton turned back to the counter and reached for a jar of instant coffee. "Milk?"

"No thank you and no sugar."

The woman was silent while she made the drinks and then handed Hannah a mug. "Sit down. You'll need to." Hannah complied and Melanie Felton sat opposite her. "I'm afraid Daniel has died."

Hannah managed to feign shock. She thought the least she said would be better. She put down her mug, searched for a tissue in her handbag and blew her nose.

"How? What happened?"

Melanie Felton shrugged. "He died in that church he sings – sang at. After choir practice, it seems. No one knew he was still there, apparently." She looked as though she didn't believe a word of it.

"I see." Hannah sipped her coffee. "Was he ill? He seemed fine the last time we met."

Melanie Felton gave her an old-fashioned look. "Not that I know of." She sniffed. "Suspicious circumstances, that's what I was told."

"And you weren't worried when he didn't return that evening?"

For a moment Hannah thought Mrs Felton was going to ask her to leave. "I don't think that's any business of yours."

"Of course not. But it must have been a shock for you. Have, had you known him a long time?"

Melanie stared into her teacup. "No, not long. A few months. He was in the area for work." She paused. "He said he worked for an insurance company. Investigating fraudulent claims, I think." She looked straight at Hannah. "You probably know more about him than I do."

"It wasn't his work we talked about." It was the best Hannah could come up with.

"No, I didn't think it was. I suppose you'd like to see his room?"

"I'm sorry I…"

"Don't give me that old chestnut. I can smell a rat when I see one. Did you lend something to him?"

It was as good as any excuse she could think of. "Yes, I…"

"Not sure you'll find what you're looking for though. Whatever it is. The police took anything of interest."

Hannah sat back down with a thump. She blew her nose again. "Even his briefcase, I assume. He went everywhere with it. I used to tease him about it."

The woman was staring at her but not unkindly. "No, they asked about his briefcase – or the first lot did. But as I told them he didn't leave it here."

"The first lot? The police came twice?" *In so short a time*, Hannah thought.

"That's what I said. And that's who said they said they were. Looking for missing documents. Come on, I'll show you his room."

Hannah followed her up the stairs. There were two rooms with a bathroom separating them. Daniel's was the back room. Melanie Felton opened the door and stood aside. "His sister took all his personal effects left by the police."

"His sister?"

"That's what I thought. He had never mentioned her. Mind you, he never spoke about you either."

"I'm not surprised. I don't suppose it's of any consequence now. Patient confidentiality and all that. But I am, was, his therapist. That's why I was seeing him regularly." It was the best Hannah could come up with.

"Fancy that." She didn't look convinced. "So what exactly are you looking for?"

"I lent him a couple of books and there was a notebook…" Hannah was thinking on her feet. There seemed to be nothing in the room of interest. Nothing to give her an indication of who

Daniel Lyons was. She tried to imagine him here. Sitting in the comfortable armchair by the window overlooking the garden. Or perhaps working at the table above which hung a print of a Parisian scene. The wardrobe and chest of drawers would be empty. But she was trying to imagine a person she'd never seen, let alone someone she'd never met. She hadn't realised Melanie Felton had left her alone in the room until she returned.

"I kept these aside as they had a different name in them. Not his." She handed three books to Hannah.

"Thank you." Books had been an inspired choice.

"Now you have to leave as I have someone coming to see me."

"Of course." Hannah surreptitiously dropped a glove. "Was his sister called Rosa? That was a name he mentioned sometimes."

"No." The landlady offered no other name and led her downstairs to the front door. There were so many questions Hannah wanted to ask but as his therapist it would have been odd if she hadn't already known the answers.

Hannah left the house, turned right and walked until she came to a small shop on the opposite side of the road. She went in and peered out of the window. From this vantage point she would be able to see Melanie Felton's visitor. She did not have long to wait and who she saw made her stop in her tracks. She certainly wasn't expecting to see that person here.

Hannah's lapel camera wasn't good enough to take a distance shot. She looked at herself in the shop window and, deciding her disguise would hold good for a brief encounter, retraced her steps to Melanie Felton's house. Even before she reached the door she could hear the raised voices within. Her knock produced an immediate silence. "See who it is then," hissed a voice she recognised.

Melanie opened the door a fraction. "Oh it's you." She did not open the door further but Hannah had at least switched on her recorder.

"Yes, sorry to bother you again but I think I may have dropped a glove while I was here." Hannah held out the other one to the pair.

Melanie stared at her. "I didn't notice one. But I'll have a look."

Hannah was surprised when she opened the door. "Come in." She left Hannah standing in the hall as she went upstairs in search of the missing glove.

Hannah looked about her. She didn't dare move into one of the ground-floor rooms. But she noticed the visitor had hung her coat over the banister within arm's reach. She slid her hand into the nearer pocket.

"What the hell do you think you're doing?" Melanie had appeared so quickly and silently Hannah was completely thrown.

"I was just admiring the fabric. Looks so warm and…"

"Here's your glove." She almost threw it at Hannah. "Now get out!"

Hannah turned and quickly opened the door, managing to conceal what she had removed from the pocket. She made it to the end of the street in record time and – a miracle – she saw a black cab and hailed it. Once inside she removed the glasses and her wig and took a few deep breaths. The driver eyed her in the mirror but said nothing.

As they pulled up in the road running parallel to her own, the address she had given, he asked, "Need a receipt, love?"

"No thanks." She smiled as she paid him. "Keep the change." The tip was just enough to be unmemorable as either mean or over the top. Hannah watched him drive away, pretending to search for her keys in her bag. Once he had gone, she turned and walked back to her own home. No sense in leaving a trail of clues behind her. Just in case.

TEN

HANNAH MADE SOME COFFEE and sat at the kitchen table staring at Ruth Robertson's purse. It had been utterly reckless, not to mention absolutely wrong, to steal it like that. Idiocy. She found a pair of latex gloves to wear, then wiped the outside of the purse with a tea towel to remove her fingerprints. She opened the purse and tipped out the contents: some loose change and a safety pin. The wallet side held an old photo of two schoolboys, several banknotes and a credit card. She was just thinking that it was a complete waste of time when she found a piece of paper, which she carefully unfolded.

Hannah copied the numbers into her notebook then equally carefully refolded the paper and returned all the contents to the purse.

She rang the bank number that had been on the credit card saying that she'd found the purse and would like to return it to the owner. The clerk at the other end was really helpful. "How kind. Why don't you take it into a local branch and they'll make sure it reaches her."

Perfect, thought Hannah, *and anonymous.* There was a branch on Lordship Lane. She could have taken it in to the police station but she had no wish to give her name and address or even, perish the thought, be recognised. She put the purse in an envelope and on the outside wrote *Found on the street. The credit card inside is for this bank.* On her way to the bank she turned over in her mind how to deliver the envelope. She didn't want to draw attention to herself and was considering how to achieve anonymity when she saw Alesha walking along towards her.

Hannah called out to her and waved. When they were close enough, she asked her to take the envelope into the bank.

Alesha gave her an odd look. "Of course, but why can't you?"

"There's a reason and I'll tell you later."

"Okay." Alesha took the envelope and disappeared into the

bank. She seemed to be gone for ages but it could only have been several minutes later when she reappeared. "Sorry, there was a bit of a queue."

"Did they ask you anything?"

"They asked where it had come from and I said one of my aunties found it." She grinned. "Now you're an honorary auntie."

"In that case, can I take my honorary niece to lunch?"

"I was going to buy a sandwich but that sounds much better. And there's something I'd like to talk about with you."

OVER LUNCH Alesha reminded her that she'd agreed to give another talk at her school.

Hannah paused. She could see how much this meant to Alesha. "Of course, shall we arrange a date for next term?"

Alesha nodded happily. "We do them on Monday evenings but obviously I wouldn't be able to babysit then."

Hannah kept a straight face. "That could be a problem." Then, seeing Alesha's confusion, she relented. "Don't worry, I'm teasing you. I'll ask Janet."

They finished their meal chatting about plans for Christmas.

"Oh and there was another favour I wanted to ask of you?"

"Yes?" Hannah was surprised by the answer.

"I've bought your book for my dad for Christmas and I'd like you to sign it for him."

"That would be an absolute pleasure. Bring it when you next babysit." In the meantime, Hannah thought, she'd have to work out a very special inscription for Sanjay Singh.

STILL THINKING about the name and numbers, she decided to ring Peter Savage to see if he had any more information.

"Sorry, Hannah, nothing really to report. I haven't heard anything from the police."

She pondered how much she should tell. "Did you know Daniel had a sister?"

"No, but not surprising. Most of us have siblings and…"

"I don't. Anyway, Daniel's landlady wouldn't tell me her name or where she lived but apparently she arrived and took whatever belongings the police hadn't taken."

"And her name wasn't Rosa, I suppose."

"No. She wouldn't tell me the sister's name. But you could phone Mrs Felton and find out."

"Yes, I should have done that anyway."

Hannah wondered how to phrase her next question. "Do you know if he had any connection with Ruth Robertson? I think she's one of your parishioners."

"She is. And also not my greatest fan. Why do you ask?"

"Does she know anything about me?"

"I've no idea. Why should she?"

"She was very hostile to me in church yesterday. But to my knowledge I have never met her before."

"Curious." Hannah could hear a pen or pencil tapping. "I think her bark is probably worse than her bite."

"But why is she barking at me?"

"Maybe she's heard of you and your investigations."

"You haven't told anyone about asking me to help you find out more about Daniel Lyons, have you?"

"I certainly have not." The vicar sounded affronted.

"No I didn't think so. Oh just one other thing before I let you go."

"Yes?"

"You said when we first met that you thought someone might be framing you for Daniel's death. Were you serious?"

"I'm not sure but I have a feeling that someone is working against me. Perhaps more than one person."

"Any names?"

"Not that I'd be happy to divulge at the moment, I'm afraid."

And that was what she had to be content with.

DI BENTON REPLACED the telephone in its cradle and walked out into the open plan office. "Listen up, guys. Has anyone come up with the name Jill Bradshaw in connection with Daniel Lyons?" Blank faces met this question. He chuckled to himself. Something about the name rang a bell somewhere. "Okay, bear the name in mind. She could be the dead man's therapist."

He returned to his office frowning. Mrs Melanie Felton had just phoned to tell him that a woman with short blonde hair and heavy-rimmed glasses had visited her purporting to be Daniel's therapist. Apparently, he'd missed their regular appointment and she'd been worried. A cock and bull story, according to the landlady. So now they had two women, Jill Bradshaw and a Mrs Charlotte Jones, supposedly a sister, checking him out. And neither of them was the mysterious Rosa the vicar had been told to contact.

"IS THAT MRS FELTON? Melanie Felton?"

"It is and who is calling?"

"I'm Reverend Peter Savage. From St John's where your lodger, Daniel Lyons, sang in the choir."

"Yes."

Mrs Felton wasn't making it easy for him. "I'm very sorry I haven't been in touch sooner. I wondered if I could call in and see you?"

There was a slight pause. "That won't be necessary, thank you."

The vicar was stumped. People weren't usually so curt with him. Except Hannah Weybridge, he thought. "Well in that case," he tried to sound conciliatory, "I wonder if you have the contact details for Daniel's sister?"

"I'm not sure I'm at liberty to divulge them. Thank you for calling." And with that she hung up.

THE VICAR'S NEXT CALL went far better. DI Benton was at his desk and sounded happy to hear from him.

"What can I do for you, vicar? Or do you have any further information for me?"

"I was rather hoping to get some from you."

"Oh?"

"I've just come off the phone with Daniel's landlady who gave me short shrift, refusing to give me Daniel's sister's contact details."

Benton laughed. "She wasn't that forthcoming with us although she did call after Daniel's therapist turned up at her house."

"His therapist?"

"My thoughts exactly. Name of Jill Bradshaw. Does that ring any bells?"

"None at all, I'm afraid." Peter wondered if this had been Hannah.

"Okay. Well Daniel's sister is a Mrs Charlotte Jones. The problem is her telephone number is disconnected and she doesn't live at the address we were given. Are you still there, vicar?"

"Yes, sorry, I was just thinking. How very strange. To give a false name and address seems…"

"Like she doesn't want to be found. Anyway I'll keep you posted. Oh by the way, we had some results from the post mortem. Definitely looks like poisoning. And could have been self-administered."

The priest felt a wave of nausea hit him. "And the blood?"

"Not his, apparently. Sorry, I have to go now."

THE VICAR REPLACED the receiver slowly. Suicide? Could Daniel Lyons have really felt so desperate that he'd taken his own life? How could no one have known how hopeless he felt? His thoughts turned to the sister. Charlotte Jones – that name seemed to ring a bell in the dark recesses of his mind but for the life of him he couldn't think why.

ELEVEN

WHEN SHE WAS DROPPING ELIZABETH at nursery, Hannah bumped into Fran Croxton rushing out. She gave her a quick hug. "I don't suppose you're free for a drink this evening? I could come round with a bottle."

Hannah agreed after only a moment's hesitation. "Yes it'd be lovely to catch up, Fran. About eight?"

Fran beamed at her. "See you later then. Must dash as I have a big order on. Who'd think it was coming up to Christmas?"

Hannah checked the parents' noticeboard as she was leaving and made a note of the children's Christmas party and the request that parents supply a present for their child valued at no more than five pounds. A new book, thought Hannah. Or a game? As she had some free time she decided to go to the toyshop in Lordship Lane before going home.

The shop was quite full for early on a Tuesday morning. Obviously, some people were making sure of their purchases before the real Christmas rush. Hannah glanced over the books section but then found the games. And there was the perfect gift: Tummy Ache. Hannah looked at the instructions; it was easy to play and required no skills as it was all down to chance, the turn of a card. Before Hannah made her purchase, she continued looking at the array of toys. She had already bought Elizabeth's main present – a red and yellow trike – and she had been collecting small gifts to go into her stocking. She'd go into town to buy her a couple of Christmassy dresses as well.

Hannah smiled to herself, as she picked up a spinning wheel. Someone brushed against her. She froze as she turned to see who it was but found herself in a bear hug. When she could move again she smiled up into James' face.

"So the hospital does let you out occasionally?"

"Just back from a night shift so I took the opportunity to do a spot of Christmas shopping. Do you think Elizabeth would like this?"

He was holding a large Playmobil camper van. Hannah smiled. "I think she'd adore it – and so will I. Although I hope you'll set it up with her."

His tiredness was obvious.

"Are you working over Christmas?"

"Only Christmas Day. I volunteered so others could spend time with their kids."

You would, Hannah thought. "Well if you're not doing anything on Boxing Day would you like to come to lunch at mine? My parents will be here but you'll be able to give Elizabeth her present then."

"I'd love to. Thank you." He tried to hide his yawn. "Sorry, I need to go home before I fall asleep standing up." He hugged her again and only just remembered to pay for his gift before leaving.

HANNAH WAS LOOKING FORWARD to seeing Fran that evening but the knowledge that Albert Croxton was her uncle made her wary. It was strange that Janet who had been at school with her viewed Fran in a more favourable light these days. Hannah could imagine how difficult life for the young Janet would have been when everyone at school knew her father was a policeman. Still it hadn't deterred her from joining the Met. Hannah smiled. Janet was certainly happier living on her own and back in a job she loved. She was delighted she could count on her as a friend, if no longer as a nanny. Of Fran she was more uncertain.

"SO HOW ARE YOU enjoying living with your uncle?" Hannah asked as they sipped their wine in the sitting room.

Fran looked thoughtful. "It's so different. Liberating. To be honest just to be living without the fear of wondering how the bills are going to be paid is such a huge relief."

Hannah nodded. It wasn't so long ago that she had been in that position. "And you hadn't had any idea about Phil's gambling?"

Fran took a large gulp of wine. "No. I didn't know the full extent but I should have guessed from his increased antagonism towards me. The escalation of his violence." Her eyes filled with tears. "Sorry, I feel such an idiot."

"You are not an idiot. Far from it. You run a successful business. You should be proud of your achievements."

Fran sniffed. "I am. But I'm aware that life could have turned out so differently. Without Uncle Albert's help…"

Hannah topped up their glasses. "We all need a helping hand sometimes, Fran. I'm sorry I wasn't much use to you…" Hannah thought back to Harry's birthday party. A photographer had paid Phil so that he could get a photo of her. Plus Phil had indirectly been involved in Elizabeth's abduction…

"Hannah?" Fran's voice brought her back to the present.

"Sorry. I'm glad your uncle has given you some breathing space. And of course I am eternally grateful that he found Elizabeth and Edith."

"Yes, I can't begin to imagine what you went through. And to think I was married to that bastard." She took a deep breath. "Still on a happier note, Uncle Albert has given me a sort of apartment in his house so Harry, Zoë and I can be relatively independent. Zoë loves living with Uncle probably because he spoils her rotten. And we won't be under the feet of his housekeeper who doesn't seem that pleased to have me in residence."

"Oh, I wouldn't have thought that was any of her business."

Fran laughed. "You'd think so. No, I'm being unfair. She's a dragon with a heart of gold."

"If you say so."

"She's babysitting the kids this evening."

"Well at least the children are asleep!" They both giggled. "By the way, I've been meaning to ask you, do you know anyone called Rosa?"

"No, I don't think so. Why?"

Hannah shrugged. "She came up in a conversation and it's an unusual name."

"Sounds intriguing. Are you working on something specific?"

"No, not really. I still have some book publicity to do and then there'll be the paperback launch, but otherwise I'm at a bit of a loose end." Mentally she crossed her fingers. "But it gives me time for all the Christmas preparations with my parents coming over."

For a moment Fran looked sad then finished her wine. "I suppose I'd better be off."

"How will you get home?" Hannah assumed she had driven over but obviously shouldn't drive now though Hannah didn't like to say as much.

Fran winked. "Another benefit of living with my uncle – I have his driver at my disposal." She took out her mobile phone and made her call. "Thank you for this evening. It's been lovely to relax with someone who understands."

Hannah wasn't sure what she was supposed to have understood. She gave Fran her coat. "Have you bought a present for the nursery Christmas party?"

"I have. In fact I've done most of my Christmas shopping, as I know I'll be frantic with last-minute orders." Her phone rang once. She glanced at it. "My chariot awaits."

Hannah saw her to the door. They hugged briefly and Fran ran to the car. *I wonder if we'll have a white Christmas,* Hannah thought as she locked the door on the night chill. As she collected the empty wine bottle and their glasses, Hannah thought about Fran's reaction to the mention of Rosa. Had she replied rather too quickly? There was no pause for consideration. Or was she reading too much into their conversation?

Later in bed, her last thought before sleep claimed her was of the mysterious Rosa and who she might be and her relationship to the enigmatic Daniel Lyons.

TWELVE

CHRISTMAS WAS GOING TO BE so different this year. Elizabeth would soon be two and much more aware of all the festivities. Memories of last year when they had gone to her parents' home in the Loire and Tom had been with them threatened to overwhelm her. It seemed a lifetime ago. A time when Liz was still alive and … And now Tom was in Australia and would be, it seemed, for the foreseeable future. And was seeing someone else, according to Claudia Turner. Hannah didn't dwell on that thought. She was looking forward to having her parents stay. She wanted this year to be extra special after everything she'd put them through.

HANNAH STUDIED THE CARD the priest had left for her on the mantelpiece: a Christmas message and a list of services over the festive season. One was a Christingle for children. Hannah had no idea what that entailed but it might be a fun thing to do with Elizabeth on Christmas Eve. And her parents would probably enjoy it. The thought of singing in the choir at Midnight Mass filled her with anxiety. Then she chided herself for being a fool. It wasn't as if she'd be singing solos. As long as she began and finished in the right places and looked as though she knew what she was doing she'd be fine. If all else failed she could mime the high notes. And before that there'd be the carol service – that was an afternoon as well so Elizabeth could go with her parents.

She searched through her collection of CDs – somewhere, she knew, was one of Christmas carols. She found it at last – King's College Cambridge Choir – and put it into the player in her study and listened as she cleared her desk, thinking that Elizabeth would enjoy them as well. On listening a second time she sang along as best she could. At least she was giving her vocal chords a workout. She thought she'd attend choir practice from the beginning as there was bound to be a vocal warm-up then, and while the others were concentrating on the regular service hymns, she could sit to one side and study them.

As she sang or hummed along to the carols and caught up with her filing, she thought about the vicar. Surely he didn't really believe that someone was trying to frame him for murder? If, of course, it was murder. She wondered if the police had had the post mortem report and what it revealed. Could she ask DI Benton? Would he tell her? Probably he'd tell Peter Savage – eventually.

She rang the vicar. "Hello, Hannah, what a nice surprise. How can I help you?"

She thought that was a bit rich since he was the one who had turned up on her doorstep asking for help. Then, feeling more generous, she realised he was probably in vicar mode ready to talk to his parishioners.

"I was just wondering if the police have told you the results of the post mortem, if they have them yet?"

There was a slight pause. "As a matter of fact, DI Benton did mention some of the results." He sounded preoccupied. "Apparently Daniel was poisoned or poisoned himself. They're still trying to source the exact poison but it must have been slow acting."

Exasperation was bubbling up inside her. "And you didn't think to tell me?"

"No, I – to be perfectly honest I wasn't sure if it was confidential."

Hannah counted to ten. "Well, I'm going to choir practice this evening. Is there anything I should know?"

There was a moment's silence. "Perhaps it would be better if you attend without any preconceptions then we could discuss any thoughts you have afterwards."

"Fine."

They ended the call. Murder or suicide? Either way the poor man was dead. Until she knew more about him she wouldn't know. Someone must know him. Finding Rosa was becoming imperative to solving the case and she herself was a mystery. Would anyone in the choir know more about either of them?

Her stomach churned at the thought of the evening ahead. She had no idea about the dynamics of a church choir. Was there a hierarchy among singers? Would they be welcoming to or resentful of newcomers or "extras" as the musical director described them? Did they socialise together and form a tight-knit group or were there the usual jealousies and competitiveness among them, as in most groups? Probably both, she thought, wondering yet again why on earth she had agreed to this.

"WELCOME, HANNAH, you're nice and early."

Hannah returned Craig Fletcher's smile. "I thought I'd probably need the warm-up exercises."

"Good. Everything you need is on the table. We'll be starting in a few minutes."

Hannah removed her coat. "There're hangers over there for coats and things." Hannah hadn't noticed the person who spoke when she'd entered the vestry. A small woman with grey hair tied in a ponytail and rather large, blue-framed glasses. Her clothes looked a size too big; she shuffled towards Hannah, holding out her hand and smiling. "I'm Lorraine. I look after all the music and sing alto. Lovely to have you join our ranks."

"Thank you. I'm Hannah, I..."

"You're Leah's neighbour," Lorraine finished for her and pointed to the music before moving away as other people started coming in.

Hannah picked up the carol books and sheet music. Plus an A4 sheet with the list of music for the carol service and Midnight Mass:

Carol Service
Choir: Once in Royal David's City 1st 2 verses
Congregation: O R D City last four
Choir: Adam lay ybounden – Boris Ord
Congregation: Silent Night
Choir: O Holy Night – Adolphe Adam
Congregation: O Little Town of Bethlehem
Congregation: Away in a manger 1st verse kids
Choir: In the bleak midwinter – Harold Darke
Congregation: O come all ye faithful
Midnight Mass

Choir: The Angel Gabriel – Edgar Pettman
Congregation: O little town of Bethlehem
Congregation: In the bleak midwinter
Choir: The Infant King – Edgar Pettman
Congregation: Hark! The Herald Angels

She hadn't realised she had sighed so loudly until she looked up and saw a young black woman, wearing jeans and a vivid red polo neck jumper, was smiling at her. Hannah recognised her from the service on Sunday. "Hi, I'm Dinah. My first time here." There was a confidence about her that Hannah envied.

"Mine too."

"Soprano. How about you?"

Hannah had considered this and thought that although she might not hit all the high notes she would be familiar with the melodies.

"Same. I've heard sopranos have all the fun."

Dinah winked at her; her expression was, *seriously? Here?*

The vestry was becoming more crowded with other members of the choir who greeted each other with various degrees of affability and threw curious glances their way. A few smiled. Hannah tried to make mental notes about each of them. Surreptitiously she took photos with the concealed camera she still had, hoping she'd be able to put names to faces later. They seemed to have set places to sit and were, Hannah supposed, grouped into sopranos, altos, tenors and bass. She and Dinah remained where they were, by the table.

"Right, everyone. Dinah and Hannah are joining us for the Christmas services. So make sure they feel welcome." *What strange phraseology*, thought Hannah. A few smiled or nodded at them. A couple cast curious glances.

"We'll begin as usual with a prayer. Please stand, everyone." There was a moment's silence. "Heavenly Father, we offer our hearts and voices to Your praise and glory." He paused and Hannah stared as his Adam's apple rose and fell. "And we pray for the soul of our departed brother, Daniel. Amen."

The "amen" was repeated by the choristers, some of whom were visibly upset. Hannah realised a chair had been left empty between the tenors and the basses. A cassock and surplice were folded on the seat.

"Right, let's start with some scales…" Craig played a cord on the keyboard and led them through several scales and vowel sounds.

Hannah managed not to disgrace herself but Dinah's voice rang out with beautiful clarity. She grinned at Hannah as they sat out the service hymns. "Used to go to a gospel church," she said by way of explanation, before intercepting a glare from one of the tenors, and made a guilty face at Hannah who leafed through the sheet music, relieved that she'd at least heard of most of the carols. Listening to her CD had paid off. But she had never heard of any of the carols to be sung by the choir. This was going to be harder than she'd imagined.

Hannah was fascinated watching the interaction between the choristers. There were fifteen, not counting herself and Dinah. One of the altos was constantly sipping from a take-away coffee cup. At one point she looked as though she was about to nod off. Hannah caught one of the tenors miming her drinking. The cup, she assumed, wasn't filled with by now cold coffee. The musical director played a loud chord on the keyboard, which jolted her from her snooze. "Hazel, you missed the entry there." For a moment she looked disorientated, then smiled at Craig and the singing continued.

As Hannah absorbed the atmosphere, it struck her that one of the people here could be the perpetrator, if indeed Daniel had been unlawfully killed. It was a distinctly uncomfortable thought and she shifted awkwardly in her chair and exhorted herself to act professionally. She was here for a reason and that wasn't to improve her musical skills. She needed to focus on the people here.

Hannah had brought a notebook with her, drew a circle and added names as they became apparent during the practice. Dinah leaned over and wrote Noel in one of the spaces. She smiled and revealed her own notebook page with a similar circle of names. *Old trick I use for work meetings*, she wrote as an explanation. Hannah didn't have time to reply as the singing stopped.

"Right, let's make a start on the carols. Dinah, Hannah – if you'd like to join us? Could the altos move up two seats?" Two of them made a great fuss of moving from one chair to another just as there was a flurry of activity as the door flew open and a large man, followed by a slim, hawkish woman, strode into the room.

"Not too late, are we?"

Two other men followed. A waft of alcohol indicated they'd probably all been to the pub first.

"No, come in and join us. We're just about to start." Hannah couldn't work out whether the musical director was pleased to see them or irritated at their exuberance.

Hawkish woman joined the altos. The men distributed themselves between tenors and basses. One went to sit on the chair marking Daniel's absence and immediately thought the better of it. Hannah didn't think she needed to concentrate on the newcomers. What she did need to do was make friends with at least one of the established choir members. The woman sitting to her right had a pleasant air about her and had smiled when she sat down. "It's the other book," she whispered as Hannah searched for the first carol. She pointed to the page number in her own copy.

Hannah hadn't realised how hard a choir rehearsed; the musical director proved to be a demanding task master and she struggled to keep up. At one point one of the extras, a tall, rather good-looking man, commented that one of the sopranos was flat in a certain phrase. Hannah could feel her colour rising but the woman next to her said, "Sorry – lost myself for a moment."

AT THE END of the session Craig said, "Right. Plenty of work to do but we made a good start. Stand please. Let us pray." Everyone stood and joined Craig in saying, "May the grace of our Lord Jesus Christ, the love of God and the fellowship of the Holy Spirit be with us all. Amen."

Hannah mumbled an amen and let out a sigh of relief.

"Wasn't that bad, was it?" said the woman sitting next to her. "I'm Marianne, by the way. I saw you in church on Sunday with your adorable daughter. She seems quite a character."

"Yes, she has her moments and not always at the appropriate

time. Do you have children?" Hannah could have kicked herself as she saw a sadness fill those deep brown eyes.

But the other woman smiled. "No. Do you need a lift? I'm going towards Peckham."

"That's very kind of you but I live in the opposite direction."

"Well, see you next week then if we haven't frightened you off." She looked at Hannah strangely. "I don't know if you are aware that one of our number, Daniel Lyons, was found dead in the church after last week's rehearsal?"

Hannah waited for her to say more. "Of course, silly me. Father Peter mentioned it in his sermon. Still, it's hit us all in different ways, I suppose."

"Did you know him well?"

"Not really. He hadn't been with us for very long but there was something about him – I'm probably just being fanciful. Have a good week." She pulled on her hat and scarf, shouted, "Night, all," over the general hubbub and left.

"Would you like a lift?" Dinah had slipped into her coat but hadn't seemed in a hurry to leave. She'd been chatting to one of the tenors. Hannah had observed them while she was talking to Marianne.

"I'm only going up the road."

"A short lift then." She smiled and Hannah accepted, thinking how cold and dark it was outside.

Dinah had parked her car right outside the church. "Okay, where to?" she asked after they strapped themselves in.

Hannah noticed how clean the inside of the vehicle was. Dinah had thrown her bag on the back seat. It was partially open and Hannah thought she saw a wallet that looked vaguely familiar.

She gave her address. "So what did you think of tonight then?" Dinah looked into the mirror and indicated. "I've sung in a few other choirs but they were a lot friendlier."

"Perhaps they weren't recently bereaved."

"True. Seemed a bit strange that no one really mentioned the dead chorister except Craig at the beginning."

"Maybe they've been told not to discuss him."

"Possibly." Dinah gave her a sidelong glance. "Still, I enjoyed the singing."

"You have a beautiful voice." Hannah had been envious of the way the other woman had integrated seamlessly into the sopranos.

Dinah laughed. "It's okay. And so's yours, you just need a bit more confidence."

"We'll see." Hannah remembered the note. "What sort of work meetings do you have then?"

Dinah indicated to turn left. "Used to be the bane of my life. Moved into another department in the civil service." She didn't say what. "How about you?"

"In communications but I'm between contracts at the moment." Two could play at that game. Hannah was playing her own cards close to her chest.

They had arrived outside Hannah's house. "Thanks for the lift. See you next week."

Dinah grinned. "Or at church on Sunday?"

"Perhaps." She noticed Dinah's appraising glance. "Yes, I suppose I should be there. Thanks again." Hannah noticed Dinah waited until she'd let herself in before driving off.

THIRTEEN

LEAH HAD BEEN BABYSITTING for her. "How did it go?" She closed the book she'd been reading and smiled.

"Challenging. Do you have time for a chat?"

"I do. Brian's out with his badminton group this evening so I'm all yours." She looked relaxed and at home in Hannah's sitting room.

"Fancy a glass of wine, then?"

"Twist my arm."

Hannah returned with the wine and glasses. "Have you been going to St John's long?"

"More or less since we moved here. I like the people – well most of them."

"So what can you tell me about the vicar?"

Leah didn't reply and contemplated her glass. "It's bizarre," she said at last. "Peter has been with us for nearly two years yet some people still call him the 'new vicar'. It's undermining, don't you think?"

Hannah shrugged. "I've no idea. He did mention that his appointment wasn't universally accepted."

Leah sipped her wine. "He's had a few run-ins with some of the PCC, not to mention Ruthless. I think she propositioned him."

Hannah nearly spat her wine. "You are joking? Isn't he gay?"

"He's single and that was enough for Ruth."

"And the PCC members?"

"Oh the usual stuff – people who don't like change and want everything to stay as it used to be."

"And how does the choir fit into all of this?"

"Craig is very accommodating. He doesn't rock the boat but he does like the choir to be given a free rein. Sometimes Peter feels the choir is given too much prominence."

"Aren't all choirs?" Hannah just assumed this to be the case.

"Possibly." Leah sipped her wine. "They're a mixed bunch, aren't they? Did you get to talk to any of them?"

"They weren't that friendly, that's for sure. Marianne, one of the sopranos, was very nice. Someone called Hazel, an alto, looked as if she was falling asleep."

"Mm." Leah looked as though she might say more but didn't. "Was Noel there? He's a nice guy. Teaches in the local secondary school. Maths, I think. He's married to Sarah, another teacher. She sings soprano. Red-headed and rather pretty."

Hannah recalled she was sitting the other side of Marianne. "Yes, fabulous hair. There was an older woman singing soprano, I didn't get her name."

"Lorraine?"

"No, she introduced herself. She organises all the music."

"Oh yes. She was a librarian before she retired. The other one must be Carol. She's not as old as she looks. A solicitor, I believe."

"The altos seemed a bit grumpy. Two took exception to moving for us to join the sopranos."

"Us?"

"A black woman called Dinah was there. I saw her in church on Sunday."

"Oh yes, always wears brightly coloured jumpers. I bet the grumpy altos were Rosie Ball and April Hunter. I think they suck lemons for fun."

Hannah laughed and refilled their glasses. Leah smiled as though at a memory that had just wafted into her mind. "Do you believe in the supernatural?"

The question threw Hannah. She stared at her. "What do you mean?" And in that moment there was a strong smell of freesia in the room. It had been some time since she'd experienced that. "Ghosts?"

Leah shook her head. "I suppose I mean something that is extra, beyond our experiences. Or rather beyond our understanding."

Hannah remained silent. She was intrigued to hear what Leah was going to say although she did have an inkling.

"You remember when my brother contacted me?" Hannah nodded. Leah's brother had been part of the Child Migration Scheme to Australia. Their parents had been told he had died.

Adam, like many of the children involved, had been told their families hadn't wanted them. They shared a smile at the memory. "It was such a relief as I had spent so much of my life over-shadowed by my parents' grief. Something was always missing but it was as though my body, my cells knew differently. And then I spoke to him and everything fell into place. My world changed, was given a new meaning. An extra or super." She paused as though embarrassed by her words.

Hannah took a deep breath. "Can you smell the freesia?"

Leah looked at her askance.

"There's a strong smell of freesia in the room. At least there is for me."

Leah looked at her wide-eyed. She reached out and held Hannah's hand. "Who d'you think it comes from?"

Hannah noticed that she didn't ask 'what', but 'who'. "I don't know. I like to think it's from Liz, you know my friend who was killed... she knew how much I adored freesia."

"And maybe it is. I sometimes get a lovely sensation when I bake a cherry cake – my father's favourite – it feels like a benediction. And I don't care if it's just wishful thinking." She sipped her drink. "Maybe your freesia is similar."

"Perhaps it is. But..." Hannah stared into the distance.

"But?"

"I feel silly saying this but sometimes I think I see people who aren't or couldn't possibly be there."

Leah concentrated on her glass of wine. "Go on."

"You'll think I'm mad."

Leah giggled. "No madder than I think of you now for all the dangerous situations you get yourself into." Just a gentle rebuke.

Hannah breathed deeply. "In the summer I was in the pub by *The News* offices and I looked across the bar and saw Paul. Well I thought I saw him but of course he was on remand then. But later that day I heard he'd died... and I wondered if his spirit was reaching out to me. Or if it was a warning."

Leah didn't dismiss her idea. "Who knows what happens when our souls leave our bodies. You ought to talk to Peter about this. He's –" she paused as though searching for an apt description – "he's very knowledgeable."

Hannah wasn't so sure and she certainly wasn't going to leave herself prey to a priest's manipulations. "He did something curious when he came here."

"Oh? What?"

"He made the sign of the cross, I think, and mumbled something I couldn't make out."

"A blessing. Or perhaps a protection."

Hannah looked at her aghast. "A protection? From what? Me?"

Leah said nothing for a moment. "Maybe it was a prayer to protect you." She saw Hannah's face pale. "I'm not saying you need protection…"

Hannah tried to relax. "Oh I think we could all do with some protection from time to time. Did I tell you someone slashed the strap on my bag in town last week?"

Leah's face was a picture. "No. Oh, Hannah, how awful for you."

"Well I was with Rory but…" She drank some wine, her mind going back over the incident and the note she'd been handed.

"But?"

"Well you never know, do you?"

Leah looked as though she was about to ask more but changed the subject. "Do you know that Peter trained as a priest as a second career?"

"Oh really, what did he do before?"

"I think he was a solicitor or something… he doesn't talk about personal things often. You have to grasp the nuggets of information when they come your way."

They both laughed. "But you do like him?"

Leah finished her drink. "He's been very good to me."

That wasn't what Hannah had asked but that was the only answer on offer.

"And now I must take my leave of you." Leah picked up her book.

Hannah saw her to the door. "Thank you so much for babysitting."

"Any time." Leah hugged her as she left and Hannah watched her cross the road and let herself into her own home. As she was closing her door, Hannah glimpsed the shadow of a fox walking along the pavement. He paused at her gate and stared in for a moment before moving on. Hannah smiled at what she considered her security patrol. Of course she couldn't be sure it was always the same fox but she liked to think it was, and she locked the door on the winter's night with a lighter heart.

FOURTEEN

THE CAR FROM THE STUDIO arrived bang on time. Hannah
had taken Elizabeth to nursery early so she would have time to
prepare herself for the interview. *Joan Ballantyne: A Life* was
garnering more and more interest. Hannah had assumed there
would be a flurry of interest then it would die down. At least until
the paperback release. However it was holding its own in the
bestseller lists, and certainly *The News* – and some other papers –
mentioned it whenever the opportunity arose. Plus there was the
matter of police corruption in the form of former DS Tony
Farnham, whose actions were linked to Joan's death. The
police investigation had also linked him to the murder of Sam
Smith. Hannah wondered if Tom Jordan had heard about the demise of his former snout. She hadn't liked to ask Marti when she
saw her at the funeral. Marti had looked broken.

"I'm so sorry for your loss." Hannah had kicked herself for
saying those silly trite words at the funeral. What a cliché. But what
do you say? "Sam was a good friend to me." Marti nodded.
A young boy, her son, was by her side looking tearful. He was
wearing his school uniform to what was presumably his first funeral.

There weren't many people there. A few from The Old Vic
had turned up. Hannah was surprised to see that Sir David Powys
was there and so was Albert Croxton. *Yes*, thought Hannah, *you
would be here*. It was a statement of his authority. Sam had been
paid by Croxton to be his eyes and ears in the theatre. Sadly, it
hadn't worked and both Joan Ballantyne and Sam had been murdered. Albert Croxton stopped beside her before leaving.

"He spoke about you, you know," he said quietly without
preamble.

Hannah felt a trickle of fear but realised there was no threat
in his words. "He was so proud of you."

Hannah was stunned.

Albert chuckled. "He told me about the time you had completely fooled him in your disguise as a homeless person. He said you had guts. I think you do too." He smiled and touched her arm. "Right, I'm going to take Marti home. Take care, Hannah." Hannah was confused. There was no implicit or explicit threat from Albert Croxton. He appeared concerned, avuncular. Maybe she was getting things out of proportion in her mind. Seeing threats where none existed.

"We're here, Miss." Hannah was brought back to the present. The car had turned into Broadcasting House and the driver got out to open the door for her. "Just over there. Through the main doors and reception will sort you out."

"Thank you." Hannah inhaled deeply. The cold air made her pull her coat more tightly around her as she made her way into the building.

"SO HOW DID YOU FEEL taking over Joan Ballantyne's autobiography?"

Hannah was ready for this, as she had been asked the same question many times before. "It was a privilege to continue what we had started working on together. Joan was an immensely private person but she had left clues as to how she'd have wanted the narrative to proceed."

"Do you think she knew she was going to die then?"

Hannah glared at the women. What a stupid question. "I have no idea. But she certainly knew someone was trying to intimidate her. I had access to all her private papers…"

"And her son, the actor Leo Hawkins, no doubt helped on a personal level."

What the… "Leo Hawkins was seriously ill as I finished the book. An attempt had been made on his life and…"

Hannah's throat constricted, and she reached forward for the glass of water in front of her and sipped as she mentally counted to ten.

"But once again, Hannah, you had a front-page story – as well as a bestselling book on your hands…"

"I hope you are not implying that I made capital out of the fact that my daughter was kidnapped?"

The interviewer changed tack. "Of course not. That is, I imagine, every parent's worst nightmare. But did you even not question yourself afterwards for putting your daughter at risk?"

Hannah wanted to scream but managed to plough on with the interview. "Of course I did. But I wonder if you would ask the same question of a male journalist who was also a father?"

Fifteen minutes felt like fifteen hours…

"Well thank you, Hannah Weybridge, for your insights. *Joan Ballantyne: A life* is published by Halstone Books and would make a great Christmas present for especially for fans of *Chicory Road.*"

HANNAH COULDN'T WAIT to get out of the recording studio. In the corridor the PR from Halstone Books, Ciara Burns, was waiting for her. "Sorry I wasn't here to meet you. Got held up. But I listened to the interview. Went well, I thought."

"Well that's where you and I will have to disagree."

Ciara looked confused. "*Ok–ay.* Anyway we have a lunch now with Ian Cuthbert, who's writing a spotlight piece for *The Bookseller.*"

Hannah looked at her watch. Midday. "Why didn't you mention this before? It's not on the schedule."

Ciara smiled. "Last-minute addition but I didn't think you'd mind."

Hannah sighed. This was the downside to writing a book. She had to jump through hoops for the publicity team. "Okay, where are we going?"

A MAN STOOD as they walked into the Dean Street restaurant. "Hello, Hannah, Ian Cuthbert. Thank you so much for agreeing to this so late in the day."

Hannah tried her best to fashion a smile on her face. He looked over at the PR and pushed his glasses up his nose. Ian's fair hair was sparse and his skin had an unhealthy pallor. A crumpled suit did little to improve her impression of him. A burst of laughter from a neighbouring table seemed to bring them all back to reality.

"Do sit down, Hannah." A waiter hovered nearby. "Shall we order then get on with the questions?"

Ciara took her time choosing what to have while Ian and Hannah decided quickly.

"Wine?" the waiter asked.

"Sparkling water for me please." The PR and journalist exchanged a look, obviously expecting, or hoping for, a boozy lunch. Hannah wanted to get the meal over as soon as possible so she could go home and collect Elizabeth from nursery.

"So," Ian said. "I've read the book – which I really enjoyed by the way – and I have the background info. All I need is a few quotes to bring the article to life."

Hannah sipped her water and nodded. Her heart was sinking lower by the second.

"You were working with Joan Ballantyne on her memoir. What was your first thought when you heard she had died?"

Hannah stared at him. Crass idiot. "I was shocked and saddened, obviously."

"But you didn't think she had killed herself?"

Hannah paused for a moment. "At first I just heard she had died. Then there was the speculation that she had taken her own life. Nothing I had learned about her would have led me to that conclusion…" Her phone rang. "I'm so sorry, I have to take this."

She turned away from the table. "Hannah, it's Rory. We've just had confirmation that Albert Croxton has been shot down outside his home. He was still alive when emergency services arrived. Just thought you ought to know."

Hannah felt a lurch in her stomach. The world tilted on its axis. Now what was going on? She'd thought Croxton had highly trained security staff. This didn't make sense. "Thank you. Keep me posted."

Hannah turned to her companions. "I've just had some distressing news and have to get home. I'm so sorry, Ian. If you need anything else perhaps you could phone me tomorrow?"

Ian stood as she did and took her arm. "I'll see you to a cab."

"There's really no need. I…"

"You're as white as the proverbial ghost." They walked out onto the street and Ian hailed a black cab. "I'm so sorry for whatever has upset you, Hannah," he said before closing the door. He sounded genuinely concerned.

Hannah gave her address to the driver and leaned back into the seat. Her phone rang again. It was Janet. "I don't know whether you've heard but Albert Croxton…"

Hannah swallowed hard. "I just had a call from Rory. Do you know how he is?"

"Still alive. I just wondered if you could contact Fran. She'll be all over the place and won't know how to deal with the media interest."

"I'm on my way home now. I'll call her."

"Okay, I'll speak to you later."

Strange, that Janet should be so concerned for Fran. Hannah wondered why. She dialled Fran's work number. Engaged. Or off the hook? She also had a mobile number for her. She rang that and Fran answered immediately.

"God, I'm relieved it's you, Hannah. It's been a nightmare here …"

"What can I do to help? I'm on my way home and then to collect Elizabeth from nursery. I could pick up Harry as well and keep him with us for a while."

"Oh would you? That would be brilliant. I'll ring the nursery to confirm."

"Right, don't worry about him – do whatever you need to do for your uncle."

HANNAH HAD THE CAB drop her at the nursery. She noticed a few extra cars around. Paparazzi waiting for Fran? Well they'd have a long wait. She drew no interest as she went inside to collect the children.

Elizabeth was ecstatic to have her friend coming home with her, making Hannah realise she should do more socially for her child. She loved playing with other children, Harry especially. She would have to think about a birthday party – perhaps.

They played happily constructing Duplo edifices and populating them with Elizabeth's collection of animals bought at their visits to the Horniman Museum.

After a meal, they curled up together on a sofa to watch Elizabeth's favourite video. Apparently it was Harry's too, and their giggles made Hannah smile.

Her mobile rang, and assuming it was Fran, she answered.

"Hannah – I assume you've heard about Albert Croxton?"

Mike Benton's voice sounded tired.

"Yes. Do you know how he is?"

"In ICU. Apparently, the op to remove the bullet went well. I just wanted to… to alert you to be careful."

Hannah could feel her whole body tensing. "Do you think I'm at risk?"

"Not sure until we find out more."

"I have Fran's son here."

The DI swore under his breath and she half-heard him say something to somebody in the same room as him.

"Okay, I'll get back to you." He hung up.

The doorbell rang and Hannah froze. She checked the video screen and saw Fran standing outside.

Opening the door, Hannah saw how exhausted the other woman looked and gave her a quick hug. "Harry's been fine. I'm sorry I didn't even think to ask who was collecting Zoë."

"She was picked up from Afterschool Club by Uncle Albert's housekeeper as usual to try to keep things as normal as possible."

"Of course. How's your uncle?"

She shrugged. "As well as can be expected. The surgeons seemed pleased. Look, I'm sorry, I can't stop. I've a car waiting outside."

"Where are you staying?"

"At my uncle's of course." Her expression gave nothing away. "It's home – we'll be safe there."

Hannah had her doubts, as that was where her uncle had been shot, but said nothing. Fran followed her into the sitting room and Harry threw himself into her arms with a screech of, "Mummy!"

Elizabeth looked sad that her little friend was leaving.

"Thank you so much, Hannah. I don't think Harry will be at nursery tomorrow but I'll be in touch."

As Fran and Harry left, Hannah saw that it was a police car waiting for her. Well at least she was being looked after.

"Let me know if you need anything."

"I will. And thanks again."

Elizabeth seemed thoughtful as Hannah took her upstairs for a bath. "Did you like having Harry here to play?"

Elizabeth kissed her cheek. "Yes." She said no more but chattered to herself in the bath and tottered into her bedroom, to choose a book. Hannah sighed. *Each Peach* again! They'd go to the bookshop soon and see if Hannah could wean her onto some new titles. For this evening *I spy Tom Thumb* would rule.

FIFTEEN

ON THE WAY BACK from taking Elizabeth to nursery the next morning, Hannah bought all the newspapers. The Albert Croxton shooting had made a couple of front pages but not, she noted with some surprise, that of *The News*. There he featured in a low-key piece – for the tabloid – on page four. They downplayed the incident and Hannah assumed that most of the news editors were holding back to see if the former gangster would survive.

When her phone rang she was surprised to hear the voice of Reverend Peter Savage asking if it would be convenient to call in to see her.

He arrived looking haggard and stressed. Again as he entered he made the sign of the cross and mumbled a few words.

"Why do you do that?" Hannah felt ill at ease and hadn't slept well, worry about the implications of the attempt on Albert Croxton's life disturbing her sleep. Fran's uncle had freed Elizabeth and Edith from their kidnappers although she had no idea of the details but she assumed he was behind the bombing at the Soho club. Did that implicate her? She should phone Edith.

"Do what?" The priest looked perplexed.

"Make the sign of the cross and mumble some words."

"The sign of the cross is a benediction and I pray for the health and safety of you and Elizabeth. Nothing sinister, I promise you." His smile accentuated the sadness in his eyes.

Hannah shrugged. "You look as though you could do with a coffee."

He followed her into the kitchen. She wondered how often he had sat in Leah's welcoming kitchen with its plants and spices and the promise of delicious cakes. He however seemed taken with Elizabeth's artwork, which adorned the walls and odd photos on the fridge door.

"What a lovely room." He paused. "I visited someone recently – a young single parent, who is doing a great job of bringing up her son on her own. But the kitchen – the house – was clinical. Pristinely clean but not a photo or picture. Nothing to indicate their life. Then while we were talking she told me she'd been brought up in a children's home. It hadn't been a terrible existence. They were warm, clothed, fed but there was no joy. It wasn't a 'home'."

Hannah was waiting for the punchline. Nothing. "How sad."

"I introduced her to someone I thought might be able to help." He laughed. "When I went back yesterday, I nearly tripped over a truck in the hallway and her little boy was having the time of his life painting a picture – and getting as much paint on himself as the paper. His mother looked flustered and started apologising then stopped herself and giggled. It made me think of the child she could have been in a loving environment…" He stared at a blotch of colours on some blue paper. "I'm sorry, I…"

Hannah was mystified. "Shall we have coffee in the sitting room?" She carried the tray through with the priest in her wake.

"So what can I do for you?" Hannah asked when they were both seated.

"I was wondering if you had made any progress about Daniel Lyons? The police seem very quiet on the subject."

Hannah decided on honesty – almost. "I went to where Daniel was living. His landlady didn't seem to know much about him. I thought it was strange that he was a lodger like that. She said he worked in insurance fraud or something. I got the feeling it wasn't a long-term arrangement. So perhaps he has a flat or house elsewhere?"

The vicar looked thoughtful.

"Apparently a sister collected his belongings. She was quick off the mark. Mrs Felton wouldn't give me any details."

"She gave them to the police."

Hannah was mystified as to why he had been holding back on information that might help her investigation. "If you would like to share them with me I could check her out."

"No point. The phone number was disconnected and she wasn't living at the address she gave."

"How curious. Someone seems to be covering their traces." Should she mention the other person who had turned up at Mrs

Felton's? Perhaps not for the moment.

"How did you get on in the choir?"

"Okay. Craig mentioned Daniel in a prayer at the beginning but other than that, nothing. Curiously what I assumed were his robes were neatly folded on a chair where he would have sat, I presume."

The priest shrugged. "Maybe it's a choir tradition."

"Maybe. I chatted to a couple of other people there. I don't think Daniel made much of an impression. A woman called Dinah seemed very nice. Beautiful voice."

"Yes." He didn't meet her eye. "Will you come on Sunday?"

Hannah wasn't sure if that was an invitation or an enquiry.

"I thought I would. Elizabeth seemed to enjoy the service. And you never know, I might pick up some information if people get used to seeing me."

"That's true and I do appreciate your help."

"Maybe you can help me?"

"Oh?" He looked surprised as though Hannah needing help was the last thing he associated with her. "Of course, if I can."

Hannah jumped up. "Excuse me, I just want to get something to show you. Help yourself to more coffee."

She went up to her study and collected the notebook in which she'd copied down the numbers from the slip of paper in the purse.

"Here," she said, returning to the room. "Have you any idea what these numbers could mean?"

Peter Savage studied the piece of paper. "Is it relevant to Daniel?"

"It could be." Hannah could hardly own up to stealing a wallet from someone's coat pocket.

"Well, if it has a religious significance, I'd say it was a reference to some biblical verses. The first number could be the book. The second would be the chapter and the third and fourth hyphenated numbers the verses." He looked up and smiled.

Hannah smiled back at him. "Easy when you know how."

"Yes, the first number refers to the book of Matthew. Chapter 7 verses 1 to 3. Do you have a bible we could look at?"

"I'll get it." Excitement was bubbling up. Would the machinations of Ruth Robertson now be revealed? Hannah returned with the bible she'd won at some competition at school, and handed it to the priest who quickly found the relevant passage:

"Don't criticise, and then you won't be criticised. For others will treat you as you treat them. Why worry about a speck in the eye of a brother when you have a plank in your own?"

Peter smiled at her. "Does that help in any way?"

Hannah considered the words. "It may do. I'm not sure." She wondered why that woman would have kept that in her wallet. Was it a code for her or to pass on to someone else? She could hardly ask her.

"Any news on Daniel Lyons' briefcase?"

"No, that seems to have disappeared." Peter finished his coffee and stood to leave. In the hall he looked at her and smiled. "There's always a delightful fragrance of freesia in your home."

Hannah could feel the blood drain from her face as she placed a hand against the wall to steady herself. "You smell it too?"

"Yes. Are you okay, Hannah?" He reached out to steady her then led her back into the sitting room.

"You're the only other person who's ever noticed it. The freesia, I mean…"

Peter Savage smiled at her. "Do you think it's anything to worry about?"

Hannah shook her head. "No not really." She looked at his face, which was full of compassion. "Actually I find it sort of reassuring."

"Why?"

"I had a friend, Liz, who was murdered at the beginning of the year. She knew freesia is my favourite flower and often bought them for me." She scratched her hands. "I know this probably sounds mad but it's like she's still with me, sending a sign."

"And it could well be so. It's a nice, comforting thought."

Hannah took a deep breath. "I've never seen her though."

The vicar looked confused. "But does that mean you think you've seen other people who have died?"

Hannah stared at her hands. "I thought I had… It could have been a trick of the light or something. I don't know." She looked up at the priest. "I think I saw Elizabeth's father in a pub but at the time he was in prison. And I learned later that he had died at about that time."

Peter took hold of both her hands. His felt warm and comforting. There seemed to be an energy. But not only that, a kindness. Compassion. "Look upon it as a gift," was all he said for a long time. She could feel herself relaxing and her eyes filled with tears. "Try not to struggle with it, Hannah." He looked down at their entwined hands. "I could say it's a blessing from God but I'm not sure I'd convince you." He smiled – sadly, she thought. "Just accept and see what happens."

IT OCCURRED TO HER after the vicar had left that neither of them had mentioned the shooting of Albert Croxton. He didn't live in the parish but Hannah thought he'd have heard from one of his neighbouring colleagues. She thought Albert was the type of man to turn up at his local church periodically. He enjoyed his status and would probably have written large cheques when it came to fundraising. Hannah sighed at her own cynicism.

SIXTEEN

EDITH WAS IN HER STUDIO in the arches at Waterloo. She stood back from the canvas she was working on and wiped her paint-covered fingers with a rag. She heard the telephone ringing in the office and thought about letting it go through to answer-phone then decided she could do with a break. Sometimes she had to let her work "settle" before she added the final touches.

"Edith Holland."

"Hi, Edith, it's Hannah. How are you?"

"Hannah! Lovely to hear from you. I'm okay. How about you?" Edith felt they had both skirted around the terrible time when she had been imprisoned in a house she'd gone to, thinking she was there on a photographic commission. And then, hours later, Elizabeth had been handed to her, wide-eyed, in shock but unharmed. Those were the darkest moments of her life, and there had been a few. She had cuddled the child and encouraged her to eat what was brought to them – sandwiches on paper plates, and plastic mugs of milk. She had had no idea of time. And listen as she might there were no clues as to who else might be in the house. She and Elizabeth had passed the time singing nursery rhymes and Edith telling the child fairy tales she barely remembered. Then there had been the rescue... Hannah's voice brought her back to the present.

"Sorry, Hannah, I didn't get that."

Edith could almost feel the smile coming to her across the telephone wires. "I was wondering if I could commission you for a portrait of Elizabeth and me together? I have those lovely photos you took of Elizabeth and I thought one of us together would make a great present for my parents. I know I've left it a bit late…"

"No, not at all. I'd love to. Shall I come and take some shots of you at home?"

There was, it seemed, no time like the present, so Edith

arranged to visit later that afternoon. She went back to her painting and considered it for a moment before removing her smock and attacking her hands with turps.

HANNAH HAD TAKEN some time with her hair and make-up and donned her favourite dress. Elizabeth chose one of her new Christmas dresses and by the time Edith arrived in a taxi, they were camera ready.

Elizabeth stared at Edith for a moment then beamed at her. She rushed over and embraced her legs. The photographer placed her bags on the floor before dropping down for a bear hug. The warm glow Hannah felt was reflected in her smile.

"Where would you like us?"

EDITH HAD BROUGHT light reflectors and her favourite camera with all sorts of lens attachments. As she assembled the tools of her trade she chatted – mainly to Elizabeth – and clicked away to sort out light readings and best angles.

"Do you have a favourite toy, Elizabeth?" Edith asked.

"Yes." The toddler went across the room to pick up her "baby".

"Perfect. Now hold Baby up for me." Edith clicked away. "Right, let's put Baby here to watch you. And you sit on Mummy's lap."

"No. Stand." She settled in the end for sitting on the arm of the Chesterfield so mother and daughter had their faces alongside each other. A few more shots and positions, and the session was over.

WHILE EDITH PACKED away her equipment, Hannah and Elizabeth went upstairs to change. "Tea? Coffee?" Hannah asked on her return. She'd already prepared Elizabeth's meal so they sat in the kitchen with her.

"So how's life?" Edith helped herself to the biscuits on offer. "I saw that Albert Croxton had been shot." Her tone was so matter-of-fact that Hannah just stared at her for a moment.

"Yes I wanted to talk to you about that." She breathed deeply. "I wonder if it had anything to do with…"

Edith had paled visibly. "D'you know it never occurred to me. You mean Joan Ballantyne's death and…"

Hannah nodded. Edith finished her biscuit. "Well I certainly hope not!" She swallowed some coffee. "I suppose that sounds so selfish considering he rescued us."

"No it doesn't, but I do think we should both be extra careful. I'm happy for you to let me know your whereabouts especially if you're going somewhere unusual."

Edith smiled. "I am actually. I'm going on a cruise to the West Indies in a couple of days."

"Wow, does this include Christmas?"

"It does. But it's a working holiday. I shall be taking photographs of the guests but also running art workshops."

"That's amazing."

Edith smiled. "Should keep me out of harm's way, don't you think?"

"Absolutely." Hannah could feel her shoulders relaxing – one less person to worry about.

"And now I must leave you. And get to work on these prints for you. I'll send over some proofs for you to choose from. Let me know how many copies you'd like." Edith ruffled Elizabeth's hair. "Thank you for being such a good model."

"And Baby."

"And Baby too."

Edith rang for a minicab, which arrived soon after, and left with all her paraphernalia. Elizabeth waved goodbye enthusiastically.

AS SHE WAS BATHING ELIZABETH, Hannah wondered if she should also give a photo to Celia and Mary. It would solve the problem of what to give them.

Avocado Baby was the book of choice that evening and Elizabeth giggled all the way through. On the third reading, her eyes closed and she murmured something Hannah couldn't make out.

Time for dinner and a grown-up book.

AFTER DINNER, Hannah decided to look at the photos of the choir she'd had developed. She placed them in a circle on the dining table. She still didn't have all the names. She glanced at her watch. After eight on a Friday evening. She rang Leah. No reply. Could she, should she, call Peter Savage? What did she have to lose? And he had asked for her help. His phone rang for some time before he eventually answered. When Hannah asked if he had time to call round to help with identifying the choir members, he was silent for a moment. "What, now?"

"Yes, if you're not busy." She crossed her fingers, willing him to agree. She thought she heard him say something to someone else in the room but she could have been mistaken.

"Okay. I'll be with you in a few minutes."

"SO HOW DID YOU GET all these photos, Hannah? Or shouldn't I ask?"

"Better not to. And I'm only using them for my personal reference. I've placed them in the circle they sit in for rehearsals."

"With a space for Daniel Lyons," the vicar noted. "I take it you didn't have these this morning when I called in?"

"No, I collected them later. Leah helped with a few names when she was here the other evening. So you can see those."

"Right. So you have all the sopranos."

"But not their surnames." That was what Hannah really needed.

The priest consulted a piece of paper he produced from his pocket. "I asked Craig for an up-to-date list after... after Daniel died. Carol Wilton, Lorraine Fenton, Sarah Hindman and Marianne Merton." He studied the next group. "Alison Gregory, she's on the PCC; Hazel James, you have; Rosie Ball and April Hunter..." He paused. Hannah remembered them as the two altos who'd made such a fuss about moving round to accommodate her and Dinah in the sopranos.

"Tenors: David Smythe, also on the PCC, Noel Hindman, John Bowman and —" His voice seemed to disappear as his hand passed over the space for the dead man. "So that leaves us with Grant Weston, Richard Lomax, Tony Smollet and Jack Gold in the bass section."

"And do any of them have a connection to Daniel Lyons, do you think?"

"I really have no idea. You can have this list, which has their addresses as well. But it is confidential." His eyes held hers. As far as she was concerned, nothing was confidential where murder was involved, but she didn't tell him that.

"I assume you have given this list to DI Benton?"

He smiled. "I have. And now I really do have to go home." He didn't say why. Hannah could only assume he had a guest waiting for him. Lucky him.

SEVENTEEN

IT WAS ONE of those crisp winter days when the sun added a magic sparkle to their shopping expedition. Hannah struggled up North Cross Road balancing a Christmas tree on the buggy with Elizabeth skipping along joyously beside her. She was singing something she had learned at nursery and was attracting quite a few smiles. By the time they arrived home, Elizabeth was desperate for the loo and a snack, in that order.

As they sat in the kitchen together, Elizabeth concentrating on her apple and cheese, Hannah asked, "What was the song you were singing?"

Through a full mouth one word emerged: "Carol."

"Who?"

Elizabeth stared at her and shook her head. "Carol, Mama."

"Oh?"

"Wayinamanger."

Hannah could sense that Elizabeth was disappointed she didn't know this. However she redeemed herself when they took the tree into the sitting room and placed it in the bay window. The evening before, Hannah had retrieved the box of decorations she'd accumulated over the years from the attic. Now she presented them to Elizabeth, who was ecstatic when she found the fairy Hannah's uncle had given her years ago. "Angel, Mama. Look at the angel." She stroked the wings and then kissed the painted face.

"Shall I put it on the top of the tree?"

Elizabeth looked as though she'd rather keep hold of it then reluctantly relinquished the doll. They carried on dressing the tree. Elizabeth loved the tinsel and the "treasures" as she called them. When they turned on the lights at the end of their endeavours, Elizabeth clapped loudly and Hannah felt her heart melting. Whatever was happening in the outside world, her time with her daughter was precious. She was even looking forward to having her parents join them. She decided they could have her bedroom – not the bed-settee in the sitting room where they'd stayed before – to give them some space and privacy, and she'd use the futon in her study.

She wanted everything to be special for Elizabeth although the chances were she would never remember it. Still, there would be photos. She would cherish the memories and so would her parents.

Thinking of photos made her wonder about what they had at St John's. She had her photos of the current choir now with full names thanks to the vicar, but presumably there was an archive. It crossed her mind that Daniel Lyons could have been there for another reason entirely. The choir could have been a cover for something quite different. She'd ask Peter Savage tomorrow whether they had a church magazine.

She was roused from her musings by a ring on the bell. The video showed a delivery person in full motorbike gear. She wasn't expecting anything. At the same time as she noticed the envelope in his hand, the phone rang.

"Sorry, Hannah, should have phoned earlier. Sending over some proofs via courier."

Hannah felt the tension in her body relax. "They're here now, Edith. I'd better open the door. Thank you."

Edith rang off with, "Let me know what you think."

Hannah signed for the envelope at the door. The courier looked peeved that she'd left him to wait. "Sorry, the phone rang at the same time."

He grunted then left.

"Motorbike!" Elizabeth had a fascination for them. She waved but the driver rode off ignoring her.

"Right, shall we look at Edith's pictures?"

Elizabeth climbed next to her on the settee. Hannah was speechless when she opened the envelope. The images were amazing. She knew what Edith could achieve from the previous photos she'd taken of Elizabeth. However she had captured their mother/daughter relationship in a unique and fascinating way. Hannah had never really liked photos of herself and tried to avoid them but these were in a class of their own. Instead of the rabbit caught in the headlights look she mostly portrayed, Hannah thought she actually looked relaxed and attractive. As she looked through the proofs she found one with a note attached.

"Elizabeth, look – Edith sent this one especially for you."

"Baby!" Elizabeth squealed. She took the photo and kissed the image of her holding her doll. It was enchanting. Elizabeth climbed down from the settee and ran over to "Baby" who'd been left unceremoniously on the floor in favour of the motorbike. "Look, Baby, look." Elizabeth cuddled the doll, sitting on the floor and mumbling something Hannah couldn't catch.

After much deliberation Hannah chose her favourites: one for her parents, one for Celia and Mary and one for herself. Each one was different but captured the loving relationship between her and Elizabeth. She phoned Edith.

"What d'you think?" Edith sounded uncertain.

"Edith, they are perfect. I can't begin to thank you enough."

Edith was quiet for a moment. Was someone with her, Hannah wondered? "You don't have to thank me. I've had loads of work through you. They are my thank-you present. Now tell me which ones you've chosen and I'll get them over to you."

AFTER PUTTING ELIZABETH to bed, Hannah was faced with another Saturday evening alone. Her thoughts kept going back to Daniel. Who was he? And why did he die? Perhaps she could ask Rory at *The News* if he could check National Insurance records and maybe crime records? He seemed a singularly unknown man. An enigma if ever there was one. What drew him to singing in a church choir? Apparently he'd had a good voice. Was it a cover for something? Perhaps nothing. Maybe he just enjoyed singing.

Her phone rang. "Hi, Hannah, it's Fran."

Hannah swallowed, hoping – almost praying – that it wasn't bad news about Albert Croxton. "How are you? And your uncle?"

"The operation went well but we'll know more later." Fran's voice cracked. "I'm so scared, Hannah."

"Is there anything I can do?"

"Have you heard anything via your news contacts?"

"No, it's been strangely quiet. How's your security?"

"Police are here." That said it all really. Hannah assumed they thought Fran might be a hostage to fortune.

"Okay, if I hear anything I'll let you know of course."

"Thanks – and thank you for being a friend." With that she hung up.

Hannah was perplexed by the shooting. She had thought Albert Croxton was virtually untouchable but obviously not. Was it to do with the Soho bombing that had been some sort of retaliatory action during Elizabeth and Edith's kidnapping? If so that led back to her – and Elizabeth. She felt sick with apprehension. She phoned Claudia Turner, now a DCI in some sort of special unit she wasn't able to talk about. Her call went through to voice-mail. Hannah didn't leave a message.

Hoping for some distraction from terrifying thoughts, she turned on the television just as a talk show was beginning.

"And my guest this evening needs no introduction, star of the BBC's phenomenally successful series *Dead Voices*..." Hannah felt sick. Her arms became leaden as she stared at the image of Leo Hawkins smiling into the camera. Why hadn't he told her he was back in the UK?

"So, Leo, you're well known to our viewers for your chart-topping TV roles especially of late in *Dead Voices*, but more recently you've been in the headlines due to the attack..."

"Attempted murder – let's not mince words." Hannah had noticed his fists clenching.

"Quite. How's your recovery going?"

Visibly trying to relax, Leo smiled. "Physically most of my scars are healing." He smiled. "And time with my family in the US has been restorative."

"Yes, family is so important. Especially since the murder of your mother which must have been traumatic." *Well that's an understatement*, thought Hannah.

"Yes, it was horrible."

"And your grief was shared by all her devoted fans."

"Yes, but what was unbearable was that initially people – the police – thought she had taken her own life."

"But the journalist, Hannah Weybridge, helped you there..." Hannah's skin tingled. In spite of the fact she was on her own, she could feel her colour rising. She needed a drink but couldn't tear herself away from the screen.

"Yes, she did. At the time she was collaborating with my mother on her memoir: *Joan Ballantyne: A Life*, and she was able to …" he coughed, "she was able to offer valuable insights. I am very grateful to her."

Hannah wondered where the interviewer was going with this line of questioning and wondered why no one had thought to alert her to this programme. Surely someone at Halstone Press would have known? Her distraction meant she missed the next question. The answer made her freeze.

"Yes, my mother and Albert Croxton had been friends for many years. I was horrified to hear of the recent attempt on his life." Leo did indeed appear horrified. He also looked as though this wasn't the interview he expected or wanted.

"Did you meet Albert Croxton often?"

Leo looked as though he might actually walk off the set. "I understood this interview was about my return to the new series of *Dead Voices* and what my future career plans are. If that isn't the case, then there really isn't anything more to add."

The chat show host smiled. It was obvious he had actually got more than he'd hoped for and he'd managed to get under Leo Hawkins' skin.

"And do your future plans include Hannah Weybridge?"

Hannah nearly fell off her seat. How many people would be watching this show? The last thing she needed was this sort of inane publicity.

Leo burst out laughing. "Nice try. Now shall we move on?"

The interview wound up and Hannah went to get herself a glass of wine. How dare they bandy her name about like that! She felt hurt and betrayed on so many levels. Not least, she had to admit to herself, that Leo had laughed about his plans including her. Well they could all go …

The sound of her mobile phone ringing broke into her thoughts. She was tempted to let it go through to answerphone then answered anyway.

"Hannah, I am so sorry. I was ambushed there and I should have …

"You should have told me about the interview? Yes, you should have. As a courtesy, if nothing else. Goodnight, Leo." She cut the call and topped up her wine. This was just what she didn't need. Her name being linked to Leo Hawkins and by association Albert Croxton. *Shit.* The phone rang again and she let it ring out. Whoever it was could do one.

Her throat tightened, then the tears flowed and she sobbed noisily. Why was there never anyone around when she needed someone? As if on cue the doorbell rang. Hannah froze. Who on earth would call round unannounced at this time of night? She checked at the video screen: Claudia Turner. A sense of relief flooded her body.

Hannah wiped her eyes, blew her nose and took a deep breath before opening the door.

"Hi, Hannah – thought you might need some company," she said brandishing a bottle of wine.

"I can't believe no one thought to warn you about the interview." Claudia looked furious on Hannah's behalf. A comforting thought.

"It does seem strange. Maybe Leo's publicist didn't think it was necessary to liaise with Halstone Press. He rang me."

"Who? Leo? When?"

"Just after the programme ended. He apologised after a fashion but I cut him off. As far as I'm concerned, there was no excuse he could have come up with that would justify…" She took a deep breath and swallowed her sadness. "I feel such a fool."

"Well, you are no one's fool. And he above all people should know that." Claudia topped up their glasses.

Hannah sipped her wine. "As a matter of interest, how did you know?"

Claudia looked uncomfortable. "I didn't – initially." She looked as though she were judging how much to say and share with Hannah. "Leo is still on our radar along with Albert Croxton. We monitor… well anyway the programme came up as an alert: Albert Croxton's shooting and his link to Joan Ballantyne and thus Leo."

Hannah nodded. She didn't really know what Claudia's new job entailed and understood it was a subject not up for discussion. Whatever it was, she was grateful for Claudia's company and support.

"Oh well, I've survived worse."

"You have indeed. You're one of the strongest women I know, Hannah. Just don't let the bastards get you down."

Hannah smiled, wondering who exactly the bastards were.

They finished their wine in silence. "Right, I'd better be off. I have a car waiting for me outside."

So was this visit semi-official then? Hannah mused.

At the door, Claudia paused. "Try not to worry about Croxton, Hannah. He has powerful friends – and so do you." She kissed her cheek and departed into the darkness.

And what does that mean? Hannah thought as she locked the door then collected the glasses and bottle from the sitting room. In the kitchen she drank a large glass of water and checked the back door was locked. She turned off the lights and stared out of the window. No shadows. No demons. Leo's actions had hurt her. She had to make herself less vulnerable. More robust. Easier said than done. Hopefully she wouldn't run into him again soon.

She smiled as she went upstairs. Claudia's visit was a blessing even if it might have been linked to work.

Elizabeth was sleeping peacefully. They were safe. She remembered Father Peter blessing her home. Perhaps it was working.

EIGHTEEN

Hannah had been disconcerted that Leah was away and wouldn't be going to church that Sunday. Reflecting that her name had been bandied about on national television the previous evening, she almost backed out before giving herself a pep talk. Regard it as a job then it wouldn't seem so worrying.

Elizabeth and she arrived just before the service started at ten. There were smiles from the people who welcomed them as they entered, and Hannah was handed a hymn book and service sheet.

"Would you like me to park your buggy at the back of the church?"

Hannah was about to reply when Elizabeth said, "Yes please," and beamed at the woman who looked like everyone's idea of a kindly grandmother – or maybe in her daughter's mind an angel without wings.

The first notes of the organ reverberated as they quickly found seats towards the rear of the pews. As the choir processed in she scanned their faces. A couple of smiles were directed at Elizabeth, who was humming along in tune. Hannah wondered if Paul had been musical as a child. So many questions, which would never be answered now. She was glad that she'd heard the choir rehearsing the hymns for this Sunday so she had some idea of the music.

The service began once again with the lighting of the candles in the Advent wreath. This time the vicar didn't leave the volunteer to chance and invited a small boy sitting with his parents near the front to do the honours. He beamed his gratitude. Hannah caught Elizabeth's expression, which seemed to be torn between pleasure and extreme jealousy.

From her vantage point Hannah could only see the backs of the congregation but Dinah was distinctive in a bright pink jumper a couple of rows in front of her. She remembered the embarrassment of her last visit and quickly dived into her bag to turn off her phone. The person next to her smiled and pointed to the place in the service book.

During some prayers led by someone Hannah had never seen before and which were called intercessions, Hannah was brought up short when Albert Croxton's name was mentioned in the prayer for the sick. She had no idea how anyone's name was added but assumed most were members of the congregation. Perhaps someone here knew Albert and had asked for his name to be included. That thought was not a comfortable one although she would not deny the man his right to divine intervention. Daniel Lyons, of course, was mentioned in the recently departed category. She wondered if his funeral would be at St John's but supposed that depended on the sister who no one appeared to know or had heard of. Then again, you could hardly say that Daniel was known or heard of. But she did wonder how much Ruth Robertson knew. Perhaps she should just come clean with the vicar – or DI Benton – about seeing her with Daniel's landlady, Melanie Felton.

Hannah was brought back to the present by Elizabeth's religious enthusiasm, shouting "Amen" just after everyone else for maximum impact and thoroughly enjoying sharing the Peace, which Hannah found excruciating though she managed a few handshakes.

As people went up to receive communion she could see more of the congregation – and the choir who went first. Their reaction during the prayers seemed resigned. She felt sorry that Daniel had made so little impact on them but it reinforced her notion that his death probably had nothing to do with the church. She looked across at the Lady Chapel and almost gasped when she saw a man in the corner staring at her, a shaft of light from the stained glass window, depicting some saint or another, illuminating him. She blinked and he was gone. Instead she was almost overcome by the scent of freesia.

After the service, Dinah approached her. "Hi, good to see you again – and you, little one." She tickled Elizabeth's tummy.

"I'm Elbet."

"Elizabeth," Hannah added for clarification.

"And I'm Dinah. Pleased to meet you, Elizabeth."

"I like pink." Elizabeth smiled as she made this announcement and stroked Dinah's mohair sweater.

"So do I." Dinah smiled at Elizabeth. "Shall we get a coffee?"

Hannah nodded and followed her to the rear of the church where the refreshments trolley had been wheeled to – rather noisily – during the final blessing.

"Welcome back, Hannah. I'm glad we didn't frighten you off last week." Reverend Peter Savage was smiling. "Good to see you, Dinah." He looked embarrassed as though there might have been something between them. Maybe there still was.

"I was going to ask you whether you have a church magazine?" Hannah stepped into the awkward breach.

The vicar looked askance. "Yes we do. I'm sure we have a pile of back issues somewhere," he said, anticipating Hannah's next question. "Ruth –" he called over to the woman Hannah least wanted to have any dealings with – "Could you lay your hands on some back issues of *St John's Way* for Hannah?"

Ruth looked daggers at her but smiled at the vicar. "Of course." With that she disappeared to the front of the church and the door leading to the sacristy. Hannah was relieved that no one had mentioned the previous evening's talk show. Possibly many didn't know her surname. Or more likely, didn't imagine someone like her would attract the attention of a TV heartthrob. Dinah had moved away to chat to someone else. She had almost finished her coffee and had said hello to Craig, the musical director, and a few people she knew from nursery when Ruth reappeared. She handed a large bag to Hannah but whatever sour comment she was about to make was lost as a shot rang out followed by a scream…

FOR A FEW SECONDS there was total silence. Faces frozen in terror. Hannah pulled Elizabeth to her and found her phone. She pressed 999 but for some reason there seemed to be no signal. She saw Ruth making her way back to the sacristy – presumably there was a phone there. In the same moment she saw Dinah make a flying leap and, in an action worthy of a professional rugby player, bring down a man onto the paved area between the two sets of doors into the church. Time seemed to have slowed to a standstill.

"Mama – can't breathe." Elizabeth was pulling away from her. She could hear other children murmuring and adults comforting them. Someone was sobbing. She heard a voice: "Is anyone hurt? Please stand back from the doorway."

Sirens sounded. Father Peter and his team were trying to reassure everyone while Dinah sat astride the perpetrator, his neck in an arm lock. She looked ferocious. Hannah, like most of the congregation, was rooted to the spot. She was stunned by Dinah's swift reaction. She didn't even know if the bullet had hit its target. If there had been one. Perhaps it was a random act although that was highly unlikely.

The sirens got louder until two police cars screeched to a halt outside. Immediately two officers relieved Dinah of her prisoner and arrested him. Hannah watched Dinah closely. There was something niggling her. Scratching at the back of her mind. A third officer went over to Dinah and presumably took details. Then Father Peter moved forward as DI Mike Benton went towards him.

"Get a chair, someone!" As Mike moved to support the vicar, Hannah noticed that he was holding his arm awkwardly and there was a lot of blood on his robes. He had been shot. Mike barked instructions to his officers, who quickly took charge of the situation, and within what seemed like minutes two paramedics appeared and, after a swift assessment, Father Peter was taken outside and driven away in an ambulance.

Dinah was beside her. Hannah couldn't divine her expression.

"That was impressive." Elizabeth, in her arms, applauded.

Dinah laughed. "I always hoped my martial arts training would be put to good use one day."

Into Hannah's mind, unbidden, came the image of the leaflet on self-defence classes Claudia Turner had given her a month or so ago. She stared at Dinah. "You're not hurt, are you?"

"No, but I don't think my jumper came out of it too well."

Hannah thought that would be the least of her worries. Mike Benton approached them. "Hello, Hannah, in the thick of it again." He winked at her and ruffled Elizabeth's hair. "And you, Miss –?"

"Dinah Bell."

"DI Mike Benton. That was some tackle, I hear. And an impressive arm lock." He looked at Elizabeth again. "I'll be in touch, Hannah. Good to meet you, Ms Bell." He sauntered away, deliberately casual.

"Why will he be in touch?" Dinah asked.

"Long story." She smiled to take any sting out of her words. "Now I must get Elizabeth home. We've had quite enough excitement for one day."

"See you Wednesday, then?"

"Wednesday?"

"Choir practice." Hannah nodded but wasn't sure she particularly wanted to set foot inside the church again. It was only as she was pushing the buggy home that it crossed her mind that the bullet might have been meant for her and Father Peter had stepped in the way. Her mind went back to when another shot had rung out on the steps of another St John's – at Waterloo. That time she had definitely been in the firing line but the man calling himself Sherlock had stood in front of her and had not budged even when the bullet hit him.

NINETEEN

HANNAH WAS DISTRACTED by her thoughts as she turned into her road, about ten minutes later. She felt sick that someone might be out to get her. But she had little evidence to go on. Maybe it was a random event. But how often do you hear of gunmen shooting into a church? Could it have been a warning? She wondered what Peter Savage thought about it all and hoped his wound wasn't serious. She had been amazed at Dinah's presence of mind. And then there was the awkwardness between her and the vicar. She had been surprised to see DI Benton. He didn't look too concerned, when she recalled his face and comments. Perhaps he'd ring her. She hoped he would. But she had no right to assume anything.

Elizabeth was chatting away to Baby in her buggy, and now and again humming the hymns from the service. She hadn't seemed upset or affected by what had happened in church. Hannah was once again impressed by how tuneful she was. As they reached their gate, Elizabeth struggled to get out of the buggy and Hannah bent over to unstrap her. As she stood up, she found herself face to face with Leo Hawkins brandishing a huge bouquet of flowers and smiling tentatively. He was leaning heavily on a walking stick.

"What the..."

"Hannah, I am so sorry." He rested an arm on the gatepost. "I wanted to let you know about the interview and thought my agent, Charles Trafford, had contacted you, as I had asked him to. I found out this morning that he had been in a minor car accident and..."

"Hello – what's your name?"

Leo leaned forward awkwardly. "I'm Leo and you must be Elizabeth."

Her treacherous daughter beamed at him. "I am."

Hannah walked past them and unlocked the front door.

Elizabeth rushed inside. Hannah was tempted to close the door in Leo's face but she was aware they were drawing some attention from some people chatting in the street and could see a few curtains twitching, so rather begrudgingly invited him inside.

He followed her slowly into the sitting room and handed her the flowers.

"Thank you." She felt drained and irritable. "Look, Leo, we've just come from church. There was a shooting there."

Leo looked aghast.

"The guy was apprehended but the vicar was shot in the arm. He was standing right next to me…"

"God, that's awful. I'm so sorry for barging in on you but when you hung up on me last night… And then I heard about Charles, well, I thought…" He seemed to be studying his feet. "I thought I could better explain in person. I'm sorry. I got a cab over and have been waiting outside for half an hour." He looked chilled to the bone.

Hannah concentrated on getting Elizabeth out of her snow-suit. Her attitude thawed slightly as she took off her own coat. "Would you like a drink? I could do with one after this morning."

THEY SAT WITH their drinks while Elizabeth sat at her little table with her lunch.

Leo watched her with a half-smile on his face. "Are you hungry, Hannah? We could have a take-away?"

Hannah was about to deny her hunger but her stomach rumbled. Not eating would only make her feel worse and even grumpier. "I was going to have pasta. The sauce is already made and there's enough for two, if you'd like to join me?" She felt shy inviting him like that – a spur of the moment decision.

"I'd love to." Leo accepted quickly as if he thought the offer might be withdrawn.

Elizabeth was almost nodding off as she finished her food so Hannah took her upstairs to bed. When she returned a few minutes later, she heard Leo speaking to someone on his mobile. He rapidly ended the call as Hannah entered the room. She wondered if he had had other arrangements, which he was cancelling.

Leo followed her into the kitchen. He topped up their wine as she took out the sauce she'd made earlier and put the pasta on to cook. She saw him looking at everything and was acutely aware that he'd never visited her house. So different from the minimalist elegance of his apartment.

"What a lovely home you have." He was looking at Elizabeth's pictures stuck on the wall – some framed – in much the same way Peter Savage had done.

Hannah made no comment.

"I remember when I was away at school I sometimes visited the homes of the day boys. I used to envy their cosiness. My mother wasn't much of a homemaker – at least not for a child. You'd have been hard pressed to know she had a child if you'd seen our house in those days."

Leo had made himself comfortable at the kitchen table. Hannah produced some olives and had popped some garlic bread in the oven and made a salad.

Her guest smiled. "A feast."

"Hardly, but help yourself."

They ate in silence for a while. It seemed curiously intimate, eating together in her kitchen. Hannah tried to relax but she felt on edge both from having Leo here and from what had happened earlier.

"Have you heard how Albert Croxton is?" she asked, hoping for some safe territory.

"No." He wiped his mouth on a napkin and sipped some wine. "I only flew in to the UK yesterday afternoon. I had very little time to do anything before the show." He stared at her. "I'm so sorry you didn't know about that. I was appalled that the interviewer brought up your name like that. I was trying – badly as it turns out – to deflect attention from you."

Hannah sipped her wine. She didn't say that she had felt ridiculed. "I'm sorry, I probably overreacted but I was so shocked. There may be some complications about Albert Croxton. And today's shooting has, quite frankly, terrified me."

He reached over, covering her hand with his. It felt warm and comforting. "I can understand that. Ever since the attack on me, I've felt vulnerable – physically and mentally. My confidence has taken a hit. I feel less of a person if that makes any sense?"

Hannah stared at him. Before she could comment her phone rang.

"I'd better answer that just in case it's the police following up from this morning."

"Hannah, how are you?" It was Claudia Turner. "I heard about what happened at St John's this morning."

Of course you would have, Hannah thought. "It was terrifying but could have been a lot worse. Dinah, a member of the congregation, made an amazing citizen's arrest…"

"So I heard." Was that a chuckle from Claudia? "I just wanted to reassure you that it doesn't seem to be connected to the Croxton shooting."

"You know that already?"

"I can't say any more than that."

How frustrating! "Have you heard how the vicar is?"

"Surface wound. A lot of blood but little damage."

"I hope he feels as nonchalant about it. Claudia, he was standing right next to me."

There was a pause. "Right. Try not to worry. Are you on your own?"

Hannah wasn't sure why but she felt reticent about the truth. "No."

"Right." Did Claudia sound irritated?

"Leo Hawkins is here."

"Okay. Be careful."

AS SHE FINISHED her call, Leo walked into the sitting room balancing their glasses of wine on a small tray. Hannah wondered it Claudia had been warning her to be careful of Leo. And if so, why?

"Hannah, I –" His mobile rang. He answered and listened. "Okay I'll get there as soon as I can." He cut the call. "I'm sorry, I have to go." He gave no reason. "Please don't think too badly of me. Do you have a local minicab number?"

THE CAR ARRIVED very quickly. If he noticed Hannah checking the video camera, Leo said nothing. He put on his coat and kissed her lightly on the cheek. "Thank you for lunch. I'll be in touch, if I may?"

Hannah nodded. As she closed the door behind him, she felt the enormity of the space he had left in his wake. She wondered if the call was about his agent who'd been in an accident. She remembered they had been friends since schooldays and Leo had trusted him implicitly. Trust that seemed in short supply recently. Who could she trust? A line from Shakespeare popped into her mind: *To thine own self be true.* She couldn't rid her mind of Claudia's reaction to Leo being with her. Did she suspect him of being involved in the shootings? Surely not. That was unthinkable.

Maybe Claudia's reaction was that of a friend. A friend who didn't want her to be hurt – possibly romantically.

THAT EVENING Hannah decided to look at the pile of church magazines Ruth Robertson had given her just before the shooting. *St John's Way* looked rather good for a publication put together by non-journalists. At least that was her assumption as she flicked through the pages. The magazines, published monthly, were in date order so she started from the oldest – April 1994. Nothing much to intrigue her. No red flags. There were a couple of profiles of people who volunteered in the church, which she'd read later.

May was more interesting. There was a profile on Craig Fletcher. Hannah skimmed the article then reached for a highlighter and read more carefully.

Craig Fletcher had been the musical director at St John's for over ten years. He was a peripatetic music teacher and ran another choir outside the parish. More interesting were his reflections on the church choir and a plea for new members to join. In another issue there was an article by Ruth Robertson about faith in the workplace, and she put that aside to read later.

The October issue contained a group photo of the choir and there in the middle of the back row, according to the caption below, was Daniel Lyons. It was a surprisingly good photo and Hannah popped up to her office to find her magnifying glass. With that she studied the image of the dead chorister.

He was taller than the men either side of him. His hair was neatly cut and he was clean-shaven. His expression, however, was inscrutable. But she had an overwhelming sense of certainty that this was the image she had seen fleetingly in the Lady Chapel during the service that morning. Others in the line-up were smiling. Hannah recognised the faces and could now, thanks to the vicar, put names to them. Marianne, the soprano who had been friendly towards her, seemed to be looking somewhere else rather than at the camera. Craig was standing to one side at the front, smiling broadly. They were all in their choir robes. That reminded her that she and Dinah would need to find robes that fitted. For the women they were royal blue and distinctly unflattering.

Her attention returned to Daniel. "So, Daniel," she asked out loud, "why did you join the choir? And who is Rosa? And what do you want to tell me?" She stared at the photo a while longer but it revealed nothing further. She flipped a few more pages and was staggered to see a beautifully written piece by Leah Braithwaite about finding out she had a brother in Australia and what this had meant to her. Hannah was amazed by the fulsome praise she read about herself and wondered why Leah had never mentioned it. There was a photo of Leah and her brother together when they met in Australia. Hannah was stunned at how alike they looked – and how radiantly happy Leah appeared. And so much younger. At least, Hannah thought, there had been one happy outcome of her investigations into the Child Migration Scheme and the murders perpetrated by Peter Edwards. This led her thoughts to Lucy. She should really visit her. Perhaps she could take her out of the care home for a pre-Christmas lunch. And she should take a copy of her book as a Christmas present as well as the other gifts she'd bought her.

Those thoughts accompanied her to bed. She needed to organise her diary. And she needed to do some more Christmas shopping.

TWENTY

HANNAH'S FIRST CALL on Monday morning after taking Elizabeth to nursery was to Rory at *The News*.

"Hannah, you beat me to it. I was going to ring to ask if you could …"

Hannah cut in. "Did you hear about the shooting at St John's, my local church?"

"Yes. The police don't seem to think there's a link to the Croxton shooting."

"I was standing next to the vicar when he was shot."

"I didn't know you were a churchgoer…"

"Rory!" She felt like screaming at him for not picking up on the implication. Instead she calmly repeated her words: "I was standing next to the vicar when he was shot."

"Hold on." She heard him walk across the new office he had as Assistant Editor and close the door. "Right, so tell me."

By the end of the call, Hannah had got him to agree to run checks on Daniel Lyons, Dinah Bell and the Reverend Peter Savage. "And if there's anything in the cuttings library, I'd be eternally grateful."

"Leave it with me. And the reason for my call…"

RORY HAD BEEN RINGING about a last-minute meeting proposed for lunchtime. Georgina wanted her back under contract and so did Lord Gyles apparently. "And my vote to have you back goes without saying," Rory had said.

Hannah changed her clothes, putting on her favourite dark red suit, which always made her feel competent and businesslike. The car sent by *The News* arrived and she was away to the offices.

LARRY JEFFERSON WAS in the boardroom alone when Hannah arrived. Rory had ushered her in and then left with an "I'll be back in a moment."

"How are you, Hannah?" He actually looked as though he was interested in her answer, as they both sat at the table.

"Fine." She was feeling anything but fine and was thrown by the company solicitor's presence with no one else there.

His smile made her think of Kaa, the huge snake in *Jungle Book*, which she had watched recently with Elizabeth.

"I have a new contract for you." He handed her some papers. He cleared his throat, looking a bit sheepish. "I took the liberty of showing the contract to Neville Rogers as I know he looks after your interests. He made one or two suggestions and I've amended accordingly."

"I'm sorry. Why did you discuss this with Neville and not me?" Hannah's hackles rose. "And why didn't he contact me?"

"I asked him not to."

Hannah was speechless. Who did these men think they were? Looks after her interests indeed! As if she wasn't capable of looking after herself. Or asking for advice if she needed it.

"It was an informal discussion that only he and I – and now you – know about." He paused. "I wanted to make sure you know that I too have your best interests at heart. If you look at section 3 paragraph 2, you'll see that..."

Hannah was shocked by the terminology and the amount of money.

"Georgina and Lord Gyles will want you to sign the contract so you are not being manipulated or ..."

"Hannah, how good to see you." Georgina swanned into the room with Rory in her wake. "I hope you approve the new contract and that we'll have you on board again."

Hannah glanced across at Larry who gave her the briefest of nods. "It just needs both your signatures," he said.

Hannah and Georgina both signed as Rory looked on.

Then they heard the pop of a champagne cork, and flutes were filled by someone from hospitality who had arrived silently. There was something familiar about him, in the way his eyes met hers as he handed her a glass, but she couldn't for the life of her place him. *Am I being paranoid?* she thought.

"Welcome back, Hannah." Rory raised his glass to her as the door opened and a trolley of food was wheeled in.

Neither Albert Croxton nor the previous day's shooting was mentioned. Georgina was full of the Christmas party that was happening on Thursday and after a short time she and Larry absented themselves, both taking a plate of food with them.

Rory refilled their glasses and produced a file. "I've been digging into the names you gave me and these are the cuttings I found. Nothing on Daniel Lyons. I'm assuming that must be an alias and his job was a cover for something else. Dinah Bell is interesting for nothing apart from having served in the army. I found one reference to her winning some trophy for martial arts and that's it. Your vicar is far more interesting."

He passed the file across to her. Hannah stared at the cuttings. So much for no connections. Reverend Peter Savage had some explaining to do.

IN THE CAR going home Hannah reread the cuttings Rory had given her. Then she called Peter Savage. The phone rang for some time before he answered.

"How is your arm?" Hannah asked immediately.

The vicar seemed subdued. "A bit painful but it could have been so much worse. I hope Elizabeth and you were not too traumatised."

Hannah pondered his words. "To be honest, the whole situation seemed to have passed Elizabeth by. However I…"

"I'm sorry, Hannah, the archdeacon has arrived. May I return your call later?"

"Of course." *How convenient.* Hannah hung up and drummed her fingers on the phone. She wished she had Dinah's number. She stared out of the window trying to make sense of conflicting emotions. She had been growing to like Peter Savage but she didn't like the idea that he was holding back on her. Still there was nothing she could do about that until he agreed to meet her.

Her thoughts turned to *The News* Christmas party that would be attended by the Halstone Press staff as well. She wondered how dressy the occasion was but when she'd asked Rory he'd just said wear a nice dress. She could do with a woman friend there. She rang her editor. When asked, she told her to "put on your glad rags".

Hannah had already asked Janet to babysit. It would be too late for Alesha on a school night and after what had happened at the church she felt reassured that Janet would be there.

"Here we are, love." The driver turned round and smiled. For a moment she saw the face of the man she'd seen in church, then it reassembled itself into her driver's older face. "Have a good afternoon."

She smiled. "Thank you, and you."

As she was unlocking her front door, Leah rushed over. "Hannah, I only just heard this morning about what happened at the church. How are you?"

Hannah opened the door and burst into tears.

LEAH HAD TAKEN HER in her arms and allowed her to sob. She didn't offer platitudes, just soothing murmurings. Gradually the tears subsided; Leah handed her a handkerchief and she blew her nose noisily.

"I am so sorry. I don't know what came over me."

"Don't you dare apologise. My goodness, what are friends for?" She smoothed an imaginary crease in her skirt. "I spoke to Peter this morning. There's to be an emergency meeting of the PCC." Her face betrayed her concern. "Another one. It's such an important time in the church year, we have decided it's 'business as usual'. The police have the perpetrator – although rumour has it that he wasn't talking…"

"Oh." Hannah felt unaccountably sidelined that DI Mike Benton hadn't contacted her. She was out of the loop. She sighed then smiled tremulously at Leah. "Would you like a coffee?"

"Love one." Leah looked round the kitchen in much the same way as Leo had done. "I'm feeling so excited with Scott and Adam coming over for Christmas but it's feeling a bit tainted if you know what I mean."

Hannah didn't reply. She knew she would have to get a grip if she were to make Christmas special for her daughter and her parents.

"My brother can't wait to meet you."

Hannah hugged Leah. "This Christmas is going to be really special and we must make every moment count, whatever has happened." She poured their coffees. Just for a moment she saw a face reflected in her cup and she almost dropped it. It faded.

"So how's choir going? Would you like me to babysit on Wednesday?"

Hannah had almost forgotten about the rehearsal. "Would you mind?"

"Of course not. What did you make of Dinah?"

"You must have read my thoughts. I was going to ask you the same question. I was stunned by how she brought down the man with the gun on Sunday. It reminded me that Claudia Turner had suggested I take self-defence classes a while ago."

"Well if that's the result, go for it." Leah chuckled. "Although from what I heard, she must have been training for years."

"She used to be in the army." Hannah could have kicked herself for being so indiscreet.

"Really? How fascinating. Shows how little we know about each other." She sipped her coffee.

"I'm sorry, Leah, I shouldn't have mentioned that. I don't think it's common knowledge."

"Oh don't worry. My lips are sealed. Anyway you haven't said how you're feeling."

"Confused, if I'm honest. By everything."

"Including Leo Hawkins?"

Hannah gave her an arch look.

"Brian said he'd seen him waiting outside yesterday. It was so cold he almost invited him in."

Hannah ignored that. "Did you see him on TV on Saturday?"

"I did. I thought he was going to walk out of the studio when that idiot mentioned you."

"Yes." Hannah felt more kindly towards Leo now. "Writing Joan's book has been a double-edged sword. I've become part of the story, which is something I've always managed to avoid up until now."

"Not quite." Leah had also perfected the arch look. "But perhaps not so publicly."

Hannah felt her stomach clench; memories of past investigations flooded her mind. Investigations in which she had inadvertently put herself at risk. And her beloved daughter.

"Something to accommodate then." Leah's voice seemed to come from a long way off.

Hannah wasn't quite sure what she meant. "I called Peter today but the archdeacon arrived. Do you know how he is?"

"When I spoke to him this morning he was shaken but stoical. The show must go on and all that. The police have been reassuring. However there is still the death of Daniel Lyons haunting us."

Haunting. Hannah was haunted by visions of the dead man she had never seen or met. But she knew who it was from the photograph in the church magazine. "Has anyone told you anything about him?"

"No, he's a bit of an enigma. No doubt you'll solve the mystery."

Hannah was about to dispute that but Leah continued, "Now I must love you and leave you. But I'll be over on Wednesday."

"Thank you." Hannah saw her out. She felt her audience had been terminated – in her own home!

It was almost time to collect Elizabeth. She'd check her emails first.

THE FIRST EMAIL she opened was from Charles Trafford, Leo's agent and friend, apologising profusely for not telling her about the interview. As she had suspected, his accident had driven it from his mind. Hannah wondered about that. What had happened to him? He didn't offer any details.

The second email, from Simon Ryan, was more of a surprise.

"My dear Hannah, how are you?

I saw that awful talk show interview with Leo Hawkins on Saturday. My heart went out to you and of course it made me realise we haven't been in touch for a while.

I shall be in London tomorrow. Is it too short notice to invite you to lunch? I have some information to share and it's always nicer to do so in person. Plus it would be lovely to see you again…"

HANNAH WONDERED what on earth he wanted to share but did a quick reply to say she'd love to meet for lunch. By return came "Strand Palace Hotel at 12.30 okay for you?" It was.

She looked at her watch, and closed down her computer. Time to collect Elizabeth.

THAT EVENING, once Elizabeth was asleep, Hannah looked at the Christmas presents she'd already bought and made a list of what she needed to buy. Before lunch with Simon, she'd go to Oxford Street and hopefully find what she needed.

TWENTY-ONE

HANNAH, LADEN WITH carrier bags, walked into the Strand Palace Hotel reception and asked for Simon Ryan. The concierge smiled at her and told her to go to the second floor, room 214. "The lifts are just through those doors, madam."

Hannah took the lift and smiled to herself; at least she knew that Simon would have no ulterior motive in inviting her to his room. He had told her that he was gay although it wasn't something he broadcast. She wondered about his parents. Two gay sons with no prospect of grandchildren. Unless they didn't know of their sons' proclivities. And one of those sons had been murdered. Her musings were cut short when the lift doors opened at the second floor.

Room 214 was a misnomer. It was a suite. Simon greeted her at the door with a bear hug. "Come in. Come in. Let me relieve you of those bags. And your coat." The sitting room had a dining table set for two and a bottle of wine in a cooler. He poured them both a glass and handed her a menu. "I thought it would be better to talk without the possibility of being overheard. Choose what you'd like and I'll phone through our order."

The food options were quickly settled as they sat in two comfortable armchairs set either side of an electric "open fire", which blazed in the grate.

"I was intrigued to hear about the dead chorister at the church near where you live."

Hannah was caught off guard. She hadn't known what Simon had wanted to discuss but she hadn't expected him to be interested in Daniel Lyons. "Oh, why?"

"I'll get to that. But a little bird tells me you've become involved." He stared at her in a way that made her grateful that she wasn't in the witness box in court. His eyes were like shards of ice … She mustn't allow the warmth of the room and the wine to soften her. Simon had always been on her side. Had her back.

Up until now, said a small voice. Things could change. She knew that.

"How on earth..?"

Simon held up a hand. "I'll come on to that." He sipped his wine. "However, I wasn't so surprised by the news that Albert Croxton had been shot."

Hannah felt awkward. "Do you know him?"

"Let's just say I've had dealings with him. Some time ago now. And, of course, I heard about him rescuing Elizabeth and your photographer friend, Edith Holland. I also know your friend the vicar who was shot at. Peter Savage."

Yes, she thought, *that figures*. He too had been a barrister.

"I wasn't really surprised when he gave up the wig for the cloth. He always had too much of a conscience. Not great when you are the defending counsel. Or prosecuting for that matter." His expression told her that he would never have such qualms. She sensed his power now which had been diminished somewhat when his brother had been murdered. It seemed his strength had returned like a regrowth of Samson's hair.

"I wouldn't describe him as a friend but he did ask me to find out about the man who died in his church."

"Oh yes, that would make sense." He stood up and walked over to a side table by the window, picked up a file and then handed Hannah a photograph as he returned to his seat.

Hannah stared at the image. She could feel herself shaking. "Who is this?" But she knew before she heard the answer. It was of course the man whose face had been haunting her.

"That is Jonathan Cartmel."

"But who is…"

There was a knock on the door. Simon rose. "That's your dead man." He opened the door and the waiter wheeled in their lunch.

ONCE THEY WERE SERVED and the waiter had left the room, Hannah said, "I don't understand. At the church, and by his landlady, he was known as Daniel Lyons."

"That as the case may be. But his real name is Jonathan Cartmel. Let's eat before it gets cold."

Hannah forced herself to concentrate on lunch. It looked

delicious but tasted like ashes in her mouth. The wine helped her swallow the food.

Simon had reverted to social chat. "I trust Elizabeth is well."

Hannah tried to relax and smiled. "Yes she is and she seems remarkably taken with going to church."

"Could be worse."

"Except Peter Savage was shot at on Sunday in front of us."

Simon's cutlery clattered on his plate. The colour had drained from his face. "Why didn't you say so sooner? How is he?"

"He has a surface wound on his arm which is sore but not life-threatening as I understand."

"Thank God for that." Now both their appetites had evaporated. Simon filled their glasses. "Shall we move back to the fireside?"

They sat, as they had earlier, facing each other in comfortable armchairs. "Could you let me have Peter Savage's telephone number?"

"Of course." Hannah reached into her bag for her Filofax, found the vicar's number and read it out to Simon. Interesting that for all his information he didn't have the vicar's number.

"Thank you." He seemed thoughtful. "I wonder what has really been happening at that church."

WHEN HANNAH LEFT an hour later, Simon took her down to reception, carrying some of her bags, and outside to hail a taxi. "Take care, Hannah. And keep in touch. Call me any time. If I'm in court leave me a message. You are not alone in this." He hugged her tightly.

As the cab set off, she turned and saw him still standing at the kerbside. She couldn't see his expression but could guess what he was feeling from his body language. Obviously there was far more to the death of the chorister than was first suggested.

Hannah thought about everything they had discussed. She needed to see Peter Savage even more now. And she would have to share what she now knew with DI Benton.

THERE WAS A LIGHT ON in one of the rooms, which faced the road, and one above the entrance at the side of the vicarage. She pressed the bell and heard the ring reverberate inside the house but it seemed a long wait before the door was opened and Peter Savage stood before her, looking slightly dishevelled, his left arm in a sling and a black Labrador by his side, wagging his tail.

"Hannah! How lovely to see you. Come in."

She glanced at the dog.

"Don't mind Moses. He's a kitten really."

He led the way into his office. It was warm in there. "You're the last person I expected."

"Oh, why?"

He didn't answer. "Would you like some tea? Or coffee? Leah brought me one of her famous cherry cakes."

That was an offer Hannah couldn't refuse and she followed him into the kitchen to help. Everything was sparkling clean; a tray was laid out with cups, saucers and plates. The kettle quickly boiled and he filled the cafetière. "Eva, my cleaning lady, has been today. She's been so kind. Even popped a casserole into the oven for my supper."

Hannah smiled. "Shall I carry the tray through?"

"Please." He followed her with the cherry cake, and the dog, looking hopeful, padding beside him.

ONCE THEY WERE ENSCONCED in armchairs, the vicar glanced at her in a way she couldn't fathom. "The police were here this morning."

"About the shooting?"

"Partly. Apparently the man they arrested seems to have been some sort of stooge. He says he was paid to fire into the church but claims he doesn't know who actually wanted him to do it or why."

"I don't suppose he bargained for Dinah's amazing tackle and citizen's arrest."

"No." He looked at her strangely. "I don't suppose he did. This cake is delicious."

Hannah was not so easily deflected. "Do the police think he had anything to do with Daniel's death?"

"They can't see any links at present."

Hannah picked at a cherry. "It seems to be rather a coincidence and I don't think you are being totally honest with me, Peter."

His face flushed. "In what way?"

"You asked me to try to find out about Daniel Lyons."

"I did."

"But I think you knew him."

"That's a ridiculous assertion. Why on earth would you suggest such a thing?"

"Because you knew him as Jonathan Cartmel."

The coffee cup rattled onto the tray. Peter looked totally shocked. Hannah was convinced he wasn't faking his reaction. His hand shook and his face had drained of colour.

"Didn't you recognise him?"

"No. I didn't. Truly I didn't." He made a sign of the cross on himself and muttered something.

Another prayer, Hannah thought. She decided to give him time to recover himself and changed tack. "Do you know Albert Croxton? He was on the prayer list on Sunday."

"I heard about his shooting." That wasn't the answer to her question. Was he being deliberately obtuse?

"Who asked for his name to go on the prayer list?"

He stared at her and just for a moment she recognised the steely expression she had noted in Simon Ryan. She thought he would reply that it was none of her business. "His niece."

"Fran attends St John's?"

"Not often." He looked distinctly uncomfortable. "But she did ring me and ask that we pray for her uncle."

Hannah nodded. "But you knew Albert Croxton years ago, did you not?"

The vicar was rescued by a ring at the doorbell. "Excuse me." He went to answer the door and returned accompanied by the archdeacon. Hannah had had run-ins with him when Father Patrick, Simon Ryan's brother, had gone missing and knew her time was up. "Ms Weybridge. We meet again. I trust you are fully recovered now from that dreadful stabbing at the airport?" He made it sound like he hoped she wasn't.

"Yes thank you." She took a deliberate look at her watch. "I have to collect my daughter from nursery. I recommend the cherry cake."

AFTER SEEING HANNAH OUT, the vicar went into the kitchen to collect another mug and plate for the archdeacon.

"I didn't realise you knew Hannah Weybridge."

Peter could sense the undercurrent of criticism. "I don't really. She helped one of my parishioners find her family in Australia and is thinking of having her daughter christened." That was only a slight prevarication. He had no intention of telling Andrew Fanshawe that he had sought the journalist's help. Or what she had just told him about their dead chorister.

The archdeacon didn't look convinced but was obviously in a charitable mood. Maybe he felt not knowing the full story was the lesser of two evils. "Actually this is a pastoral visit. Just checking up on you after that unfortunate incident." He made it sound as if Peter had tripped and hurt himself in church, not been shot at. "How's the arm? Not too painful, I hope."

Peter thought the other man's expression gave the lie to his words. He looked as though he hoped it was painful – for bringing the church into disrepute.

"A bit sore but nothing to what could have been." Privately he thought – no, his gut instinct told him – that the bullet had been aimed at Hannah. He hadn't wanted to frighten her. Nor did he want her gratitude. What she had just revealed to him had thrown him into confusion but he was determined not to reveal anything to the archdeacon. Not yet.

"Quite. God spared you. Just as well as the last thing I need is another parish in vacancy."

Peter nearly choked on his coffee. The archdeacon's lack of compassion and empathy was legendary but Peter was shocked that he didn't even feign some semblance of concern. "More cake?"

"No thank you. I have a dinner this evening and must watch the waistline." He placed his cup on the table. "Anyway, good to see you are coping. If you need anything let me know. But I expect the good ladies of St John's will be flocking to keep you nourished." He made it sound rather rude. "Anyway I have another visit to make so I'll take my leave of you."

They both stood, and at the front door the archdeacon paused. "Do take care, Peter. The past is not another country…"

And what the hell did he mean by that? Peter thought as he went back into his study and sat in his armchair, closed his eyes and prayed for guidance and for the soul of Daniel now known to be Jonathan Cartmel. Why in God's name hadn't he recognised him? Had he changed so much? Jonathan used to wear glasses, had a beard and dark hair, which used to curl over his collar. Daniel's hair was lighter, and neatly cut. He was clean-shaven and might have worn contact lenses now. He'd also lost weight. But why would he be in his church incognito so to speak?

The telephone interrupted his thoughts.

"Simon. I wondered if I would hear from you."

THAT EVENING, after Elizabeth had been put to bed, Hannah wrapped the presents she'd bought in the morning and the finished photos Edith had sent over. She'd even framed them for her. She found doing a physical task like this allowed her mind to wander, to think about what she should do about Jonathan Cartmel. As she wrapped the present for Celia and Mary, the smell of freesia was almost overwhelming. Tears filled her eyes. Was Liz sending her a message? Approbation? Love? It would be good to think so.

When she'd finished her task, she came to one decision. She would have to contact DI Benton to tell him Daniel was in fact Jonathan Cartmel.

TWENTY-TWO

AS SOON AS she returned from dropping off Elizabeth at the nursery, Hannah phoned Mike Benton. His phone was answered by a voice she didn't recognise so she asked him to pass on a message for the DI to contact her as soon as possible.

Now she was back on board at *The News*, Hannah had direct access to the cuttings library. So she sent an email requesting any cuttings on Jonathan Cartmel and any links to Peter Savage, and Simon Ryan – then she added Albert Croxton. As an afterthought she added the names of choristers. Maybe one of them had a history worth knowing about. She copied the email to Rory, letting him know what she was doing.

She wondered about contacting Ruth Robertson but that would blow her cover. However, Ruth had been at Jonathan Cartmel's digs. Did Ruth know him as Daniel Lyons or Jonathan Cartmel? It was obvious to her that the vicar was shocked by her revelation but that didn't mean that Ruth would be. Maybe she was involved in the deceit. Perhaps she had an inkling of what Hannah might be trying to find out. But she certainly didn't know about her visit as Jill Bradshaw. Or the fact that Hannah as Jill had purloined her wallet.

Her thoughts were interrupted by the phone ringing. It was Angie from the cuttings library.

"That was quick," Hannah said when she was told the cuttings were ready.

"Command from on high," said Angie. "Rory asked me to do the search personally and as a matter of urgency."

"Well, thank you."

"The reason for my call is to check you'll be at home as it's easier to bike the cuttings over rather than to fax them. And I'll have to go through the microfiche library for your choristers as I found nothing in the cuttings."

FORTY-FIVE MINUTES LATER a courier stood at the door with a large envelope, which she signed for. Now that she had the dead man's real name, she hoped she would learn more about his life.

Angie had been meticulous in her cuttings search and the pile was in date order, oldest first dated … Hannah flipped through them to see the date on the most recent one. Then began at the beginning of Jonathan Cartmel's story.

While she was reading, DI Benton rang.

"What can I do for you, Hannah?"

She decided on the direct approach. "I've discovered that Daniel Lyons was actually called Jonathan Cartmel."

"Oh, how's that?"

"I had lunch with Simon Ryan and he told me."

There was a pause at the other end of the line. "Well that should help our enquiries, thank you. Anything else?"

"I'm just going through the cuttings *The News* got for me on him…"

"Right. Would you mind if I popped over to have a look as well?"

"Not at all. I'd welcome your thoughts."

MIKE BENTON ARRIVED with some rather nice sandwiches he'd bought from the local deli. "Not as posh as your lunch with the QC, I fear." He grinned at her.

"I'll put the kettle on."

He followed her into the kitchen. She had already decided to come clean about her visit to Daniel's digs. "Mike, can we be straight with each other?"

His expression gave nothing away. "I hope so."

She concentrated on pouring the boiled water into the cafetière. "I went to see Daniel Lyons' landlady. I sort of went in disguise and told her my name was…"

"Jill Bradshaw, his therapist."

"You knew!"

"I guessed." He grinned at her. "You forget I know your penchant for dressing up."

"You're not mad at me?"

"Should I be?"

Hannah deflected the question with one of her own. "Why did the police search his room twice?"

Benton looked furious. "Mrs Fenton didn't think to share that information with us. But it makes sense. There was absolutely nothing there of interest. Someone else did a clean-up operation. Anything else?"

Hannah concentrated on the coffee. "Mrs Fenton asked me to leave as she was expecting someone. I … I watched her house from a nearby shop and saw Ruth Robertson from St John's arrive. I'd dropped a glove in Daniel's room to use as a pretext…"

"Go on."

"I could hear raised voices when I knocked but … anyway Mrs Fenton found my glove and that was that. I had no excuse to stay." She didn't need to tell him about stealing Ruth's purse. "The thing is Ruth Robertson was really unpleasant to me on my first visit to St John's. Threatening even. But to my knowledge I have never met the woman before so I don't know how I can have upset her."

"Strange, but thank you. In return, I can tell you that a park-keeper found the missing briefcase hidden in some bushes – empty of course. So we're no further forward there."

Hannah handed him the tray of mugs and plates. "Well let's see if the cuttings reveal anything." She followed him out of the kitchen with the cafetière.

THEY SAT AT the dining room table with their sandwiches and the cuttings spread before them. "There isn't very much on Cartmel. It appears he was a clerk in the chambers that Peter Savage worked at."

Benton looked at her blankly.

"He was a barrister before training as a priest."

"Right – something he didn't think to share with us."

"Possibly he didn't think it was relevant." Hannah was aware she was defending the vicar and should try to be more objective.

"And he didn't recognise Daniel Lyons as Jonathan Cartmel?"

"It would appear not. When I told him he looked genuinely shocked."

"And what else did he say?"

"Nothing. The archdeacon arrived and I had to leave."

"Convenient."

"I thought so too. Anyway it appears that during a case when Savage was representing a company that was partly owned by Albert Croxton…"

"You are joking?"

Hannah's face showed him she was not. She had her own reasons for being cross at the vicar's deceptions.

"Anyway the fact is Jonathan Cartmel was sent down for apparently taking a bribe to fix some of the evidence. It's not very clear but it looks as though he 'interfered' with witness statements and intimidated a key prosecution witness."

Mike finished his sandwich and drank some coffee. "So what's the motive for killing him?"

"That's the big question."

MIKE HAD MADE copious notes and copied the timeline Hannah had made.

"Well that gives us a lot more to work on, thanks, Hannah. I'll check out Cartmel's prison record and see what that reveals. And I'll be having a word with your vicar and Albert Croxton when he's well enough."

"How is he?"

Mike sighed. "Put it this way, he's getting the best medical treatment money can buy. But his doctors are shielding him. We also have placed a twenty-four-hour armed guard on his hospital room." He looked at Hannah. Her expression must have given away her thoughts. Someone had still managed to get to Father Patrick and kill him when he'd had police protection at St Thomas' Hospital.

"I think Croxton has his own security there as well." He packed up his notes and stood ready to leave.

"I presume you ran police checks on all the people in the choir?"

"Of course. Nothing of note. Why?"

"*The News* cuttings department is doing a search through the microfiche library. But I haven't had the results yet. It's a long shot but you never know."

"Indeed. Let me know if there's a person of interest." Hannah nodded. "Take care and make sure your security is high as well."

Hannah paled. "You don't think…"

"Just a precaution." He smiled. "I'll let you know if there are any developments."

AS SOON AS the DI left, Hannah went to collect Elizabeth. She felt exhausted by the day's revelations. Her mind was full of conspiracy theories and subterfuge. She wondered how Simon knew what he did. And why? At least Mike Benton seemed on the level. At least she hoped he was.

THAT EVENING she went through the cuttings again. Had she missed a vital clue? She thought about the empty briefcase. What had been in there? Did the contents incriminate someone who would kill to maintain silence? That thought took her back to Albert Croxton. He hadn't been directly involved in the case in which Jonathan Cartmel had perverted the course of justice. But one of his companies was. The directors of that company were on trial but they wouldn't reveal where the money they were laundering was coming from. Presumably organised crime. Were Jonathan Cartmel's death and the shooting of Albert Croxton linked? And what had Jonathan done that made him vulnerable to blackmail?

All these thoughts continued to spiral in her mind as she went to bed, and her dreams were haunted by the face of Jonathan Cartmel.

TWENTY-THREE

THE NURSERY WAS looking more and more Christmassy. Hannah felt quite envious as she left Elizabeth there to be absorbed into decoration making, which was that morning's activity. Elizabeth rushed in to sit with Harry and a little girl she didn't recognise. Hannah's wave goodbye was all but ignored.

Back home, Hannah decided to go through the cuttings Angie had gleaned from the microfiche library and had printed out. Angie had annotated the list she'd sent over. By each name was a "nothing found" or the number of cuttings. There were quite a few for Craig Fletcher. No great surprise as he often arranged concerts, which were reported on by the local press. Hannah leafed through them, highlighter in hand just in case she saw something of note. Those that were about him personally were complimentary. Some of the concerts didn't get brilliant reviews but that probably said more about the critic than the performance. Nothing to connect him with anything illegal.

Sarah and Noel Hindman's wedding was featured in a local paper. Hannah was deeply saddened to read an announcement of death of Marianne Merton's only daughter, aged six and the funeral arrangements. Nothing about how she died. Hannah made a note to check that out.

A very old cutting revealed that John Bowman had been something of a child prodigy, singing with a fairly famous choir – a career which ended when his voice broke.

There was a lovely piece on Lorraine Fenton when she retired from the local library after a lifetime of service – Hannah wondered if her contact there, Natalie Vines, knew her. She was about to make a note then decided to call her.

Someone else answered the phone but she was eventually put through to the chief librarian. "Hannah – how lovely to hear from you. I was going to contact you for a favour."

"Oh nothing too onerous, I hope."

Nathalie laughed. "I was wondering if you would sign a copy of your book for me. I loved it by the way."

"That would be a pleasure." It always surprised Hannah that people wanted to have books signed by her. But at least it was a favour she could easily fulfil. "If you have it with you, I could pop in later."

"I do actually – I've kept it here just in case you came in." They agreed to meet in The Plough at lunchtime. Strangely she didn't ask why Hannah had rung.

Hannah returned to the cuttings. The only other was of Richard Lomax running the London Marathon in 1990 in record time. The rest of the choir had made no mark in the local press.

THE PLOUGH WASN'T BUSY; Nathalie and Hannah arrived at the same time. They ordered the soup of the day. Hannah had a glass of wine, Nathalie a pineapple juice. She handed over the carrier bag containing two books. The librarian looked sheepish. "One for me and one for my mum for Christmas."

Hannah completed the task as their lunch arrived. "Actually I wanted to pick your brains."

"Yes?" Nathalie and Hannah had met when an Australian man had died in the library. Nathalie had shared vital information that instigated Hannah's investigation into the Child Migration Scheme.

"Do you know Lorraine Fenton?"

Nathalie returned her soupspoon to the bowl. "Well, that's a question I didn't expect." She looked as though she was considering what to say. "I knew her as a colleague in the borough and I had a two-week handover period, just before she retired. She was a legend in the library world. Why d'you ask?"

"She sings in the choir at St John's and I've just joined as an extra for the Christmas services."

"Really?" Her expression was a picture of disbelief. "Nothing to do with the fact that a chorister died there? And the vicar was shot at?"

"I'm not working at the moment."

"Just as well after…" Her concern was obvious. "After what happened with that awful man." She finished her drink. "Does her daughter still sing there?"

Hannah looked at her blankly. "I've no idea. What's her name?"

"Rosie something or other. Lorraine told me about her grand-child being killed by a hit-and-run driver."

Hannah felt a frisson of déjà vu. "When was this?"

"Probably about ten years ago. I'm not sure really. Rosie, according to her mother, went to pieces. It finished her marriage."

Hannah could understand how that could happen. "What a tragedy. And the driver was never found?"

"Not that I know of." Nathalie looked at her watch. "Sorry, I have to get back. Thanks for signing my books. Happy Christmas if I don't see you before."

AS HANNAH WAS WALKING back down Barry Road, she considered Nathalie's abrupt departure. She wondered why. She also wondered why Peter Savage hadn't told her that Lorraine and Rosie were mother and daughter. And presumably Leah knew too. Why the secrecy? Who would know about Rosie's loss?

She phoned DI Benton when she arrived home and was in luck as he was at his desk. "So what can I do for you, Hannah? Or have you solved the mystery surrounding Jonathan Cartmel?"

"Sorry, no. But can you access any info on a hit-a-run incident that killed a child locally? The mother is Rosie Ball and she's in the choir, as is the grandmother Lorraine Fenton, although you wouldn't know they were related."

She didn't have to explain further. "Okay. I'll get someone onto it and let you know if we come up with anything."

HANNAH HAD BEEN in two minds about going choir practice. The church didn't seem such a safe place to be, whatever the vicar and DI Benton said. She was half-minded to send her apologies but if she was going to get anywhere with discovering more about Daniel/Jonathan she felt she needed to be there, and she had also made a commitment. She was keen to see Dinah again as well. There was something about her that didn't quite ring true. That she had been in the army could explain her fitness and the way she tackled the gunman, but Hannah felt there was something more to her presence at the church. And she definitely had the impression that the vicar and she had some connection.

She hadn't found the vestry particularly warm last time so wore trousers and a thick jumper. Leah arrived on time to babysit but there was no time to ask her about Rosie and Lorraine. "Have fun."

"Leah, have you heard me sing? I have to concentrate so hard to finish at the same time as everyone else, let alone end on the right note."

"Get away with you." She ushered Hannah out of the house.

HANNAH ARRIVED EARLY. So had Dinah. Craig Fletcher welcomed them, and Lorraine smiled as she organised the music on the table. "Great to see you again, ladies. Everything you need is on the table. I just need to check something in the church." No mention of Sunday's shooting. No one, it seemed, ever talked about the elephants in the church.

Hannah picked up the various pieces of sheet music and books. "Not too many bruises, I hope?"

Dinah hesitated. "What?"

"Bruises – from your flying tackle on Sunday?"

She chuckled. "No just a bit of a sore hip where I landed badly. Must be out of practice." She grinned. "It was all rather dramatic, wasn't it?"

"Yes and thankfully the vicar only got a surface wound. Could have been a lot worse and I was standing right next to him." Hannah had wanted to see the other woman's reaction but just then several choir members came in. They stopped talking when they saw them. Or rather when they saw Dinah.

Alison went up and hugged her. "Hope you're okay? That was quite a performance on Sunday."

As the attention focussed on Dinah, Hannah noticed that one man, Richard Lomax, had studiously avoided them. Others came in in twos and threes. There was an undercurrent of conversations that Hannah couldn't hear properly. It was as though she were under water. No one spoke to her although she noticed that some looked in her direction. She wondered if they were always this unfriendly to newcomers. Had they ignored Daniel – as they knew him – as well? If so, little wonder he had found himself dying alone in the Lady Chapel.

However he hadn't been alone all the time. Had someone been

waiting for him, hidden away, or had he arranged to meet someone there? If so, was it a member of the choir? Someone who was here now?

She had asked the vicar to find out from the musical director if anyone else had joined the choir recently. Apparently another man had joined at around the same time as the dead man but he had only lasted a couple of weeks before leaving, seemingly not happy with the way the musical director conducted rehearsals. A lame excuse but the man wasn't a member of the congregation and had just disappeared.

Craig returned looking out of sorts. Hannah wondered why. Rosie had come in a bit late but hardly acknowledged her mother – or anyone else.

"Right. Let's begin with a prayer." Everyone stood. "Almighty God, we bring before You our hearts and voices to the glory of Your name. Amen." They moved on to the scales to warm up. Hannah noticed that Daniel's robes had been removed from the chair. She watched the men she was sitting opposite. Could one of these have lured their fellow chorister to his death? *And what makes you think it was a man?* The voice in her head seemed so loud she wondered if anyone else had heard. She sang the last notes of the scale, relieved she could sit back and listen for a while. But no such luck.

"So let's start with hymn 495 'God is working His purpose out'." There was a rustle of books as the singers found the hymn. "Hannah and Dinah – do join us. I know you won't be singing in the choir on Sunday but it's all good practice."

The two women sat at the end of the sopranos. One of the altos, April Hunter, a middle-aged woman with mid-length mousy hair and wearing a long tweed skirt and a huge, shapeless grey cardigan, huffed noisily about having to move her music from a chair. She glared at Hannah and Dinah for no reason Hannah could think of.

"NO, NO, NO!" Craig rapped his pen on the keyboard. "We need to phrase the music... shades of light and dark..." He sighed. "Let's try again from bar 21 and don't forget that B-flat, sopranos."

Hannah realised that her thoughts had been miles away and she hadn't a clue what the director of music was talking about. She wasn't the only one.

"Sorry, where are we?" There were groans in reply to Hazel's question. Hannah looked across the room. One of the tenors, David, was miming that she'd been drinking. Another, Noel, was shaking his head in disbelief. She caught Richard Lomax, the man who had avoided them earlier, staring at her. Not in an unpleasant or intimidating way. He looked curious as though he thought he knew her from somewhere. He looked away as soon as Hannah smiled. He was one of the regular choir members so probably would have known Daniel. But how well?

Hannah tuned back into the room. *Concentrate*, she admonished herself.

"Right, let's 'la' through the music." But it wasn't right. "Please watch me for direction." Craig was sounding more exasperated. "You need to come in together – and strongly." The second time it went better. "Good, now let's add the words."

BY THE END of the session they'd made some inroads into the hymns – some to be sung on Sunday afternoon service of carols and readings and some at Midnight Mass. She wondered if her mother or father would come along to the service. One of them would have to babysit Elizabeth.

They all stood. "Before we leave just a couple of admin points. Our extras will need robes. Marianne, could you organise the ladies and Noel, the men, please. Plus as you know we have our choir party to look forward to –" his gaze took in all the 'extras' – "and we'd be delighted if you could all join us on Friday 16th. Our vicar is adamant that it should go ahead at the vicarage as planned." He smiled at everyone. "As usual please bring a dish or a bottle – or both." There were a few titters as Craig bowed his head. "Let us pray. As we continue to remember our departed brother Daniel, we give thanks for the time we spend together. May the Lord be with you."

"And also with you." The response was followed by the grace.

"I do hope you'll be able to join us, Hannah." It was Marianne addressing her.

Hannah returned her smile. "I'll try." In fact she had every intention of being there.

"Fancy a lift?" Dinah had packed away her music and was struggling into her coat.

"I'd love one."

As they were leaving, Dinah checked a mobile phone. She looked irritated. "Sorry, I'll just have to make a quick call." She opened the car door for Hannah then moved away to make her call. It seemed very much a one-way conversation with Dinah listening.

"Sorry about that." She smiled but looked worried.

"Not bad news, I hope?"

"Nothing I can't handle." She put the car into gear and they drove off. "Do you fancy a drink tomorrow evening if you're free?"

"I'm not actually but I am on Friday evening if that's convenient for you? I'd need to check out a babysitter." She paused. "Or we could have a drink at my house?"

Dinah grinned at her. "Perfect, what time suits you?"

"Eight?"

Dinah pulled up outside her house. "See you Friday." Once again Dinah did not drive away until Hannah had entered the house.

LEAH SEEMED KEEN to leave as soon as she arrived. Hannah would have liked to have had a chat about the choir but didn't want to impose on her neighbour's generosity.

"Let's catch up soon." Leah gave her a brief hug then made her way across the road. Her sitting room light was on so presumably Brian was waiting for her. Hannah sighed. Sometimes, she thought, it would be nice to have someone to come home to. Someone waiting for her news.

In the absence of that someone, Hannah went upstairs to her study to check her emails. Nothing. She was just going to log off when she thought to check her junk mail. What she saw made her flesh crawl.

SHE PRINTED OFF the email. It came from a Hotmail address. The sender went by the name of avengingangel…

The message was written in quotation marks.

"But don't be afraid of those who threaten you. For the time is coming when the truth will be revealed: their secret plots will become public information." Matthew 10:26

For a long time she stared at the words, reading them over and over again. Then she pressed reply and wrote, "Who are you? Who is threatening me?"

All she received was a notification that there was no such email address. Whoever had sent the email had then deleted the account. What was the point? Why such subterfuge? It all seemed very melodramatic. But was its purpose to frighten her or to intrigue her? Hannah tried to convince herself it was the latter but she went to bed with a heavy heart. In her experience, anonymous messages did not bode well.

TWENTY-FOUR

Her first call was to Reverend Peter Savage. He really was going to have to talk to her. However her call went through to the answerphone. She didn't want to leave a message so hung up. She'd try later.

Hannah decided to dig back and find out if anyone connected with the case – the vicar's last – would be likely to seek revenge or retribution. Peter Savage QC was the barrister for the defence of a company – part owned by Albert Croxton who had a portfolio of business interests – accused of money laundering. Albert wasn't on trial but the company directors were. The case appeared to be a foregone conclusion – the Crown would win. But in the end the case was dropped on a technicality. Presumably this had something to do with Jonathan Cartmel's interference. There was nothing much to go on in the cuttings she had, so she emailed Angie and asked her to check out anything to do with the case but not necessarily the names she had given.

While she was waiting she doodled a time line for the vicar. He had been at St John's for two years so arrived presumably in 1992. He would have spent three years – possibly less – as a curate and two years at theological college so that took him back to 1987 or thereabouts. The case in question was tried earlier that year. That was seven years ago – surely a long time to harbour a grudge, although what motivates such a powerful emotion?

Love. Obviously. Loss. The more Hannah thought about it the more she convinced she was. Perhaps the loss of someone so precious that... Hannah could relate to that in terms of the loss of a child. When Elizabeth had been kidnapped, when she didn't know what had happened to her... Supposing the worst had happened. It didn't bear thinking about but ...

Her phone rang. "Hannah, I've only got a couple of cuttings so if you switch your fax machine on I'll pop them over to you."

"Will do. Thanks, Angie."

A FEW MINUTES LATER, the fax machine came to life with the promised cuttings. Three. One that she almost passed over was from a local paper – a short article about the death of a young woman who had been a witness in the case. It had not been seen as suspicious as she had died in hospital of a viral infection. The second was about a witness, an employee of the company accused of money laundering, who had withdrawn his statement. Presumably this was the person Jonathan Cartmel had intimidated. She wondered how. The third mentioned someone who had stood as a character witness at Jonathan Cartmel's trial. And the name wasn't really a surprise: Ruth Robertson. That might explain her visit to his landlady.

She phoned Mike Benton. "Yes, Hannah?" He sounded stressed.

"I've just found a cutting that states Ruth Robertson stood as a character witness for Jonathan Cartmel at his trial."

"Did she now? Right, thanks, I'll get someone to check on this."

Hannah felt sidelined again. But at least she couldn't be accused of withholding information. She looked again at the timeline she'd constructed for Jonathan Cartmel. He had served time for his part in the case. Was he, she thought, out for revenge for having been sent to jail? Maybe he was looking for retribution. But if that were the case, why hadn't he made himself known to Peter Savage? Perhaps he had been going to and that was why he had lost his life. No there was something missing. Did he, she wondered, take the rap for someone else? Maybe he was paid to confess? By all accounts in the cuttings she'd read, Peter Savage had been a successful barrister. Could it be that he'd had enough of defending people who he thought could have been guilty? Especially if he'd always been inclined towards the church. How close had he been to Patrick Ryan? Simon certainly seemed horrified that he'd been shot. Had they been close? Closer than colleagues?

Thoughts were whirling around her head and she was no closer to solving the mystery. Although in one way she had done what she'd been asked to do by the vicar.

But who was Rosa? Hannah had found no reference to anyone of that name. Had Peter Savage misheard what the dying man had said? She tried to imagine what else it could be but nothing was forthcoming. Was it an acronym? She doodled the letters and wrote possible words:

R – Royal? Regional? Rosary? Revelation? River? Then… Ruth?

O – Of? Organisation? Obituary?

S – Society? School?

A – Architects? Artists? Alcoholics?

Nothing struck her as pertinent. Could it be short for Rosamunde? If there was such a person called Rosa why hadn't she come forward when Daniel, now known as Jonathan, died? It just didn't make sense. Unless, the vicar had made it up to deflect attention? No, that was unthinkable.

IN HIS STUDY, the Reverend Peter Savage's thoughts were spiralling out of control. After his conversation with Simon Ryan and having learned of Daniel's true identity he had been going over and over in his mind the question of Rosa. He had gone down so many cul-de-sacs and dead ends in his mind. His memory of the time was hazy, probably because he didn't want to remember what had happened and his part in it. Although, in truth, he had very little to do with the outcome of the case. He had already begun exploring the idea of joining the church. He closed his eyes and let the echoes from the past wash over him. Past and present merged. He shivered although the room was warm and could feel himself sinking…

"PETER. PETER." He could hear the call coming from far off. There was a bright light drawing him in. Then a darkening shadow blocked the light. Someone was shaking him. He managed to open his eyes.

"Oh thank God. I thought I was going to have to call an ambulance."

He stared into the face of Jonathan Cartmel. "You're not dead."

"I sincerely hope not." The face came into sharper focus. It was Trevor Compton, his churchwarden, staring at him, his face full of concern. "Sorry, vicar, I used my set of keys to get in as there was no answer when I rang the bell and I was worried…"

Peter took a deep breath and tried to move. His arm was painful and the throbbing in his head made him feel nauseous. His hands were trembling.

"Take it easy." Trevor handed him some water and the pain-killers he'd been prescribed at the hospital.

Peter swallowed the pills and struggled to sit upright. He hated to have been found in such vulnerable situation. "Thank you." He smiled weakly. "Sorry for giving you a fright."

Trevor's face was unreadable. "You sounded as though you were arguing with someone. But I couldn't really make out what you were saying. I think you must have been delirious. Your face was burning."

Gradually the room came back into full focus, its proper proportions reassembling around him.

"Do you think you need to see a doctor?"

The vicar didn't answer. He was staring straight ahead and looked terrified. The crucifix on the wall had come alive bearing the face of Jonathan Cartmel. Blood seeped from his eyes. Tears of blood. Peter blinked rapidly and the vision faded. "Sorry, Trevor, what did you say?"

"Do you think you need to see a doctor?"

Peter did his best to smile reassuringly. "I'll be fine once the meds work their magic. But I could murder a cup of tea."

Five minutes later, Trevor returned with tea for them both. "Do you think you ought to be on your own? Should someone come and stay with you?"

And who would that be? Peter asked himself. "No I'll be fine, thank you. Honestly." He sipped his tea. "Now what did you come to see me about?"

TWENTY-FIVE

HANNAH HAD NO APPETITE for attending a party. Least of all one hosted by *The News*. Their Christmas party was traditionally held early in the season, she had been told, so that the journalists would be free to attend any PR celebrations they were invited to. Her new contract with them meant she was back in the fold so to speak and would be attending editorial meetings again. The contract gave her a lot of freedom – not least from financial worries. However it seemed her employment with them was motivated, as ever, more by a need to keep her away from other possible jobs rather than to engage her as a journalist. On a positive note what it did give her was access to the cuttings library and research assistants, an office desk and backup from other staff should she need it. The party was part and parcel of what was to come. The money would give her time to rethink her future.

The present was more demanding. Hannah had done her best to dress for the occasion. She was wearing one of the new outfits she'd bought to wear over the Christmas season. Janet had looked her up and down. "You look great."

"Thanks. I never know how dressy these things will be."

"Does what you're wearing make you feel good?"

"*Ye-es.*"

"Then you have it. Now off you go and have a great time."

HANNAH HAD BEEN SURPRISED that the party was being held at the offices. However, she supposed it made sense. The boardroom complex on the top floor had sliding partitions, which opened up to accommodate a large gathering. It was staff only – no partners – plus a few guests. She was staff now but had received the invitation as a guest. When she had signed the contract she'd been given a new pass, which she used when she arrived at the building and went up in the lift.

"Shall I take your coat, Ms Weybridge?"

Hannah turned to see that one of the juniors had been delegated to cloakroom duties. She smiled. "Thank you, Sadie."

The girl beamed at her. It was one thing Hannah had always done. Learned people's names wherever they were on the hierarchy. It oiled wheels. She was touched that Sadie recognised her.

Taking her coat, Sadie pinned on a ticket. She handed it to Hannah with a strange hesitancy. "You look lovely by the way." She flushed crimson.

There was something about Sadie, Hannah half-remembered. Something she should know. A connection to the newspaper? Was Sadie someone's daughter? Niece? "Thank you. I hope you get to enjoy some of the party too."

THE FIRST PEOPLE Hannah saw and recognised were Larry Jefferson and Neville Rogers chatting together. What on earth was Neville doing here? Careful not to let her surprise show, she approached the two men. A waiter offered a tray of drinks. She took a glass of champagne en route. The room was already full, most staff having changed their clothes at work and so being already on site.

"And what are you two Machiavellians plotting now?"

Neville kissed her cheek. "Never say no to a fancy party, Hannah."

Larry inclined his head. "Neville is my guest."

"And why doesn't that surprise me." Hannah raised her glass just as Georgina honed in on her.

"Hannah, you look lovely."

Hannah took in the editor's outfit, which was totally amazing, shrieking haute couture. Her own dress faded into obscurity beside it. Georgina moved aside slightly to reveal Leo Hawkins, leaning slightly on a walking stick. He looked tired but a smile lit up his face. "Hello, Hannah, I was hoping to see you here."

Her usual kindness overcame her irritation. "Lovely to see you, Leo." Georgina had moved on, leaving them together. "Shall we sit at that empty table?" He took her arm, although she was sure he didn't need the extra support as they walked the couple of yards across the room.

They sat and Leo visibly relaxed. "Thank you. Not sure how

much more standing around I could endure. I'm alright at the beginning of the day but by the evening I wilt."

Hannah looked askance. "You should have told Georgina. No one would expect you to…" She paused. "Why are you even here?" She didn't care how rude that sounded.

He looked confused. "Same reason as you, I suppose. As a guest of Halstone Press – representing my mother."

Hannah tried to relax. Of course Leo would have been invited. Plus he added to the glamour of the occasion. "Well it's good to see you. I…"

She didn't finish the sentence as the room went silent. Lord Gyles was on a small podium. "Ladies and gentlemen. I'm so glad we could meet this evening at our usual pre-Christmas celebration. I'd like to take this opportunity to thank you all for the sterling work you've been doing. Our sales figures are very healthy so 1995 should be a good year for us all. Please enjoy the food and drink –" he paused and looked around the room – "and the company." He raised his glass. "Happy Christmas! And that's enough from me. Enjoy!" There was a smattering of applause and the sound levels rose.

Hannah was wondering how quickly she could leave when a waiter appeared with a tray of food for them as well as a bottle of champagne.

She smiled at Leo. "Do you always get this attention?"

"Not always but it's very welcome at the moment. Please stay and eat with me. I really only came because I hoped I'd be able to see you on more or less neutral ground. I'm sorry I had to rush away on Sunday especially after you'd had such a traumatic time at church."

Hannah sipped her wine.

"Did you find out any more about the shooting?"

Hannah paused. She could hear Claudia's voice telling her to be careful. Could she or should she trust Leo, tempting as it might be? "No, the police are still investigating, I think."

"And how are you feeling about it?"

Hannah wasn't quite sure where he was coming from. Did he also think the bullet was meant for her? Or did he know? "Oh, I'll live to tell the tale."

"That's reassuring." Leo took her hand and stared at her palm as though reading her future. He looked up. "I really enjoy your company, Hannah. And I would love us to get to know each other better." His eyes locked with hers.

"That's very flattering but…" Before she could say anything else, Neville and Rory sat in the empty chairs at their table.

"You don't mind if we join you, do you?"

"Of course not." Leo was charm personified and Hannah was amused at how he and Rory were soon chatting away about football fixtures.

"You okay?" Neville asked very quietly. "You seem subdued."

"No, I'm fine. I don't really like large parties. You look in your element."

"Oh I'm a people watcher. I rarely get such an opportunity to attend large office gatherings. Fascinating watching the political manoeuverings." He chuckled.

"You and Larry seem very pally of late."

"Common interests." But Neville wasn't looking at her. Something had caught his attention across the room. Hannah's gaze followed his. A man was standing in the doorway, dressed as Father Christmas and brandishing a large sack. 'Jingle Bells' rang out through the PA system. Guests were smiling, some, fuelled by champagne, singing along but something was amiss. Hannah experienced a frisson of fear. Goosebumps rose like bubbles in an Icelandic geyser on her arms. She looked slightly to Santa's left and saw the figure that had been haunting her. He raised a finger to his lips. He seemed to be mouthing something but at that distance she couldn't see what. Behind him Hannah could see the movement of silent shadows. His reinforcements, or help for them? Then he faded away.

The room gradually became quieter as Father Christmas dropped his sack, revealing a gun. She felt sick. Under the table, Leo's hand gripped hers. Rory, she noticed, was punching a number into a phone. He looked up and caught her gaze.

The armed man shouted, "Lord Gyles, where are you?"

There was no reply. "One last chance."

Into the silence a shot rang out and the lights in the room were extinguished. Someone screamed.

Hannah could feel her whole body shaking. Another gunman in the space of a few days. In the darkness she could make out shapes moving silently. Suddenly the lights were on again and the guests could see Santa being led away by security. Rory must have had an emergency number. But why? Were they expecting some sort of incident like this? And, if they were, why go ahead with the party?

Lord Gyles was back on the podium. "Ladies and gentlemen – so sorry for that unfortunate interlude. Please be assured that the situation is totally under control. There is no need to worry. Everything has been taken care of. Please enjoy the rest of the evening."

Waiters were moving around topping up people's glasses as Lord Gyles stepped down from the podium and mingled with his guests. Hannah realised she was still clutching Leo's hand. She turned to him. "Sorry. Hope I haven't broken any fingers."

He didn't laugh. "I wouldn't have minded."

Rory had wandered away. Hannah saw him deep in discussion with Georgina. Lord Gyles approached them. Hannah would have given anything to be a lip reader. Then she remembered her apparition. Had anyone else seen him? Not the sort of thing you could casually drop into a conversation. Hannah glanced at her watch, wondering if she could slip away.

Leo interrupted her thoughts. "I'd suggest leaving but I feel I ought to stay."

"I suppose so. It probably won't go on much longer…"

"Hannah… Leo, I do apologise for that little debacle." Lord Gyles was standing before them. "Especially after both your recent experiences. I was hoping for a quiet Christmas after the year we've had." He smiled. "I have cars ready for you downstairs whenever you're ready to leave. You must be exhausted, Leo, and, Hannah, you look as though you've seen a ghost."

I have, Hannah thought, as Leo replied, "I'd like to take you up on that offer, Lord Gyles. If you don't mind."

"Not at all. Have to look after my bestselling authors, eh, Hannah?" He nodded to someone across the room as Larry arrived at their table. "Everything's sorted, sir."

"Thank you. I've arranged cars for Hannah and Leo." He

looked as though he was going to say something else but changed his mind. "Good to have you back on board at *The News*, Hannah. Have a happy Christmas." He gave a bow and moved along to another table.

Neville appeared, looking flustered. "Well, I think I'll reassess my thoughts on office parties."

"Never a dull moment," Larry murmured. "Hannah and Leo are just about to leave. Actually Hannah's car could take you on to your home afterwards, Neville, if you don't mind sharing, Hannah?"

It would seem churlish to say she'd rather be alone.

As the three of them left to collect their coats they were handed a goodie bag. Sadie, Hannah noticed, was no longer on cloakroom duty. In reception, Leo kissed her on both cheeks before leading her to the first car with Neville. "I'll phone you," he said as he closed the car door and waited for the next car to draw up.

THEY BOTH RELAXED back into the comfort of the limousine. Hannah sighed deeply.

"That sounded heartfelt." Neville yawned.

"It was. What did you make of this evening?"

Neville was quiet for a moment. "I thought it seemed staged. For what reason I don't know. Something wasn't right."

"Good Lord, that never occurred to me. Why on earth would someone do that?"

"Why on earth would someone arrive dressed as Father Christ-mas and then brandish a gun?"

Hannah absorbed this idea. "Yes and it was all dealt with so quickly, including the lights, that it seemed expected. Rory appeared to have an emergency number."

"Well it's a new line on Christmas crackers, I suppose." In the darkness of the car, she couldn't tell if Neville was joking.

"Indeed. But why would Lord Gyles stage something to frighten people?" Hannah couldn't believe that the proprietor would do something so cruel.

"Oh, I don't think Lord Gyles was in on this. He looked appalled."

Hannah said nothing.

"You're very quiet, Hannah. Do you think I'm mad?"

Hannah turned to face him. "Actually I was wondering – if Lord Gyles was capable of setting up such a stunt, could he also have been responsible for the shooting at St John's?"

It was Neville's turn for silence. "I don't think so, Hannah," he said at last. "Someone was hurt at the church. No one was targeted at the party."

"You're right, of course. I just wanted a neat explanation."

Neville patted her hand. "I know. Life's a bitch sometimes."

They drew up outside Hannah's house. "Night, Neville. Give my love to Yvonne and the girls – and baby Peter."

Neville grinned. "Will do. Take care."

BY THE TIME HANNAH had filled Janet in on what had happened at the party, she was incredulous. "Do you really think Lord Gyles would do that?"

"Who knows? It didn't occur to me but Neville was convinced someone had set it up. Mind you, he didn't think it was Lord Gyles."

Janet sipped the wine Hannah had offered her. "Seems pretty sick to me. However – someone else may have set it up. Someone with a grudge."

"Perhaps. But they did seem ready for it."

"A tip-off?" Janet suggested.

"Possibly. I wonder if they ever uncovered the 'mole' in the organisation? And if they didn't, why not?" Hannah yawned. "Sorry, too much excitement is exhausting."

"What, like sipping champagne with Leo Hawkins?" Janet grinned at her.

Hannah laughed. "Yes, it could have been worse." She reached over to look in her goodie bag, hoping Janet wouldn't see her blushing.

"So what's in there?"

"The spoils of war."

"The what? More like how the other half lives. Look at that."

Hannah took out the contents of the bag. She had to laugh, seeing a copy of her own book there. She handed it to Janet. "Would you like another one? You could give it as a Christmas present."

"Yes, thanks. I'll put it in our Secret Santa."

They both giggled as they looked through the rest of the goodies, which ranged from perfume and cosmetics to theatre ticket vouchers and gloves. "Take whatever you'd like. You never let me pay you for babysitting so there have to be some perks."

"Are you sure?" Janet helped herself to a few things.

"I am. As long as you don't keep harping on about Leo Hawkins." Hannah yawned again.

"It's okay, I'm going. I know when I've outstayed my welcome."

In the hall, Janet hugged her. "I'm sorry your evening was ruined. Try not to let the bastards get you down. See you soon."

Hannah locked the door after her and took their glasses into the kitchen. She checked the back door, drank a large glass of water, and went upstairs. Elizabeth was mumbling in her sleep. Hannah stroked her face then left her to dream.

Before drifting off to sleep, she went over and over the night's events. She thought Janet's suggestion that someone with a grudge had staged the 'Santa with a gun' sounded more probable than the proprietor doing so. Although he did seem keen for her and Leo to leave. Why was that? And then she remembered the apparition of Daniel/Jonathan standing there. As a warning? Why did she keep seeing dead people? It wasn't as if they ever helped in any way. Maybe she should discuss this with Peter Savage?

Her thoughts turned to Leo – would they ever achieve an uninterrupted conversation? He'd looked sad, she thought. Maybe he was missing his daughters. And his ex-wife? Plus he was grieving for his mother. Not a good time to be thinking of forming new relationships.

Is there ever a good time? she asked herself. An image of Tom suddenly, forcefully, imposed itself on her mind. No. Tom was the past but Leo was definitely not the future.

TWENTY-SIX

"I'M SORRY, HANNAH, Rory isn't available at the moment. Can I take a message?"

Now why doesn't that surprise me, she thought. "No, it's okay, thanks, I'll try again later." Her next call was to Neville.

"Morning, Neville, I was wondering if you'd heard anything more about what happened at the party, given your friendship with Larry?"

"You make it sound almost improper, Hannah." Neville chuckled. "But I have heard from him as it happens."

"And?" Patience was not her strong suit this morning.

"And... apparently that unpleasant interlude was staged. But not by Lord Gyles. 'Santa' was from an agency and he had been hired to appear with the gun, which wasn't real by the way. Someone else switched off the lights – a member of staff apparently who thought it had been organised by management."

"Right – and do they know why this happened? And who booked Santa?"

"If they do they're not saying. Try not to let it worry you, Hannah."

"Well I don't think it was set up for my benefit. But I do wonder who has a grudge against Lord Gyles, and presumably *The News*. Anyway, thanks, Neville."

Her phone rang almost as soon as she hung up.

She was surprised to hear the vicar's voice. "I wonder if you would mind coming over, Hannah? The police want to ask me about Jonathan Cartmel and as I'd asked you to find out about him I thought you should be here. Sorry it's at such short notice."

Hannah agreed to be there in half an hour.

"SO, REVEREND, this is an informal discussion for the moment although not off the record." DI Benton smiled at Peter Savage. Hannah thought he looked saddened rather than annoyed at the revelation that the vicar had known Daniel Lyons as Jonathan Cartmel but apparently had not recognised him. "Hannah is here at your request as you had asked her to find out more about him when Daniel – as he was then known – died."

Peter Savage leaned back in his chair as though to distance himself from the proceedings. A female officer who introduced herself as DC Young left the room to make coffee. They awaited her return in an uneasy silence. The journalist in Hannah was eager for the revelations but her heart went out to the priest. Compassion and empathy had often got her the best – no, the most explosive – news stories in the end. This morning she had little to say but was in a way bearing witness. She hoped this interview wouldn't lead to the priest's downfall.

"Coffee, and I found a cherry cake." DC Kathy Young beamed on her return. Hannah immediately thought of Leah. She had probably made and brought the cake for Peter.

Once they all had sustenance before them, and the DC had her notebook ready, Benton leaned forward. "So let's begin with Jonathan Cartmel turning up at your church as Daniel Lyons. You didn't recognise him?"

Hannah doodled on her notepad.

The priest sighed deeply. "No, I didn't recognise him. He joined the choir but never approached me. I don't think he ever spoke more than two words to me. Craig Fletcher was overjoyed to have another tenor join the ranks and that was it."

"And when you found him in the Lady Chapel?" Hannah was surprised at how gently Benton was proceeding.

"I still had no idea."

"You'd have thought he would have said something, wouldn't you? Given that he obviously knew he was dying?"

"That's the strangest part really." Peter looked perplexed. "If he had been drawn to this church because of me… but he acted as though he didn't know me. There was no warning, no accusation and, I suppose, even stranger, no confession. There was so much he could have revealed but didn't. All he said was to tell Rosa, whoever that is. He never mentioned a sister."

"Yes, we'll get back to that. What do you remember of those circumstances?"

Peter sipped his coffee. The cup rattled as he placed it on the side table. "Very little as it happens. I was involved in what was to be my last case as I had already decided my vocation was not law. I had found a higher calling." Peter clutched the cross he wore. Hannah wondered if he were seeking strength or comfort. Perhaps both.

"Jonathan was one of the clerks in chambers. He looked different then. Younger obviously. Longer, darker hair and a bit on the chubby side. He wore rather large tortoiseshell glasses. He seemed to do everything by the book, as it were, so I, all of us really, we were astounded when it emerged he had deliberately lost witness statements. But worse, he had apparently threatened – maybe that's too strong a word – warned someone not to give evidence. However, the case against my client was dropped on a technicality, not because of what Jonathan did. He, however, was found guilty of perverting the course of justice. I'm afraid I don't know much of what happened to him. I know he served a prison sentence. But as I said my mind was really elsewhere." He looked as though he would like to be elsewhere right now. "Mentally I was already on the road to priesthood." Hannah thought she heard him conclude, "Thank God."

"So his actions seemed out of character?"

"Totally. When he was caught and charged he immediately pleaded guilty and offered no defence."

Benton finished his coffee. The DC poured him some more and then cut slices of cake for them all. "Didn't that seem odd to you?"

"It did, but as I say…"

"Your mind was on higher things," Benton finished for him. He changed tack. "How well do you know Ruth Robertson?"

The vicar seemed surprised at the question. "Not well at all, really. I know she was against my appointment but I have no idea why."

The DI nodded before asking, "When did you realise that Daniel Lyons was, in fact, Jonathan Cartmel?"

For a long moment, the priest said nothing. "When Hannah told me after she'd met with an ex-colleague of mine, Simon Ryan, who'd shown her a photo of the poor man. Just after his release from prison, I think."

Hannah felt everyone's eyes on her. Benton's smile was tinged with sadness. Was he too remembering how they had first met at St John's Waterloo where Simon's brother Patrick had been the vicar?

"And what did you do then?"

"Our meeting – Hannah's and mine – was cut short by the arrival of the archdeacon, who doesn't know about any of this, by the way." He shrugged. "I know I'm lying by omission but he doesn't need to know until we get to the bottom of this mystery."

"I think you're right, Peter." What little Hannah knew of the archdeacon and the church hierarchy told her that no good would come of his interference at this stage.

"Thank you, Hannah." He touched the arm that was in a sling. "And then I had a call from Simon."

No one responded to this for a moment. "And?" the DI prompted.

"He asked me about the shooting and if I thought it was in any way involved with any of my past cases as a barrister. And did I think there was a link to Jonathan Cartmel."

"And do you think there's a link?"

The priest glanced at the crucifix on the wall opposite where he was sitting. "Well I didn't when I thought he was Daniel Lyons. Now I'm not so sure." He shifted in his chair and reached for his coffee.

Hannah stared at him. She was sure he was lying! He knew, or at least he suspected, that bullet was meant for her; she knew it and so did he. Then it occurred to her that if it was a warning and connected to Jonathan Cartmel's death maybe it didn't matter which of them took the bullet.

There was an uneasy atmosphere as though the air had changed direction. An ill wind. Benton finished his cake, making a little mound of crumbs to pop into his mouth. "So did Simon Ryan offer any thoughts on the subject?"

"Yes. He thought Jonathan had probably been blackmailed into doing whatever he did – given his previous good character."

"Plausible. But he would have to have done something seriously wrong … or maybe he was protecting someone else."

"Yes, that's what Simon said."

Benton coughed and looked slightly embarrassed. "He wasn't

protecting you?"

"Good God, why would you say that?"

"Just a thought. He may have known something that would have prevented you becoming a priest."

Hannah realised she'd been holding her breath and exhaled on a whisper. Peter's expression was furious. "I assure you, inspector, the Church of England is scrupulous in its background checks. I have absolutely nothing to hide." His tone was icy. He stood. "Now if you'll forgive me, I have work to do as I'm sure you do too." He opened the study door and they were unceremoniously ushered out, grabbing their coats as they left.

At the door, Benton paused. "I'm sorry if I offended you, reverend. Thank you for our discussion today. You may need to come down to the station to make a full statement but we'll leave that for the time being. Time for us all to reflect."

What they all had to reflect on, he didn't say, but the implication was that Peter might need to establish his part in all this a little more coherently.

"WELL, WHAT DID YOU make of that, Hannah?" Benton asked as soon as the front door closed behind them.

"You seemed to have touched a raw nerve with the last question. And yet…" She stared across at the church.

"And yet?"

"As we all know there have been cover-ups in the past by various religious denominations. You never know…"

"Well if we knew who this Rosa was we might get somewhere," the DI said as they walked down the path to the squad car. "Can we give you a lift home, Hannah?"

She was tempted but wanted her thoughts to settle before any more discussion about the vicar and any involvement in Jonathan Cartmel's death. "Thanks, but I've got a couple of things to get on Lordship Lane."

Mike touched her arm. "I heard about what happened last night. Are you okay?"

"I am, I think. Did Janet tell you?"

"She was one of my sources."

"And did she tell you about Neville Rogers' theory?"

"She did. It's plausible. Try not to dwell on it."

"Well it turns out Santa was hired from a party agency, the gun wasn't real and someone, a staff member, cut the lights."

Benton's face betrayed no previous knowledge of these facts but Hannah was convinced none of this was new to him.

They said goodbye and Hannah made her way through Goose Green. It was a perfect winter's day. Cold and crisp. She was looking up at the majestic trees, now mostly bare, and smiling to herself when a sharp voice brought her back to the present.

"Mind where you're going, why don't you." It was Ruth Robertson, red-faced and rushing towards the church, her arms laden with winter blooms. It was she who should have heeded her own warning.

"Oh hello, Ruth. You look a bit breathless. Are you okay?"

"Of course I am. Just a winter sniffle." Then she paused. "Thank you for asking. Anyway better get these flowers to church. Bye."

Hannah watched her rush off, shrugged and carried on her way.

HANNAH HAD BEEN looking forward to seeing Dinah that evening. The woman intrigued her, with her hint of mystery, her confidence and her amazing unarmed combat skills. However, when she returned home, there was a hand-delivered envelope on the hall mat.

"Sorry something's come up at work and I won't be free this evening after all. Perhaps we could rearrange on Sunday. My mobile number is 07234 39999 if you need to contact me. Dinah."

It was an oddly worded note: *"if you need to contact me."* Why would she? Hannah wondered if her reason had anything to do with the phone call Dinah had taken on Wednesday evening that had seemed to annoy her. It wasn't that she didn't trust the woman but she did feel she wasn't being totally honest. *And nor are you*, she thought. Maybe it was for the best Dinah wouldn't be coming that evening. No awkward questions – for either of them.

Hannah rang Rory and this time he answered his phone. He sounded harassed. "Don't ask me about last night."

"I wasn't going to. Well I was this morning but I've spoken to Neville since then."

"Right."

"Have I done something to offend you?"

"Of course not. Hold on…" Hannah heard him thank someone then he was back on the line. "Sorry, it's been a bloody farce here today but out of my hands now. So how can I help?"

"I just wanted to run some thoughts past you on the dead chorister."

"Go on."

"I think he may have been killed for something he did – or maybe didn't do – years ago. What if being in the church was a tragic coincidence?"

Rory was quiet for a moment. "But supposing him turning up in the church reminded his killer of what had happened? Or I suppose he could have arranged to meet someone there after the choir practice."

"True. I'm just getting nowhere fast with this."

"Well, no pressure here. Will you be at the editorial meeting on Monday?"

"Yes I shall. Need to get myself re-established. It's been a while."

"It has indeed. How about lunch afterwards? We can talk then."

"Love to. Enjoy your weekend."

SHE WAS JUST ABOUT to leave to pick up Elizabeth when her phone rang. "Hi, Hannah, it's Leo," he said as if she wouldn't have known his distinctive – seductive – voice.

"How are you?"

"Better for a good night's sleep and fortunately no nightmares about gun-toting Santas." He laughed. "And you?"

"I'm fine." She didn't know whether to say anything of Neville's suspicions.

"Good. How do you feel about lunch tomorrow? You and Elizabeth," he said quickly, as though to forestall any refusal. "I know it's short notice but Thank God It's Friday has a special lunch for kids and there's face-painting and the like. As long as you don't mind getting to Covent Garden."

The thought of a relaxing afternoon with fun activities for Elizabeth, in the company of an attractive man who was good company, made her smile. "Love to. What time?"

Leo suggested midday so Elizabeth wouldn't get too hungry, immediately reminding her that he was used to family outings with his own daughters. *And a maybe not-so-ex-wife*, she told herself as they ended their conversation.

TWENTY-SEVEN

LEO HAWKINS LOOKED so much better than the last time they met. He looked energised as though some weight had been lifted from him, cutting a dashing figure in his jeans, open-necked shirt and leather jacket. Hannah was amused to see the admiring glances in his direction from both women and men. His was a popular character in *Dead Voices,* which had huge audiences that increased with each new series. He stood as she and Elizabeth arrived at the table.

"Hello, Leo." Hannah had told her daughter who they were going to have lunch with. "I like Leo," she had told her mother. "He smells nice." As he leaned forward to kiss her on both cheeks, Hannah couldn't agree more. His nearness reminded her of the passionate kisses they'd shared after their first meal together, outside The Ivy. It seemed a lifetime ago but was only a few months.

"Lovely to see you again, Elizabeth." Elizabeth was given a booster seat at the table. "Are you hungry or would you like your face painted first?"

"Eat first."

Leo laughed. "A young woman after my own heart."

The waiter brought over some crayons and a picture to colour in for Elizabeth while they studied the menu. "Would you like some chicken, Elizabeth?" She nodded while she coloured her picture and hummed along to the Christmas carols a pianist was playing from a small stage.

A balloon burst, making them all jump. Leo squeezed Hannah's hand. "It's so lovely to see you again. Thank you for coming."

Hannah felt like a tongue-tied teenager. She wanted to say so much but she also wanted to protect herself. She felt vulnerable. "Thank you for inviting us." She sounded like a schoolgirl.

"Well that's the awkwardness over with." He grinned at her. "Let's order." The waiter came to their table with a juice for

Elizabeth and margaritas for them. "I ordered them in advance. Hope you don't mind?"

"Of course not." It had been so long since she had been taken out like this, Hannah was out of practice. Being so near to Leo sent her stomach butterflies into overdrive.

They decided on some starters followed by fajitas.

The food and Elizabeth's happy observations about the balloons and paper hats provided a cover for Hannah's uneasiness of being seen in public with Leo. He seemed oblivious. Theirs was such an odd relationship, which had started with him engaging her to find out who had killed his mother and why, and almost ended with the serious attempt on his life. He had joined her at the launch of *Joan Ballantyne: A Life* and then almost immediately afterwards departed for the States to recuperate. And then there was the disastrous chat show interview…

"Penny for them." Hannah stared at him. "Oh if it's that serious, I'll up the fee."

"Not at all. I was just remembering…"

"Hello –" A fairy had arrived at their table and addressed Elizabeth, whose eyes were enormous. The magical creature waved her wand, sprinkling sparkles around her. "Would you like to come and have your face painted?"

Her daughter had slid off her booster seat without a second glance at her mother. "Yes please."

As though sensing Hannah's reticence, the fairy smiled at her reassuringly. "We're just over there." Indeed the face painting station was only a table away. Hannah willed herself to relax.

"So where were we?"

Hannah was confused. "I'm sorry."

His smile was beguiling. "Before the attack I had been rather hoping we might have something going for us."

Hannah could feel the blush creeping up her neck. Her treacherous body remembered the passion his kisses had aroused but there was one question she had to ask. "Leo I … I thought you might have got back with your wife while you were in the States."

He looked at her blankly. "Why on earth would you think that? I thought I told you my ex-wife –" he stressed the ex – "has a new partner. And my daughters are very happy living with them."

"No, I don't think you did." But there was a memory. It was Joan, his mother, who had told her that, before she'd ever met Leo.

"I'd love to get to know you better, Hannah. Can we move on – as slowly as you like?"

Hannah nodded. There was a screech. Startled, she looked over to the face painter but it wasn't Elizabeth. Her daughter was quietly being transformed into a tiger. She picked up her wine and took a gulp to steady her nerves. People had stopped looking over at them. It was a family day and the children came first.

"We both have pasts, Hannah. You never mention Elizabeth's father."

"He's dead." The words came out far more bluntly than she intended.

"I am so sorry…"

"No, please don't apologise. Elizabeth's father –" she struggled to say his name – "Paul was never part of her life although he did meet her before he died. In fact he saved her life and I –" she fought to keep her voice from breaking – "I never got to thank him." She blinked rapidly. As she did so she smelled freesia so strongly she almost asked Leo if he could smell it too. It felt like a blessing. "Sorry."

"Good God, don't apologise. I'm sorry for blundering in on your emotions."

A waiter came over and refilled their glasses. Leo took her hand and kissed the palm, sending waves of desire through her body. The moment was broken by Elizabeth – now a ferocious tiger – returning to their table with the fairy who waved her wand sprinkling more sparkles. "Bye, Elizabeth."

"Bye, fairy." Elizabeth gazed in awe after the magical creature.

"Would you like some ice cream, Elizabeth?"

The tiger turned to Leo. "Yes please."

BY THE TIME the ice cream was eaten, Elizabeth looked as though she might nod off. "I think we ought to make a move, Leo."

He smiled at Elizabeth's weary face. "Of course." He caught the waiter's eye and asked for the bill. When he brought it, the young man who had served them looked at Leo shyly. "Would you mind signing an autograph, Mr Hawkins?"

Leo was happy to oblige. "What's your name?" Edgar got his autograph and Leo paid the bill. "Let me help you find a taxi." Without waiting for a reply, he picked up Elizabeth and then his walking stick, leaving Hannah to follow in their wake. Outside a black cab was dropping someone off. Leo saw them into the taxi and waved them off after a brief kiss on the cheek and a, "see you soon".

LATER THAT EVENING Hannah went over her conversation with Leo. There was no doubt about their mutual attraction but she wasn't sure she'd be up for a relationship with a famous actor. It was one thing getting to know someone slowly – and after all, what did she really know about him – but would that be possible given his celebrity status? They hadn't mentioned the shooting at the church or that of Albert Croxton. She hadn't thought to ask him about his friend and agent Charles either. So many imponderables.

Another was the situation regarding Jonathan Cartmel. Technically, she had fulfilled her role for the vicar but he showed no sign of wanting her to stop investigating. Why? And for her own satisfaction she wanted to get to the bottom of the mystery which, she was convinced, would eventually make a good exposé for *The News* – as long as Albert Croxton wasn't involved. If he was, she feared Lord Gyles would spike the story.

TWENTY-EIGHT

"'LET YOUR GENTLENESS be known to everyone'." A
dramatic pause. The vicar knew how to play to his audience and
took a moment to look around the congregation. A few shuffled
in their seats. Peter Savage rested his arm, which was still in a
sling, on the edge of the pulpit. He looked sad, Hannah thought,
although he smiled at his parishioners. "'Do not worry about
anything, but in everything by prayer and supplication with
thanksgiving let your requests be made known to God'." He paused
again but was chuckling to himself. "And I don't mean requests
for Christmas presents. That's Father Christmas' jurisdiction."
Several people laughed, including Leah who was sitting next to
her. Hannah saw a little girl nudge her brother. As usual, Elizabeth
seemed to be absorbing it all – silently.

"Our second reading this morning, from Philippian's Chapter
4 verses 4 to 7 was short but absolutely to the point. I hope you'll
take time to read it again at home. Remember, God knows what
is in our hearts. He knows our weaknesses, flaws and foibles but
He also knows our strengths, talents, and kindnesses. As Christmas
approaches many of us will feel stressed out, caught up in the
busy-ness of preparations and getting everything done in time.
But when you come here, to God's house, I want you to relax and
find peace in this place…"

Someone commented loud enough for everyone to hear. "Not
much peace and goodwill last week, vicar, when you were shot at."

Hannah noticed a few appalled glances. Someone had dared
to mention the elephant in the church. Leah looked furiously at
the speaker. However some people were muttering in a similar
vein. Peter put up his hand. "The culprit was caught –" he glanced
across the pews – "thanks to the amazing action of Dinah Bell."
He inclined his head towards her and there was a spontaneous
burst of applause, Elizabeth joining in enthusiastically.

"It's always good to have some guardian angels around us."

Peter grinned. "And in conclusion and, I paraphrase, may the peace of God, which surpasses all understanding guard your hearts and your minds. In the name of Jesus Christ, Amen."

"Amen," chorused Elizabeth.

As the service continued, Hannah allowed her thoughts free rein. Earlier, walking to church with Leah, she had broached the subject of Peter's past.

"I know very little about his life before he came to us." Leah looked pensive. "He was amazing when I consulted him about my brother. He's a very private person and equally he's totally discreet. And, of course his legal background is useful. But anything told to him in confidence would remain so. He's not a gossip as some are."

Hannah, pushing Elizabeth in her buggy, pondered this. "You don't think anyone could be blackmailing him?"

Leah stared at her. "Good heavens no! What on earth gave you that idea?"

"Just something I heard." They had arrived at the church, putting an abrupt end to their conversation.

HANNAH'S ATTENTION REFOCUSED on the service. "Let us offer each other a sign of the Peace." Hannah inwardly cringed but Elizabeth was in her element shouting, "Peace," and clapping. Father Peter came over to hug Leah in an awkward one-armed way and shook her hand. "Peace be with you, Hannah."

She smiled. "And with you." She noticed him make a beeline for Dinah. They exchanged a few words she couldn't hear, and then he returned to the Sanctuary where the curate helped him with preparing the bread and wine. Hannah didn't go up to receive communion but noticed that one of the servers stood by the priest holding the chalice containing the wafers so that he could administer them one-handed.

Eventually the last hymn came to an end followed by the blessing, and the service was over. Almost immediately Dinah was by her side. She greeted Leah before she moved off to speak to someone. "I'm so sorry about Friday. I was looking forward to our drink."

"So was I," Hannah said as she lifted Elizabeth out of the throng of people milling about.

"I don't suppose you're free this evening?"

Hannah almost laughed at the thought of her social calendar being so full – even Sunday evenings. "I am, actually. Shall we say eight?"

"Perfect." Dinah waved to Elizabeth and left the church. Maybe she didn't want to get into conversations about last Sunday's flying tackle and citizen's arrest.

She wasn't the only one anxious to leave. Elizabeth pulled at her sleeve. "Mama, home."

Hannah was surprised. Elizabeth loved holding court here. She looked flushed and her head felt hot. "Okay, let's tell Leah we're going."

They found Leah talking to Marjorie. Hannah touched her arm lightly. "Leah, we're going to make a move. Elizabeth seems a bit off colour so I'll get her home."

"Oh, you poor darling." She caressed Elizabeth's cheek. "You go home and get better soon. Phone me if you need anything, Hannah."

AFTER A QUIET AFTERNOON watching Elizabeth's favourite video, her daughter was so tired she went to bed as in a dream. Hannah hoped she wasn't sickening for anything but she didn't have a temperature and ate well at lunch and dinner. She was looking forward to seeing Dinah and prepared a few snacks for them to have with wine. Presumably Dinah wouldn't drink much if she was driving, and Hannah didn't want a late night given that she had her first editorial meeting of her new contract the next day.

Promptly at eight the bell rang. Hannah checked the video to see Dinah staring back at her. She opened the door, smiling. "Come in. You look frozen.

"I walked over to get some much-needed exercise." She handed over a bottle of wine and took off her coat before following Hannah into the sitting room. "Lovely and warm in here. Great tree. Must be fun doing Christmas with a child."

"It is. Last year we went to my parents in France but they're coming here this year." Hannah opened the bottle and poured the wine. "Help yourself to nibbles. What are you doing for Christmas?"

"I'm living with my gran at the moment as she hasn't been well, and all the family are descending on the day. Gran will be in her element and I'll be questioned nonstop about why I haven't found myself a good man."

Hannah laughed. "Families eh?"

Dinah drank some wine and looked over at the photographs of Elizabeth. "What did you make of church today?"

"Difficult to judge really as I haven't been going there for long. The vicar handled his heckler very well."

"Didn't he. Still, goes with the job, I suppose." She helped herself to some olives. "So what brings you to St John's?"

Hannah had anticipated the question and had thought of a suitable reply. "I met Peter via my neighbour and friend Leah Braithwaite – she lives across the road – and he suggested having Elizabeth christened. To be honest I hadn't really considered it. But I thought I'd go along to the church to see if it appealed. Elizabeth seems to love it."

"And joining the choir?"

Hannah laughed. "Yes, that wasn't in my plans at all but Leah more or less inveigled me into it. She and her husband, Brian, seem to think I need more local friends and activities." She took a gulp of wine. "And you? How come you joined so recently?"

"Oh I love singing. Plus I've only recently started attending St John's. It seemed a good way to test the waters, so to speak."

"Well you're a great asset to the choir – and the congregation! What did the vicar call you? A guardian angel?"

It was Dinah's turn to laugh. "I've been called worse." She didn't elaborate.

"Do you miss it? The army, I mean." Dinah stared at her briefly. Hannah could have kicked herself. She shouldn't have known that. Dinah had only mentioned martial arts training.

Her expression was unreadable. "I don't miss the racism – or the sexism for that matter. I worked bloody hard to achieve my rank but…" She shelled a few pistachios rather than finish her sentence.

"But?" Hannah prompted.

"But that's the past. We all have pasts, don't we?" And the way she looked at Hannah made her feel she knew far more about her than she was willing to reveal about herself, which was confirmed by her next question. "Any more books in the pipeline?"

"No. Books aren't really my forte. Especially memoirs. But I've signed a new freelance contract with a newspaper I'd been working for."

Dinah nodded. She didn't ask which newspaper so presumably she knew that too. "Is it hard bringing up a child on your own?"

Hannah was surprised by the question. "I suppose so, but I don't know any different. Thinking of trying it?"

"No way. I enjoy my independence too much."

Hannah changed the subject. "I wonder what the choir party will be like. You are going, aren't you?"

"Not sure yet. I'd like to but that depends on work."

"On a Friday evening?"

Dinah smiled. "I'll make an effort to be there."

"It'll be interesting to see the choir members off duty so to speak."

"Perhaps." She drank some more wine. "I can't help wondering how Daniel Lyons ended up being left on his own in the Lady Chapel."

"No, it is strange. Unless he was meeting someone in there."

"Why would he?"

"Million-dollar question. And one we may never know the answer to."

Dinah gave her a strange look but didn't pursue the subject. "Have you lived here long?"

They chatted about the various places they'd lived in until Dinah glanced at her watch. "I'd better make a move. Early start tomorrow. Do you have a minicab number?"

As she was leaving, Dinah hugged her. "Thanks for this evening." She looked at the reinforced door and security locks. "Impressive." But she didn't comment further other than to wish her a good night.

AS SHE WAS CLEARING AWAY, Hannah wondered why she hadn't been more upfront with Dinah. What harm would it have done? But she couldn't betray Peter's confidence. Dinah reminded her of Claudia Turner in a strange way. They were both so self-contained. And Claudia had certainly alluded to the misogyny in the police. One thing she was sure of, Dinah wasn't at all your typical civil servant. What past was she hiding? Or perhaps more to the point; what was she concealing about her present?

TWENTY-NINE

THE BOARDROOM wasn't as full for the editorial meeting as Hannah remembered them. Georgina wasn't there and the deputy editor, Terry Cornhill, was in the chair. His warm smile reminded her of how often he had helped her in the past. How she had valued his advice. "Welcome, Hannah. Good to have you back on board."

"Thank you." Rory had saved her a seat beside him. She glanced at the agenda before her and doodled on it as section editors updated the meeting. A major story was Russian troops entering Chechnya and the attack on the city of Grozny the previous day. Hannah allowed the rise and fall of the conversation around her to lull her senses. There was little she had to offer. Her mind drifted to her dead chorister. Would she ever discover why he had died…

"So, Hannah, do you have anything for us?"

Hannah was startled out of her reverie by Terry addressing her directly.

"I have been looking into a suspicious death of a chorister at my local church, St John's East Dulwich…"

"Where the vicar was shot at last week?" The news editor was making notes.

"Yes. And he had asked me to find out what I could about this Daniel Lyons who I've since discovered was …"

Rory kicked her gently under the table. "I think Hannah should run with this as she's already involved."

Terry nodded to the assistant editor. "Good idea. Hannah, just ask Rory if you need any backup." His smile included everyone at the table. "Right, chaps, let's hope for a quiet run-up to Christmas as we've got all the usual features ready to run. And that, as they say, is a wrap."

Everyone collected their papers and left the room. "What was the kick for?" Hannah asked once they were alone.

"I didn't want you to go into too much detail in an open meeting – you never know. We'll carry on with some digging here, and keep me up to date. Let me know who you're meeting and seeing." He chuckled. "Nice pic of you and Leo Hawkins in the Sunday rag whose name we cannot mention."

"What?" They had reached his office. He picked up a newspaper from his desk to show her. Someone in the restaurant had managed to take and presumably sell a photo of her and Leo looking intimate. Elizabeth wasn't in the photo, thank goodness.

"That's what you get for dating a celebrity." Rory's light-hearted tone belied his concern. "Just be careful. Seriously, when you're working keep me up to date." He handed her a sheet of paper with the names Terry and Tony Burtron.

"What's this?"

"The Two Ts. They were the gangsters involved in the money laundering case. They presumably threatened to kill members of the directors' families to make them keep quiet. They're both dead now but there are two sons, cousins, who still run the firm. So tread carefully."

Hannah sighed loudly but she knew Rory had her best interests at heart. Her investigations had led her into situations out of her control and with life-threatening potential. Her daughter had also been put at risk…

"And I'm sorry, but I can't make lunch today after all. But we'll catch up soon. Remember to keep me in the loop. And DI Benton – he's one of the good guys."

In the open plan office, there were quite a few empty desks. People on holiday or out on stories, she assumed. She used the phone on one to book a company car home. As she was leaving her mobile rang with an unexpected invitation she couldn't refuse.

THIRTY

THE HEAT FROM the blazing log fire was welcome. The mantelpiece and surrounds were ornate – marble probably – and the antique brass fire tools reflected the flames. The room had the air of a private room in gentlemen's club, or her idea of one, with a faint whiff of cigar smoke. The walls were indigo blue or at least the parts not covered by photos. Instead of politicians and actors that might adorn a club's walls, these were obviously of family and looked as though they spanned several generations. Above the mantelpiece was a portrait of a woman in an evening gown, smiling coyly at the artist. It reminded Hannah of the portrait of Joan Ballantyne. Same artist? In both alcoves were bookcases and, although she couldn't see the titles in the lamplight, from where she was standing, it appeared to be an eclectic mix of paperbacks and leather-bound tomes.

A dark Doberman growled half-heartedly from his position at the side of the man in the high-backed armchair, his legs raised on a footstool and covered with a plaid rug. His face bore traces of the trauma he'd endured but his smile was genuine as he welcomed her.

"Come in, Hannah. Welcome to my den. Take a seat near the fire. It must be brass monkeys out there."

Hannah sat facing him. She had left her coat in the hall with the person who had opened the door to her, a housekeeper with an expression to sour milk.

"How are you, Mr Croxton?"

He raised an eyebrow. "Albert, please. And what can I offer you to drink?"

She was about to decline, reluctant to stay any longer that she had to, but she didn't want to seem unfriendly and she needed him on her side if she was to discover anything at all. "What are you having?"

He chuckled. "I think I'll have a brandy, but you have whatever you'd like. Would you mind doing the honours –" He pointed to a side table replete with bottles, glasses, and an ice bucket. "Don't want to incur the wrath of Mabel. She's irritable at the best of times."

Hannah couldn't image employing someone in your home who you didn't get along with. Her thoughts must have been evident in her expression.

"She was my late wife's companion. They were friends for donkey's years. I don't feel I can turf her out." He laughed. "Although young Harry might be her undoing."

"But Harry's a sweetheart! Elizabeth adores him."

"And the feeling is mutual, I hear. But Mabel isn't used to children, although she gets on better with Harry's sister, Zoë." He sighed. "My wife and I didn't have children." He stared into the blazing logs. "Fran is the daughter I never had. Especially after her parents died."

"I didn't know…"

"Why should you? My sister and her husband were killed in a car accident. I became Fran's guardian."

Hannah brought over the drinks and placed his on a coaster on the table beside him, next to a copy of *Joan Ballantyne: Her Life*.

He caught her glance. "You did a good job. There were times when I could hear Joan's voice. So many memories."

She ignored that. "You didn't answer my question."

He looked askance.

"How are you feeling?" He looked so relaxed it was difficult to believe an attempt had been made on his life. Then she noticed the tremor of his hand as he raised his glass to his lips. For a moment she saw his torment flash across his face.

"Lucky, if the truth be told. Lucky to be alive."

A cold fear clasped her. Had she too been a target?

"And that's what I wanted to talk to you about. I wanted to reassure you that … that what happened to me had nothing to do with you or the kidnapping of Elizabeth and Edith Holland."

Hannah stared at him. Obviously he wasn't going to own up to the bombing of the Soho clubs. A retaliatory action? He sipped his brandy. "I didn't want you to worry."

"But what about the vicar of St John's? He was shot at." *If the bullet wasn't meant for me*, she added to herself.

"Was he?" Albert looked totally shocked. Could he really not have known?

"Yes. I was standing next to Peter Savage when it happened."

Albert almost spluttered over his drink. He fished in a pocket for a handkerchief. "I'm sorry, did you say Peter Savage?"

Hannah knew how to play her cards close to her chest. "Do you know him?"

"I knew a Peter Savage who was a barrister. Some time ago. I had no idea he'd made such a drastic change of career. If it's the same person."

Was he covering his tracks or being honest? She couldn't tell.

"I believe he was a barrister before ordination." She waited for him to ask if he survived. Or did he already know?

"How is he?"

"Fortunately he suffered a surface wound on his arm. Painful but not life-threatening. Unlike yours."

His stare unsettled her. Then his mood lightened. "Actually it wasn't. Life-threatening."

"But I thought…"

"What you were meant to think."

"But Fran…"

"Played a blinder. But she didn't know the real extent of my injuries either at the beginning."

Hannah now knew why *The News* had been so circumspect in reporting the shooting. Lord Gyles again. He knew the truth and had his newspaper downplay the event even though other papers, especially the red tops, were screaming about turf wars. She stood. "I hope she's proud of herself. I thought we were friends."

"Sit down, Hannah, and get off your high horse." It sounded like an order but he was laughing at her. She didn't know what was worse. "I invited you here as I said, to reassure you. And also…" he sipped his brandy… "to thank you."

"For what?"

"For being a friend to Fran."

She ignored that. "Do the police know the extent of your injuries?"

"Need-to-know basis. And the reason I can reassure you is that they have caught the gunman."

Hannah sank down into her chair and took a gulp of her drink. Why hadn't Mike Benton contacted her? He knew how worried she was. Albert Croxton was considering her in a not unkindly way.

"Who was it?"

"The gunman? Someone hired to settle an old score. You don't need to know the whys and wherefores but you do need to know you are not involved."

"Was it anything to do with Terry and Tony Burtron?"

He stared at her then smiled. "Rest assured you are not involved."

She breathed deeply and tried to smile. "An early Christmas present."

He raised his glass to her. "Indeed." He looked at her empty glass. "Would you like another?"

She glanced at the grandfather clock in the corner. "Better not. Have to collect Elizabeth from nursery soon. By the way, did you know Peter Savage in a professional capacity? As a barrister?"

"No." He didn't elaborate. Hannah said nothing. "Well, only indirectly. He defended a case against one of the companies I had shares in. I wasn't involved. It was dropped on a technicality."

"So nothing to do with you being shot at to settle an old score?"

"No, nothing."

She let that pass. "Did you hear about the fiasco at *The News* Christmas party?"

"Yes I did actually. Unfortunate affair. Jim was livid when he called to see how I was." He saw Hannah's questioning look. "Lord Gyles – we're third cousins or some such nonsense but we meet socially from time to time. Small world."

The telephone on the table beside him rang. He picked up the receiver. No greeting. He listened, his expression revealing nothing. "Thank you." He terminated the call. "Would you like a lift? My driver isn't getting much employment at the moment." His smile did nothing to relax her. He was Fran's uncle but he was also a man who had once been at the centre of organised crime, and still could be for all she knew.

Play along, she thought. "That would be great, thanks."

He tapped an internal number on the phone. A few moments later Mabel knocked and entered, Hannah's coat over her arm.

"Thank you for coming, Hannah."

She smiled at the memory of the summons she'd received that morning. "I'm glad you're over the worst now, Albert. Happy Christmas."

"And to you and your family."

FOR A LONG TIME after she'd gone, Albert Croxton sat quietly reminiscing. He was thinking of Joan Ballantyne. Her death had cut him to the quick. If only… Life was full of if onlys. His thoughts turned to Leo Hawkins, Joan's beloved son, still recovering from the attempt on his life. He had plans for him. He'd seen the photo of him and Hannah in the Sunday paper and had watched the interview Leo had given on that awful chat show. The host wouldn't be having a happy Christmas. In the old days he'd have sent one of his heavies to sort him out. These days his portfolio of legitimate shares made him a major player in the entertainment world, a force to be reckoned with. And he was a majority shareholder in the company that produced that show. That man would be receiving his marching orders. Albert smiled. The warm glow of power was better than sex. Then Joan's face stared at him from the flames of the fire. Well, not always. Not always. Joan's face faded.

THIRTY-ONE

THERE WAS AN ENORMOUS Christmas tree in one of the corners by the television in the residents' lounge where Hannah had been directed to wait for Lucy. She had phoned a couple of times and spoken to Noah, one of the staff she had met before, about what was appropriate to take in and to ask what Lucy might need and to arrange a day to take her out to lunch. Once again she was impressed by his knowledge of those in his care. She remembered how kind he had been to her when she'd heard the news about the attack on Leo Hawkins while she had been visiting Lucy.

Hannah rang the day before her lunch with Lucy and asked to speak to Noah. "Did you manage to find out where she'd most like to go to eat?"

Noah's chuckle was a delight to hear and warned Hannah of what might be to come. "If you're feeling flush – Lucy's words – she'd like to go to the carvery at the Strand Palace Hotel."

"And if I'm not?"

"She suggested you bring the booze and eat here."

Hannah laughed. "Strand Palace it is then."

HANNAH WAS BROUGHT BACK from her thoughts by a loud wolf whistle from an elderly man sitting opposite the door. "Ee, you're a sight for sore eyes, girl."

Lucy beamed. She was wearing an amazing array of colours – Hannah wondered if she'd taken a leaf from Edith's book. She was wearing a pink and green striped roll-neck jumper over a dark tartan skirt below which yellow and black tights could be seen. Her boots were a demure grey. "Special date with my friend." She hadn't noticed Hannah but when she did she blushed. "Not overdone it, have I, luv?"

"You look amazing. And I see you've had your hair done as well. Very chic. A car's waiting outside so shall we go?" She linked arms with Lucy and they waved goodbye to Noah.

THE WALWORTH ROAD was busy but eventually they arrived at Waterloo. Hannah glanced over at St John's and felt Lucy's hand cover her own. They each had their sad memories. Once on the bridge, their mood lightened.

"This is so kind of you, luv."

"Not at all. I wanted to celebrate with you. I'm back on *The News* now – as a consultant editor."

"They're lucky to 'ave you, if you want my opinion."

"Not so sure about that." They both laughed.

The car turned into The Strand and the driver did a U-turn so that they could alight outside the hotel. A few heads turned as he opened the door with an exaggerated flourish and helped Lucy out. "I'll see you at 2.30, madam," he said to Hannah.

"Yes, thank you." Hannah took Lucy's arm and smiled. "I hope you're hungry."

THE DINING ROOM was packed as you'd expect for this time of year, and was decorated for the season. They were shown to their table then offered some mulled wine along with the menu for the choice of starters. Hannah watched Lucy and saw how much she was enjoying the ambiance. She looked around her with a child-like delight.

"Blimey – look who's over there." Lucy nodded towards a table across the dining room and to the left of them. Before Hannah could stop her, Lucy was up from her seat and made her way over to the table where two men were sitting. Hannah had no idea who they were but both stood and shook her hand. As Lucy pointed across to her, one man turned towards her and gave a little bow. Hannah raised her glass – how the hell did Lucy know him?

Lucy returned to their table looking flushed and pleased with herself. "Well, that's a turn-up for the books. Fancy bumping into Charles Trafford." She took a sip of her mulled wine and pulled a face. "Can I have a Guinness, love?"

"Of course you can." She motioned to a waiter and ordered Lucy's drink and a glass of Chablis for herself. "So tell me, how do you know Charles Trafford?"

"He's Leo Hawkins' agent." She concentrated on her beer, which had just been placed in front of her.

"I know that – but how or why do you know him?"

"He came to see me when I was living in Drayton House." She had all the appearance of being caught out in a lie. "Well not really. He came to see Edith but she wasn't at home so I invited him in to wait for her."

Hannah was stunned that ex-public schoolboy Charles (as she thought of him) deigned to accept a random invitation like that. *Good on him*, she thought. "And did you know who he was then?"

"'Course not. He looked a bit unsure at first but put a card through Edith's door to say where he was waiting for her." She sipped her Guinness and dabbed the froth from her mouth with the napkin, making Hannah smile. "'E explained who he was and that Leo had asked him to check some photos she'd taken."

"When was this, Lucy?"

The older woman shrugged. She was artful. She wouldn't have survived all those years on the streets otherwise. Hannah smiled. Lucy had also managed to wrap Simon Ryan QC around her little finger, and Noah at the home obviously adored her. Hannah was pleased for her; it was about time she was getting some attention.

"Must have been just before I moved out." For a moment she looked forlorn.

Hannah desperately wanted her to enjoy herself and not be haunted by the past – especially the traumatic meeting with her son, Peter Edwards. "Well he certainly looked pleased to see you."

"Yes, he did, didn't he? Shall we start? I could eat a horse."

Lucy hadn't been joking. When they got to the buffet, she sampled as much as she could get onto her plate and then went back for more. The waiters loved her enthusiasm and the maître d' treated her as though she were his most valued client – in fact, Hannah mused, he seemed to know her. When Lucy popped out to the Ladies, Hannah managed to attract his attention.

She ordered them some more drinks. "I hope you don't mind my asking but do you know my companion, Lucy?"

The man looked slightly disconcerted. "Yes, madam, she used to be one of our regulars." He gave a slight bow of his head. "I'll have your drinks sent over."

Well, that's put me in my place, she thought as Lucy returned.

"Thanks, love," Lucy said when their drinks arrived.

"Lucy – why did you choose to come here for lunch?"

"Why, somethink wrong with the place?" Lucy's tone was defensive, belligerent almost.

"Not at all. I'd have …"

"Excuse me for interrupting, ladies, I just wanted to say good-bye." Charles' smile included them both.

"Luverly to see you again, Charles. Give me best to Leo."

"I will indeed, Lucy. Hannah, I hope we meet again soon." There was something in the way he said it that make her hackles rise although she couldn't think why.

"Yes, and I was sorry to hear about your accident."

"An inconvenience at most." Hannah felt slighted. Because of that 'inconvenience' she hadn't been forewarned about Leo's TV interview. Still, this was neither the time nor the place…

He shook her hand, and then kissed Lucy's cheek. "Take care of yourself, Lucy." And then he was gone.

Lucy had gone quite pink. "Now where were we?"

Hannah laughed. "I have my answer. You're a star here."

"Nah. Tell you what though. That maître d' is a good man. We used to come here – out the back by the staff entrance – when they'd finished serving of an evening and they'd give us food boxes. Ate like kings we did. Not every night or there might have been a problem…" Lucy looked as though she'd slipped back in time.

"Shall we have a dessert?"

Lucy grinned. "Try an' stop me."

Hannah had a portion of strawberry gateau but Lucy returned with several portions of different desserts on her plate. "Couldn't decide, luv," she said with a grin.

Hannah was pleased the meal had gone so well – even if there were surprising moments. She asked for the bill and when it came she left an extra-large tip.

THEIR CAR PULLED UP as Lucy and Hannah left the Strand Palace Hotel. The drive back was much quicker but Lucy nodded off, only to wake with a start when the door was opened for her. "Thanks so much, luv. That was smashing." Noah met her at the door and waved to Hannah as the car drove off. Reflecting on their conversation over lunch, Hannah thought about what Lucy's life might have been like if her mother had supported her when she had been pregnant at thirteen, and not lied to her about the baby. Lucy had a native intelligence which might have … such thoughts led her to Peter Edwards, the intelligent, cruel priest who had killed several Australian men as well as his uncle/father. Lucy had done well to survive herself. But he had stabbed Hannah, and his suicide meant she'd never know if he had meant to kill her as well.

"Here we are, home safe and sound, Ms Weybridge."

Hannah tipped the driver. For a moment he stared at her as though he wanted to say more but he drove off while Hannah unlocked the door to her personal sanctuary.

BEFORE HANNAH LEFT to collect Elizabeth from nursery she phoned Angie in the cuttings department at *The News*.

"What can I do for you, Hannah?"

"I was wondering if you'd seen anything recently on someone called Charles Trafford? He's Leo Hawkins' manager and was in a car accident, I think, on Saturday 3 December or maybe the Friday?"

"I'll check and ring you back."

While she was waiting, she considered what to do about Ruth Robertson. Should she confront her with what she knew? Or leave it to the police? Or maybe even the vicar would have a word with her? She didn't want to show her hand too soon.

The phone rang. "Hannah, there was nothing reported in the press. But I went through our police reports and Trafford's car was involved in a minor collision near Lancaster Gate during the early hours of Saturday morning. He was taken to hospital just as a precaution."

"Thanks, Angie, you're a star."

Hannah was just about to hang up when Angie said, "There's just one other thing. I discovered, via another search I was doing this morning, that Jonathan Cartmel was adopted. I don't know if that has any bearing on the matter?"

Another jigsaw piece fell into place. "It could well do. Thanks, Angie."

THIRTY-TWO

HANNAH SPENT an unproductive day, feeling frustrated that so many pieces of the puzzle about Jonathan Cartmel's death were missing. The empty briefcase suggested that the perpetrator – or perpetrators – had found what they wanted. But then there was the first visit to Melanie Felton's house. The landlady said they were police. What if they weren't? Whoever killed Jonathan might still be searching for whatever he had carried with him. So who had those documents? Peter Savage had said the briefcase wasn't there that morning. However he could have removed and hidden it. Especially if Jonathan had been protecting him when he was blackmailed…

She didn't want to believe Peter Savage was implicated but she had to keep an open mind. Just because he was a priest didn't mean he wasn't capable of deceit. She considered contacting Simon Ryan then dismissed the idea. Instead she went through all her notes and ideas in the hope that something would emerge. Nothing did.

By the time Alesha arrived to babysit, Hannah was feeling despondent. The girl looked at her quizzically but said nothing for a while as she unpacked her books for revision.

"Sometimes answers come when you're thinking about or doing something else. Perhaps singing will help."

Hannah smiled. "Perhaps," she said with no conviction.

"WELL, WHAT DO YOU THINK she's doing here then?" Hannah paused outside the vestry door, which was ajar. She didn't recognise the woman's voice but she sounded agitated.

A deeper voice replied. "To state the obvious – singing in the choir. What else would she be doing?"

"You don't think it strange that she suddenly rocks up so soon after Daniel's death?"

"No I don't, and quite frankly I've got enough going on without worrying about people's motivations for joining the choir." She recognised that voice. It was the musical director, Craig Fletcher.

"Well I think you're being naïve."

"And I think you're being overdramatic and seeing conspiracies where none exist. It's bad enough that…"

The voices became quieter as they presumably moved further away, and she could no longer make out what they were saying.

"What are you doing hiding away here?"

Hannah nearly jumped out of her skin.

"Good grief, you look as guilty as hell. What have you done?" Dinah was laughing at her discomfort. "Sorry, I'm only teasing you."

Hannah tried to smile. "I just overheard a conversation which I think was about me."

"And you jumped to that conclusion because?"

Hannah bit her lip. "A woman was questioning the motivations of someone joining the choir just after Daniel Lyons died."

"So that could equally apply to me."

Hannah acknowledged that was true. Paranoia was affecting her judgement.

"If I know you're the journalist whose investigations have been key to solving several murders, other people are likely to."

Hannah stared at her.

"Come on, Hannah. You're not that anonymous, you know." Dinah smiled then lowered her voice. "And would you be totally shocked if I told you I am a serving police officer?"

Hannah realised they were whispering. She swallowed hard. That made sense: Dinah's army background, her citizen's arrest. Maybe even her presence in the church choir?

"Excuse us." A group of choristers pushed past into the vestry. Dinah and Hannah followed them. Hannah now couldn't tell who had been talking to Craig. There was a strange atmosphere in the vestry.

"Right, settle down, everyone. Lorraine has a cold so won't be joining us this evening. And nor will Richard, who has to work late. So let's get on. Stand please." Craig said his usual prayer and then started the scales, at the end of which Hazel hiccupped loudly, causing David to smirk. "Let's start with the hymns."

The musical director seemed subdued, and the atmosphere was not exactly hostile but certainly unfriendly. Hannah realised that Dinah was attracting a lot of curious glances. Had the gossip been about her and not Hannah? Either way it felt uncomfortable. Marianne smiled at her. "You okay?" Hannah nodded. She'd just be glad when this evening was over. It occurred to her that she could just bow out of the services. The coward's way out. No she'd see it through, whatever.

Eventually the rehearsal was over. Just before the usual prayer, Craig spoke quietly. "I'm sorry I've been out of sorts this evening. I had some sad news today and – well I'm not feeling great. Normal service will be resumed asap and I look forward to seeing you all on Friday evening. So let us pray…"

Everyone left quietly after that. Dinah mouthed, "Lift?" across to Hannah and she nodded. They left immediately, not hanging around.

Once in her car, Dinah let out a long sigh. "Well that was awkward. I think we can safely assume that what you overheard was about me, not you."

Hannah had been thinking along the same lines. "But it doesn't make sense unless they all have something to hide."

"Perhaps they do." Dinah drove off, and minutes later they were outside Hannah's house.

"I hope you'll still be going to the party."

"It would take more than that to dissuade me. See you then." Again she waited while Hannah had opened her front door.

ALESHA PACKED AWAY her textbooks. "How was the singing?"

"A bit off-key this evening." Hannah paid her and smiled as Alesha rang her father. "Thanks. And you're okay for next Monday?"

"I am."

The bell rang and, expecting Sanjay, Hannah opened the door and was almost thrust aside by an angry Richard Lomax. "I want a word with you," was all he said before collapsing on the floor, revealing Alesha's father brandishing a rounders' bat, and behind him stood Dinah looking for all the world like an Amazon warrior.

RICHARD LOMAX WAS SITTING on the sofa with a bag of frozen peas on his shoulder where Sanjay Singh had hit him with the bat. Hannah was relieved the target hadn't been his head. It had taken some time to move Richard into the sitting room and convince Dinah not to arrest Sanjay. First aid was, apparently, another of Dinah's skills so she'd examined the injury to make sure nothing was broken before recommending the ice-pack treatment.

"I'm so sorry, Sanjay, this is all my fault for not checking the entry video. Please take Alesha home – she has school in the morning – and I'll ring you tomorrow."

Sanjay looked uncertain. As her self-appointed security guard, he was reluctant to leave the two women alone with this intruder.

"Come on, Dad, Hannah will be okay with Dinah here."

Hannah wondered if she'd heard about Dinah apprehending the man who fired the shot into the church. "Alesha's right, Sanjay. Thank you."

Father and daughter left, the former glaring at the injured man.

"SO, RICHARD, what was that word you wanted to have with me?"

Lomax glanced at Dinah, obviously unsure about her credentials. Hannah would have found this situation funny if it hadn't been for the man's anger when he arrived. He hadn't been at the choir rehearsal. So where had he been, and what had he discovered to make him this furious?

"Mr Lomax, if it would help you, I am a police officer." She showed him her warrant card.

"So two women working undercover in our choir?" For a moment he looked infuriated then lost his belligerence. "I'm sorry. I'm sorry for barging in on you like that. It's just…" He wiped his free hand over his face and inhaled deeply. "Please keep what I'm about to say confidential."

Dinah looked as though she was going to dispute that but Hannah nodded at her. "Of course."

He stared at her for a moment. "I know who you are."

Hannah shrugged. "And?"

"I knew Daniel Lyons – as Jonathan Cartmel." Dinah shifted in her seat. Hannah presumed she knew that from her police connections although she wasn't sure what she actually did or her rank in the Met. "My aunt knew him as well. And she was convinced that not only had he been murdered but that his death was linked to organised crime."

"And what made her think that?" Dinah asked.

"For what he did during a trial that led to him being imprisoned," Hannah suggested.

"Exactly. But Jonathan wouldn't have done that for money. He was such a bloody upright citizen. It must have been something else. When I visited him in prison, he was a broken man…

"Wait, you visited him in prison. Did you tell the police all this?" Hannah knew he hadn't. She was the one who had told DI Benton about Daniel Lyons' true identity.

He stared at the floor for a moment. "No. I didn't mention it when we were all interviewed. I wasn't sure if it was relevant…"

Dinah looked fit to burst. "That really wasn't your call, Richard."

"I know. But I was told not to by my aunt."

"And your aunt is?" Dinah looked sceptical but Hannah's instinct was on high alert. She already knew the answer.

"Ruth Robertson."

THIRTY-THREE

HANNAH WOKE EARLY the next morning, knowing she had to figure out what to do about what she now knew. Perhaps she should run an idea for a news story past Rory? Richard was convinced that Jonathan wouldn't have killed himself and Hannah agreed. She understood why Richard had agreed not to say anything about Daniel's true identity.

"He said he had wanted a new start and so had changed his name. To be honest, I thought that was a bit weak. I felt it was more likely that he didn't want to be discovered by someone specific. Presumably the people who had blackmailed him into doing what he did."

"But he never told you what he had done to be vulnerable to blackmail?"

Richard shook his head. "No, he said he was too ashamed."

"And how does your aunt fit in to all this?"

"I'm not sure." Jonathan looked away, his feet tapping an unknown rhythm. Everything about his body language told Hannah he was prevaricating.

"Jonathan and I went to primary school together and sometimes she collected us. She worked from home as a freelance translator. She was fond of both of us. When Daniel appeared in the choir, she asked – no, told me not to say anything. So I didn't. We did have a drink together a couple of times. I got the impression he was trying to find a way to make amends. Presumably for whatever he'd been blackmailed about."

Hannah was furious. All this time… "I still don't understand Ruth's part in all this. I know she visited Melanie Felton after Jonathan died."

Richard stared at her. "Why and how do you know that?" Hannah remained silent. Dinah nodded as if she was aware of this. He winced as he changed the position of the pack of peas. "She had also kept in touch with Jonathan."

"And?"

"I'm not sure I should be telling you any of this. What authority do…"

"You're quite right, Richard," Dinah interrupted. "You can tell all this to DI Benton tomorrow."

Hannah glared at her. "Just one thing, Richard. Did Jonathan mention the vicar at all?"

"Yes, he didn't realise Peter Savage was the vicar here until it was too late. Said he'd been worried he would recognise him. But he didn't. Obviously."

"You could have saved a lot of police time and effort if you'd told the inquiry team all this." Hannah felt Dinah would have arrested him then and there if she could have. Hannah wanted to ask her more about her role in the investigation but she couldn't do that in front of Richard.

"But why did you barge in here?"

Richard stood up. "That can wait. I've had enough of this now. I'm tired and in pain. I'm going home."

"I'll drive you."

Richard looked about to decline the offer then changed his mind.

Hannah wanted to swear – loudly. Dinah would now be able to talk to him without her there. She had a suspicion that that suited her. Dinah was a law enforcer first and foremost; her fragile friendship with Hannah didn't even come a close second.

THE WALK TO THE NURSERY took longer than usual, with Elizabeth pointing out Christmas decorations outside people's houses and chattering about Santa Claus. The actual drop-off was mercifully quick. Hannah returned home in record time. She'd only just opened the door when her mobile rang.

"Hannah, are you at home?" Mike Benton's voice sounded harried.

"Yes, I …"

"Good. I'm sending a car to pick you up. We have Richard Lomax here. Long story short, he's insisting on having you present for an informal interview."

"Right. I'll see you soon then."

Now why, she wondered, *did Richard Lomax require her presence?*

"CAN I BEGIN by stating that my aunt, Ruth Robertson, doesn't know I'm here."

The DI, sitting with DC Kathy Young in an interview room that Hannah thought looked as though it was more often used for children, given the décor and toy box in the corner, looked perplexed. "Okay, Mr Lomax, and thank you for coming in. Just tell us in your own words your relationship with Jonathan Cartmel and what you know about his death."

"I don't know anything about his death. That evening I had been going to suggest going for a drink but he disappeared from the vestry really quickly so I assumed he had another arrangement."

"Did he have his briefcase with him?"

"Well I didn't see him depart but he didn't leave it in the vestry. He always had it with him."

"Do you know why?"

For a long time Lomax didn't reply. "I think it contained something to do with the people he had ruined his career for. And maybe…" He looked wretched. "Maybe there was information about whatever he'd done which had made him vulnerable to the blackmail."

Mike Benton wrote something in his notebook and passed it to DC Young. She did not react in any way. Hannah had been surprised and relieved that Dinah Bell wasn't there. She assumed she had briefed Mike last night or this morning. The DI had said little to her when they met outside the interview room. Whatever frustration he felt that Lomax had not volunteered his information when first asked, he kept to himself.

"Jonathan and I lost touch after we left school. Well not completely. We'd sometimes see each other at my aunt's."

"Ruth Robertson's?"

"Yes. I only have one aunt." He sounded irritated.

"And what about Jonathan's parents? Do you know where they are now?"

"His mother, Jean, died when we were still at school. His father remarried and they moved away."

"Shall I get us all some more coffee?" Hannah wondered if that was what the note was about.

"Good idea. And see if you can drum up some biscuits."

During Kathy Young's absence, Mike stood up and stretched. He smiled at Lomax. "How's the shoulder?"

"Sore. That guy didn't hit me too hard but he tripped me so if Dinah Bell hadn't been there I don't know what would have happened."

Hannah felt she ought to say something here. "Sanjay Singh is very protective of his daughter, and me for that matter. He heard how angry you were, saw you push me at the door and reacted."

"Well, I won't press charges."

"Just as well as I have it all on my CCTV."

Fortunately the DC returned with a tray of coffee and chocolate biscuits. "Help yourself," she said, placing it on the coffee table.

"SO TELL ME about your aunt, Ruth Robertson. How does she fit in to all this?"

Lomax dunked a biscuit in his coffee and ate it before answering. "My aunt never married. I used to wonder why. As I said, she often collected Jonathan and me from primary school. And when we went to secondary we'd make our own way to her house. She was like an unofficial child minder while our parents worked." He stared over at the toy box. "But she certainly had a soft spot for Jonathan."

"And why do you think she told you not to reveal his identity?"

"I think she knew what Jonathan had done."

"Nothing more than that?" Hannah asked.

"No, why?"

"Jonathan was adopted. I think Ruth was his birth mother."

Richard looked stunned. "Are you sure?"

"SO WHERE DID the adoption business come from?" Mike asked as he walked Hannah out of the building. He had offered to drive her home as he was going that way.

"A contact." Hannah wasn't going to say too much.

"And Ruth Robertson being the birth mother?"

"A hunch. It makes sense of her involvement."

Mike unlocked his car; they both got in and he started the engine. "Something else to ask her about, then. Although Richard didn't look convinced."

Hannah couldn't dispute that. "Still it would have made your life a lot easier if he'd spoken sooner. And he still didn't say why he was angry with me."

"Ah that I can tell you. Or I can repeat what he told me before you arrived."

"Go on."

"He works in PR and his company had some sort of launch. A journalist from *The News* was there and mentioned you were back and working on a local story. It sounded as though the journalist wasn't your greatest fan. Anyway Lomax put two and two together…"

Hannah remembered Rory's warning about not discussing the story. What did he know? "Do you think he'll tell the rest of the choir?"

"I don't think so. If he did, he'd have to own up to what he knew. And I think Dinah Bell read him the riot act last night."

"And is she in the choir undercover as Lomax suggested?"

"No. Pure coincidence that she's started going to St John's."

Hannah wasn't sure that was the complete answer but they had arrived at her house.

"You don't think Ruth sent me that email from 'avengingangel', do you? She had a note of another biblical verse in her purse."

Mike laughed. "And when did you see that? Did Miss Bradshaw show you?"

Hannah blushed.

"But you could be right. Anyway we definitely need to interview the lady. I tried ringing her earlier but there was no reply."

"Well she has a lot to answer for. Thanks for the lift."

SHE RANG RORY but he was out somewhere. So while she mulled everything over, she got her room ready for her parents' arrival on Saturday and sorted the futon in her study.

When that was done she checked her emails. Nothing. She sent one to Rory updating him on the situation and how she was planning the story. Then she checked her junk mail. Another one from avengingangel, which she printed out. Then sent a reply, which couldn't be delivered. No such account – again.

She read the text from Matthew Chapter 7 Verses 1 & 2:

"Do not judge, or you too will be judged. For in the same way as you judge others, you will be judged, and with the measure you use, it will be measure to you."

Well at least it wasn't about threats this time. But maybe the sender wasn't Ruth but her nephew giving her a taste of her own medicine?

THIRTY-FOUR

THINKING ABOUT THE CHOIR PARTY, Hannah hadn't wanted to ask Alesha again so soon after the Richard Lomax incident. She had phoned Sanjay to explain as much as she could and to thank him for his protection.

"Janet, are you sure you don't mind babysitting on a Friday night?" Hannah had asked when Janet offered.

"Not at all. I can watch your TV just as easily as mine."

"Well I'll leave you a meal, then."

HANNAH COMPLETED the preparations for the arrival of her parents and prepared a meal for Janet. The ex-nanny collected Elizabeth from nursery to give Hannah the time to change for the choir party, which was due to start at six o'clock. She'd made a pasta salad to take with her and had a bottle of wine to go with it.

Janet and Elizabeth were giggling over something in the kitchen where her daughter was having her dinner.

"Right, I'm off. Be good for Janet." She kissed her on the top of her head.

"Always good," came the reply through a half-full mouth. Elizabeth waved her goodbye. Hannah would have preferred to stay.

WALKING TO THE VICARAGE, Hannah wondered if Dinah would turn up. Or Richard Lomax for that matter. Although it would seem odd if he decided not to attend as he was one of the organisers.

The noise level was high when the door was opened for her. Peter Savage seemed relieved to see her, and Moses, his dog, wagged his tail. Peter's arm was no longer in a sling.

"Hang your coat over there; food in the kitchen and drink in the sitting room."

She followed his instructions. Lorraine was in the kitchen organising the food. "Lovely to see you, Hannah. Have you labelled your bowl?"

"Sorry, I didn't think to do that."

"No problem." She wrote on a sticker and placed it on the base of the dish. "Now go and help yourself to a drink and mingle. Dinah's already here."

HANNAH HAD NEVER been into the sitting room, which ran from the front to the back of the house. The perfect size for a party. She took her wine over to the drinks table where Richard was manning the bar. He gave her a questioning smile. "White, please."

"Coming up." He handed her a glass. "I'm sorry about Wednesday evening."

"What are you sorry for?" Rosie was standing next to Hannah and held out her glass. She looked as though she'd already had a few.

"Missing the rehearsal," Hannah said for him.

"And who's asking you?" She slurred her words.

Hannah moved away, not wanting to cause a scene, and almost bumped into Craig Fletcher. "Great to see you here. How are you finding the choir?"

"Interesting," was the first thing she could think of. He nodded and walked away. "Not to mention rude," she said under her breath. She saw Marianne and made her way over to her, passing Noel Hindman and John Bowman discussing something about a vacancy in the maths department. Presumably John taught as well. Hazel was sitting in an armchair – at least she didn't have to conceal her drinking at a party.

Marianne smiled at her. "You made it! Is your husband looking after Elizabeth?"

Hannah smiled at the assumption she was married. "No, my ex-nanny is babysitting." Moses came over and nudged behind her knee. She turned to stroke him and was face to face with the vicar, a glass of red wine in his hand.

"Marianne – how are you? In good voice, I hope. It's always a joy to hear your solos in church."

"Thank you." She beamed at him. "And how are you managing? Such a busy time of year."

Whatever he was going to answer was lost as a voice screeched,

"I will drink as much as I like. You and no one else have the right to criticise me. What I've been through, what I've lost –"

"Rosamunde!" It was Lorraine Fenton who shouted back at her from the doorway then led her away from the bar, almost cradling her. Her face was flushed but not from anger. "Come along, Rosa," she murmured, leading her over to a corner out of the way of prying eyes.

Hannah and Peter stared at each other. Was this the Rosa Jonathan had referred to when he was dying? The vicar ushered her out of the room and into his study, shutting the door. "I don't suppose you know this but some years ago, Rosie's daughter was killed in a hit-and-run accident. Her marriage didn't survive the loss. Sometimes tragedy brings couples closer together. But not for Rosie."

"I do know actually. It would have been just before your last case when Jonathan acted completely out of character." She let that sink in for both of them.

Peter looked horrified. "You surely don't think Rosie had anything to do with his death?"

"I had some other information that I can't share with you. But I can say that Jonathan may have been trying to make amends for…"

"Holy Mother of God." Hannah wondered if that was a priest's equivalent of swearing. She looked at her watch. Seven o'clock. "I think I'll call DI Benton."

"He can't talk to Rosie while she's in that state."

"Of course not. But he needs to be kept informed. If only we knew where the contents of his briefcase were, we might be nearer to solving this."

Peter left her in the study while she made the call. Mike Benton wasn't at his desk but he was still at the station and rang her back almost immediately.

"I think we've found our Rosa."

HANNAH FOUND DINAH, who she noticed was drinking orange juice. "I'm going to drive Rosie and Lorraine home now. Best she sleeps it off before she gets any more embarrassing."

Hannah stayed for another hour but her mind was elsewhere.

She found Craig and thanked him for inviting her. Peter walked her to the door. "Thank you for coming, Hannah. See you on Sunday. Take care."

"And you, Peter."

IT WASN'T LATE but it was cold and dark. She had thought of getting a minicab but it didn't really seem worth it for such short a distance. She crossed the road at the lights, continuing down Crystal Palace Road. There were houses both sides. Too late, she heard someone had come up right behind her. He pushed something into her back. "Keep walking. Don't make a sound." The voice was gruff as though trying to be unrecognisable.

She nodded. "This is a message from someone you really don't want to upset. Keep your nose out of business that's nothing to do with you. Right?"

Hannah nodded. She couldn't identify the voice but the after-shave he was wearing was distinctive and made her want to heave. "Forget about Jonathan Cartmel." She heard him light a cigarette, which he held close to her cheek. "Be a shame if your little girl got a nasty scar, wouldn't it?" He pushed her forwards. "Now keep walking and don't look back. I'll be watching you."

Nausea threatened to overwhelm her. She willed herself to carry on walking at a steady pace, although all she wanted to do was scream into the night and run. The cigarette had singed her hair. She could hear someone whistling behind her. He was still there. She heard a car stop, then a door slam shut.

The whistling stopped. She still carried on. Nearly at her turning now. A car pulled up alongside her, then kept pace with her.

"Hannah." The car door opened. "Get in."

HANNAH ALMOST FELL out of the car as it stopped outside her house. "Thanks, Fran."

"I'm coming in with you. Don't argue."

Janet switched off the TV as soon as Hannah and Fran came in. "Hannah, what happened? You look awful! Sit down." She guided Hannah over to a settee and sat next to her.

"Some lowlife threatened her as she was walking along the road."

"But…" Janet looked confused.

"I had just been making some deliveries and as I left one of the houses, the hall light illuminated Hannah's face. I caught up with her and brought her home. I think you'll…"

The bell rang and they all stared at each other. Janet was the first to react and looked at the video screen. "It's DI Benton."

"EVENING, LADIES." Mike joined them in the sitting room, followed by Fran who'd let him in.

"What on earth are you doing here, guv?"

Mike smiled at Janet. "Good to see you here, officer." He sat down next to Hannah. He took her hand. "I'm so sorry, Hannah."

"Why are you sorry?" She was still shaking.

"After your call, I thought about where you were and how it might not be such a safe place. When I got to the vicarage, I was told you'd left. On your own. I followed on but not soon enough to stop that goon terrifying you. However he has been arrested and taken to the nick for questioning. I'll leave him to stew overnight. But I just wanted to reassure you, Hannah. We've got him."

Fran looked as though she'd walked into a film halfway through and didn't know what the hell was going on. "Good thing you were in the area, Miss Croxton." Mike beamed at her. "Now I must get home to my family. I'll be in touch, Hannah. But please try not to worry."

Actually Hannah was more worried than ever. If whoever who sent her attacker found out, they – she was convinced it was the Burtron cousins – might send someone else to get her. But she didn't air her views. Mike left. After making sure Hannah would be okay, Fran offered Janet a lift home and they too departed.

Hannah locked the door behind them, checked the back door was secure and went upstairs. She'd have to pull herself together for her parents' arrival. They mustn't learn about the threat. What a bloody awful night, and not just for her. Rosie Ball was going to wake up with a killer hangover and a lot of questions to answer.

THIRTY-FIVE

"MY GOODNESS, you've brought enough food to feed an entire army! Were you worried I wouldn't cook for you?" Hannah was laughing in disbelief. "Thank goodness you put all the cheese in a cool box – it's cold enough to leave that outside in the garden."

"And the white wine."

Hannah hugged her father. "Especially that!"

"Anyway we brought some of this to take to Lady Rayman's."

"Oh, I think Celia will have …"

"No, I spoke to her on the phone and suggested we brought some of our local cheeses and she accepted."

Hannah managed to hide her surprise. She hadn't known her mother had Celia and Mary's telephone number, let alone that she would call them. But she could understand that her mother wanted to contribute to the Christmas meal, and that was fine by her. This would be the first time they would be celebrating with people outside of the family. Tom was with them last year – a lifetime ago – but then her parents hosted.

"Well in that case I'll be careful what I nab." She hugged Daphne, who actually hugged her back. It was good to have her parents with her. Especially after yesterday evening. "Anyway, it's lovely to have you here. My room's ready for you – I thought you'd be more comfortable there than on the sofa bed so why don't you unpack and I'll go and collect Elizabeth. She's at a birthday party, otherwise she'd have been here to meet you. Although seeing all these parcels it's probably a good thing she wasn't."

Her father chuckled. "Where will you be sleeping, love?"

"I have a futon in my study. Don't worry, it's perfectly comfortable. Now I'm off to fetch your granddaughter."

ELIZABETH WAS CLUTCHING a party bag. Apparently Santa had made a surprise appearance at the party. Harry was whispering to her. Hannah wondered what two-year-olds chatted about, just as Fran arrived in a flurry. "Hannah, glad I caught you. Are you okay? Work's been frantic today otherwise I'd have called."

"I am okay. Thank you so much for last night." Hannah smiled.

"Glad I was there. Uncle Albert was furious when I told him."

Hannah's heart sank; the last thing she needed was further complications, but Elizabeth was tugging at her hand. "Mama…"

"I'd better get her home. My parents have just arrived but perhaps we could get together over the holidays?"

"Definitely."

They parted at the gate after Harry and Elizabeth hugged. Hannah noticed Fran's new car had her company logo on the side. Things were definitely looking up for her.

AS SOON AS they got home, Hannah's phone rang.

"You go ahead, love, we'll catch up with Elizabeth. Won't we, darling?"

His granddaughter gazed up at him. "Yes, off you go, Mama."

Hannah raced up to her study and shut the door. "Mike, what have you found out?"

"Sorry, Hannah, that will have to wait. There's been another death. At the church."

"What? Who?"

"Ruth Robertson." There was a silence. "Hannah – are you still there?"

She pulled herself together. "Yes, I'm just stunned, that's all."

"Do you know much about her?"

"A little. I found her intimidating and threatening… hope that doesn't put me on the list of suspects? Sorry, bad joke. Leah Braithwaite knows her."

This time there was a short silence at the DI's end. "Yes, she found her. She's really not making much sense."

"Poor Leah, and her family is arriving from Australia today. Brian, her husband, has gone to collect them from Heathrow."

"Yes, I know. She's at her house now with an officer and I'm sitting outside in my car. Could you come over to be with her?"

Hannah was torn. Her own family had just arrived. Then she heard the laughter from downstairs; she wouldn't be missed for a short while. "Yes, of course."

MIKE BENTON WAS WAITING for her at the gate. "Just to let you know we've interviewed your assailant. It's an ongoing situation." Hannah nodded. "And thanks for this. Leah needs a friend with her."

"Anything I should know?"

"I'd prefer not to influence your reactions …"

"Okay." She rang Leah's bell. A uniformed officer opened the door. In the sitting room decorated for the festivities ahead prepared with love for the family she hadn't known until recently, Leah sat hunched on the settee. Never had Hannah seen her looking so distraught. She looked up and then burst into tears as Hannah sat beside her and held her close. Gradually her sobs subsided. "Forgive me. I…"

"Please don't apologise, Leah. I know what it's like."

"I know you do, dear." She blew her nose noisily. "It was such a shock and I don't even like the woman."

"So what happened?" Hannah looked over to Mike Benton and he nodded almost imperceptibly.

Leah sniffed then paused to sip the water the officer had brought in for her. "I knew Ruth was in charge of the flowers this week and I wanted to make sure she had followed my specifications."

Hannah looked at her blankly. "Why would she?"

"I paid for them."

"I still don't understand."

Leah sighed. "Each week we have flowers in the Sanctuary and the Lady Chapel which people pay for and dedicate to a special occasion, in loving memory, that sort of thing."

Hannah nodded; this was a painfully slow explanation.

"I had asked for very particular flowers to go into the Sanctuary to celebrate the arrival of my family from Australia. The flowers I chose were very specific. They would mean a lot to my brother Adam. So anyway I know how Ruth likes to meddle." She wiped her eyes. "I know I shouldn't speak ill of the dead but I thought she might deliberately change my flowers."

"But why would she?"

"We've had a few run-ins in the past. Anyway none of that matters now, I suppose."

"And were the flowers the ones you ordered?"

Leah blew her nose and wiped her eyes. "Yes – and she'd arranged them beautifully. I saw her in the Lady Chapel and went to thank her. Before I reached her she collapsed and looked as though she was having a fit. Something was frothing out of her mouth and she couldn't speak. She looked terrified. I don't think I'll ever forget her eyes…"

"So what did you do?"

"I tried to make her comfortable and went into the sacristy to phone for an ambulance. I also called the vicarage but Peter wasn't there so I left a message."

"What time was that, Mrs Braithwaite?" It was the first time the DI had spoken and Hannah wondered why he was asking about timings.

"It must have been a few minutes after I'd arrived. I got there for eleven as I know that's when Ruth likes to get there but she must have arrived earlier today."

"Go on."

"By the time the paramedics arrived, she was dead. And they called the police."

"Was anyone else in the church?"

"I didn't see anyone. The main doors were closed but unlocked."

They seemed to have exhausted the conversation. Mike stood up. "Thank you, Mrs Braithwaite, you've been very helpful. If you think of anything else, please give me a call."

"I will, inspector."

Hannah wondered why they were both being so formal. "Leah, why don't you go upstairs and refresh your make-up before Brian and your family get here."

"God, I must look a sight."

For the first time Mike smiled. "You don't actually. Anyway, we'll see ourselves out."

"Would you like me to stay?" Hannah had divided loyalties here.

"No, my dear. I'd like some time to myself and I know your parents will have arrived by now."

"Well if there's anything you need, just ask." She hugged Leah and left with the police. As they left, Mike took a call. He put his hand up to Hannah.

"Right, the pathologist has just confirmed that, as the paramedics suspected, Ruth Robertson died from an anaphylactic reaction." He shook his head sadly. "There was an epi pen in her handbag." He left that information to hang in the air. "Thanks for coming over, Hannah. I won't keep you now but I'll be in touch. Stay away from flowers." And with that he and his officer drove away.

Hannah couldn't put her finger on it but something was most definitely not right. Where was Ruth's handbag, and why hadn't she been able to reach it?

THIRTY-SIX

TO HER SURPRISE Daphne and Donald were keen to go to church on Sunday morning even though they would be there again in the afternoon for the carol service. Unsurprisingly, Brian had called to say Leah wouldn't be going.

At the beginning of the service, the vicar announced the tragic death of Ruth Robertson. "Ruth was a devout and loyal member of St John's for many years. She was a member of the PCC and our flower arranger par excellence. Tragically that is what killed her – she was allergic to one of the plants and went into anaphylactic shock." He paused and looked across to the choir. "We shall all miss her, especially her beloved nephew Richard, and our thoughts and prayers and sympathy are for him and all the family and friends in the days ahead. And, of course, we pray for the repose of Ruth's soul, that she may rest in peace and rise in glory. Let's keep a moment's silence for her together."

The vicar stood, head bowed, alone, the rest of the team in the Sanctuary behind him. As he raised his head there was a murmur that moved around the church like a Mexican wave. All Hannah's instincts were on high alert. Donald and Daphne exchanged a glance. Hannah noticed her father had squeezed her mother's hand. Elizabeth, delighted to have her doting grandparents with her, smiled at them. Donald hugged her.

Before Hannah realised what she was doing, Elizabeth had slid from the seat, walked up the aisle and taken the vicar's hand. Hannah debated following her then decided to see what would happen. What Elizabeth said to Peter, Hannah couldn't hear. He bent down and lifted her up somewhat awkwardly.

"Elizabeth has just told me that as I'm sad we – she and I – should light the Advent candles together." He took a deep breath. "If that's okay, Hannah?"

She nodded mutely. Once again her daughter's reactions in church had astonished her. Peter was talking very quietly to

Elizabeth and she was looking at him intently. They lit a taper and the priest guided her hand to each of the four candles. When they had completed the task, Peter gently placed her back on the floor. She kissed Peter's hand, beamed at everyone then walked back to her family to resounding applause. Donald and Daphne, like the rest of the congregation, clapped loudly.

Hannah could see Richard Lomax in the choir wiping his eyes. Lorraine Fenton looked so sad. Was she remembering her own granddaughter and her loss? Hannah assumed that she and Rosie had been interviewed by the investigation team, and wondered what had transpired. Hannah's thoughts were a whirl-pool of questions without answers. Not the least of her worries was the man who had threatened her after the choir party. At least he was in custody. But if she was right about who sent him, she wasn't safe.

The service eventually came to an end, to Hannah's profound relief. She turned to her parents. "They serve coffee afterwards but I'd rather go straight home, if you don't mind, as I have to be back for the rehearsal this afternoon."

As they were leaving, Dinah came over. Hannah introduced her. "Dinah is another of the choir extras – and she, unlike me, has a beautiful voice."

"Lovely to meet you, Dinah." Daphne's expression reflected that sentiment.

"Shall I pick you up this afternoon?"

"Oh there's no need, it's…"

"Cold and you need a warm voice." She gave Hannah a mean-ingful look.

"In that case, I accept. Thank you."

OVER LUNCH, Hannah contemplated her daughter. "Why did you go up to the front of the church today, Elizabeth?"

"Peter sad," she said after she swallowed a mouthful of her lunch. "And I wanted to light the candles today."

"You little minx." Her granddad chuckled. "You'll have to watch this one."

"Just like her mother."

Hannah couldn't work out if her mother's comment was a

compliment or not, but there was little time to ponder this as she prepared for the afternoon ahead.

DINAH DIDN'T GET OUT of her car but tooted from the road. Hannah joined her. She'd shown her parents the security arrangements and how to use the door video. They seemed to take it all in their stride. "Don't worry, we'll be fine with Elizabeth and look forward to hearing you sing later."

Hannah laughed and kissed them all goodbye. She ran out to Dinah's car.

It was obvious, she had something she wanted to say and got straight to the point. "You didn't seem surprised about the fact I'm a police officer."

"No." Hannah felt there was more to come. Slowly a suspicion was forming in her mind. "Does anyone else know?"

"Peter does. We've known each other a long time since…" She paused as though uncertain how much to divulge. "Since before he was a priest."

"When he was a barrister?"

"Have you been checking him out?" She sounded irritated, almost annoyed. "I suppose that's what journalists do. Dig."

Hannah was affronted. "No, actually I have a friend who's a QC. They know each other."

Dinah nodded. "Plausible."

"True. His name is Simon Ryan."

"Simon! Now that's more than a coincidence."

"Is it?" They had arrived at the church.

"Listen, we'd better join the others. How about we continue this conversation after the rehearsal?"

THERE WAS A BUZZ in the choir stalls, which had been |transferred to the Sanctuary, as more seats would be needed for such a popular service. One or two had obviously been imbibing the Christmas spirit. Hannah's heart sank. She was in the front row with the sopranos and altos. Dinah was next to her. On her other side was Marianne. Hannah thought it must be an awful penance to have to sit next to her miserable contribution. Her throat felt tight. A tenor sitting behind her, Noel Hindman, leaned forward. "Here, have one of these for your throat. They work a treat."

Hannah turned and smiled. "Thanks." She popped one in her mouth and sucked, hoping it would work a miracle.

For this rehearsal they had a brass quartet as well as the organist. Craig rapped his baton on the music stand. Dinah nudged her and smiled.

"Settle down. We have a lot to get through. Let's start with …" Craig Fletcher was fractious. "No, no, no. You're not following my direction. Watch me. We need to get the nuances of the music."

At the end, Marianne turned to her. "You know what they say. A bad rehearsal means a great performance."

Hannah was feeling sick. There seemed to be a lot of activity in the church. People checking things. She thought she saw someone checking under the seats with a mirror on a stick. Strange. Dinah seemed relaxed.

"Come on, you two, I have robes for you and there's tea and coffee in the vestry." There was no time for Dinah and Hannah to continue their earlier conversation.

AS THE ORGAN stopped playing, the congregation stood in silence. Marianne sang the first verse of 'Once in Royal David's City' solo, and unaccompanied; the choir came in for the second verse, then everyone joined in as choristers and clergy processed around the church to the altar. Hannah was terrified of tripping. Holding the music, singing and walking was, she feared, a juggle too far.

Eventually they arrived at the altar and the vicar greeted the congregation:

"In the name of the Father, Son and Holy Spirit. Grace, mercy and peace from God our Father and the Lord Jesus Christ be with you."

"And also with you," came the response.

Peter welcomed everyone and then led the Lord's Prayer before the first lesson followed by the choir singing 'Adam lay ybounden'.

Hannah began to focus and take in the scene before her. The church was full to capacity. There were men standing at the back.

Ushers directed latecomers to the last remaining seats. She could see her parents with Elizabeth near the front, and in the same row were Fran, Zoë and Harry with Albert Croxton. Janet joined them. She looked across to the Lady Chapel, expecting to see Jonathan Cartmel, but there were no apparitions or flowers.

She could hardly breathe, and willed herself to relax. The main lights dimmed and she was aware of movements. The ushers were standing strangely… She looked up to the old organ loft. There were people standing up there as well. How strange. But she'd never been to a carol service here before and had nothing to compare it with.

The reading of the lessons and the carol singing continued. Not long to go. The introductory chords for the final hymn, 'O Come All Ye Faithful' rang out as there was a resounding crash and some muffled oaths. Hannah felt Dinah tense beside her. Marianne reached for her hand.

"Sing!" Craig ordered.

Hannah could see people being led out of the church in handcuffs. At least five of them. She looked across to where her family was sitting. They appeared fine. As were Fran and her children. But there was no sign of Albert Croxton and Janet. When they got to the final verse – in descant for the sopranos – Hannah thought her legs would give way. "O come let us adore him, Christ the Lord," reverberated around the church.

Peter stood to give the blessing and they processed out to an organ voluntary.

In the vestry Noel Hindman, looking visibly shaken, put into words what they were all thinking. "What the hell just happened in there?"

No one answered as the door burst open and two armed men burst in.

THIRTY-SEVEN

DINAH MOVED TO the front of the choristers, brandishing her warrant card. "DS Bell." At the same time there was a crackle over their radios and the order to, "Stand down. All clear." The two men lowered their guns and backed out of the door.

"Well if I didn't need a drink before, I certainly do now." Marianne walked over to Dinah. "Thank you. Again."

Once more the door opened and in walked DI Benton. "Ladies and gentlemen – sincere apologies for that." He smiled. "SO19 got their coordinates wrong. Well done, Mr Fletcher, for keeping the music going during our arrests." Craig looked bemused. "The church is clear. And I understand there are mince pies and mulled wine on offer." He nodded to Hannah and Dinah, and left.

"I could do with more than mulled wine," muttered one of the extras, and a few of them left immediately after they had disrobed.

Rosie was standing next to Hannah. "I'm sorry about my behaviour at the party. I have given a full statement to the police but if you need any background information, call me." She gave her a piece of paper then she left with her mother.

Gradually the room cleared. Hannah passed Dinah. "I'm going to check up on my family."

THE BACK OF THE CHURCH was buzzing with excitement. Hannah couldn't see her parents and daughter. She felt sick. Then Janet was in front of her. "Your parents have taken Elizabeth home and said not to worry about anything if you need to stay here." Seeing Hannah's pallor, she added, "They were taken in a squad car."

"Thank you. Where's Albert Croxton and why were you with him?"

Janet moved her aside and out of earshot of people standing nearby. "He was part of the bait. He put himself up for it and made sure word got out. The DI will fill you in. I escorted him to his car and some of his own security team were here."

Hannah nodded. It was over. Maybe Jonathan Cartmel – and Ruth Robertson – could rest in peace now.

"Hannah." The vicar stood before her looking as though he had the weight of the world on his shoulders. "DI Benton asked me to invite you over to the vicarage for a debrief. We're going there for convenience. Janet will take you across and I'll join you when everyone has gone."

HANNAH WONDERED WHY two uniformed officers were standing at the gate. Surely it was over now? Janet smiled at them. DC Kathy Young answered the door, Moses at her side, and then led them to the sitting room where the choir party had been held. It looked peaceful and festive with the Christmas tree lit up and the lamps casting a warm glow. Kathy handed her a glass of brandy. "I've been told you might need this. Guv said you could probably do with one too, Janet, as you're now officially off duty."

Hannah sipped her drink. Memories of what was going on in the church while they were rehearsing now made sense. Her mobile rang. It was Rory. "Hannah, are you okay?"

"That was quick, I was about to phone you."

He laughed. "Lord Gyles hauled me in. Terry Cornhill is here too as well as the weekend subs. We're drafting the front page story for tomorrow's edition and we'd like you to add any pertinent details. Is that okay with you?"

"It's what I'm paid for."

"I'll email you the draft for any adds you may have."

MOSES SUDDENLY GOT UP and scratched at the sitting room door, which opened to reveal his master and Mike Benton. Kathy poured more drinks. Peter and Mike both drank deeply.

"So a quick update, as I'm sure we'd all like to get home. We interviewed Rosie – Rosa – Ball and her mother, Lorraine, yesterday. The reason we didn't pick up on her child's death by a hit-and-run is that she changed her name after her divorce. She didn't know Jonathan Cartmel. We also searched Ruth Robertson's house. And there we found what we must assume were the contents of Mr Cartmel's briefcase. Obviously he'd taken the precaution of not keeping the documents with him. We found his birth certificate, and you were right, Hannah, Ruth was his mother hence the interest and her involvement at his trial. He also had the details of the people who had blackmailed him after he had run over a child and carried on driving as he was over the limit. I won't go into any more details but I want to reassure you that Albert Croxton had no involvement with Jonathan. But, as Janet has probably told you, he has worked with us to flush out Cartmel's killers."

Hannah took no pleasure in knowing she had been right on so many levels. She stood. "I think I'll go home, if you don't need me here."

Benton looked concerned. "Of course."

He walked her to the front door and out to the gate. A squad car drew up. Janet had followed them out. She got into the back with Hannah.

The DI stood watching their departure before returning to the vicarage.

JANET FOLLOWED HANNAH into her house. "Janet, good to see you." Daphne had obviously changed her opinion of Janet since her barbed comments when she'd been the nanny. Donald stood as they entered. He hugged his daughter and then Janet. "What a to-do!" Daphne had gone out of the room.

"How's Elizabeth?"

"She's fine. She had her dinner and went to bed without a murmur."

Daphne came back in carrying a tray. "I expect you're hungry too." Her mother had made a selection of sandwiches with dishes of olives and nuts. Donald popped out and returned with a bottle of wine and glasses.

"Who was that rather imposing man you were sitting with, Janet?"

Hannah answered for her. "That's Fran's uncle." Her mother nodded, and she had the feeling she knew far more than she was letting on.

"These sandwiches are just what I needed, thank you." Janet beamed at Hannah's parents. "You must be looking forward to Christmas."

"We are. What are you doing – not working, I hope?"

Janet laughed. "I almost wish I was. My sister is getting married in Essex. I finish work on Tuesday and the wedding is on Thursday." She sat back and sipped her wine.

Donald looked thoughtful. "After today I imagine getting through a family wedding will be a piece of cake."

Daphne glared at him. She'd obviously decided they should say nothing unless Hannah did.

"What did you think of the church, Mum? I might have Elizabeth christened there." She glanced at Janet. "Janet agreed to be a godmother if I go ahead with it."

"Splendid idea." Donald topped up their glasses.

"Oh damn, I need to check my emails."

"Surely you're not working this evening, Hannah."

Her daughter paused at the door. "It's what I get paid rather a lot of money for."

"Have another sandwich, Janet." Daphne smiled. "Lord Gyles has been good to us as well when Hannah …" She couldn't bring herself to say the words. "Anyway he flew us over on his private jet."

"That may be the case," Donald said, "but I'd prefer it if…"

Hannah returned. "Panic over. Nothing's come through yet."

Janet stood. "Well I'd better get going. Thank you for supper, Daphne. And happy Christmas to you all."

"And to you, dear."

"Would you like me to walk you home?" Donald offered.

"Thank you, but the squad car is waiting for me."

Hannah stared at her. Nothing was being left to chance, it seemed.

HANNAH HELPED DAPHNE clear away. "Thank goodness you were here, Mum."

Her mother sniffed. She still found it difficult to express emotions but her daughter was aware how much she was trying, and hugged her. Daphne relaxed against her and sobbed. They clung together, the stress of what had happened in church releasing in waves.

HER PARENTS HAD gone to bed, and, after a long hot shower, Hannah was in her study when her phone rang.

"Hannah – oh my God, how are you? And Elizabeth?"

"Elizabeth's fine, Leo. I'm still trying to process it all, to be honest. But my parents are here. But how do you know?"

"Albert rang me." The way he said it gave Hannah the impression that this wasn't the first time they'd been in contact recently, but she let it go. "I'm glad you're not alone. If you need anything at all just call me. Please."

"I will, night." Brief as it was, the conversation left her with a warm glow.

SHE READ RORY'S DRAFT, which included some background on the perpetrators, whose intent was to tie up all loose ends related to the first death in the Lady Chapel that had been gleaned from the outlines she'd sent Rory. The vicar was apparently also a target. She wondered if Richard Lomax was as well.

However she was surprised at the detail of what had happened during the carol service. Another journalist had obviously been there. The church was so packed it would have been easy to miss someone. Then a suspicion struck her. Rory had been there! He had rung her so quickly after the incident it made absolute sense. Albert Croxton knew what was happening. He would have contacted Lord Gyles, and Rory had been sent to St John's. Always an eye to the main chance.

This was confirmed for her when Rory faxed over the front page – complete with photographs. It made her wonder about the timing of her new contract. It seemed a bit of a leap but they knew she'd been asked to find out about Daniel Lyons… If that was so, the chances were someone at the newspaper knew much more. That led back to Lord Gyles and Albert Croxton.

When sleep eventually triumphed, no dreams troubled her.

THIRTY-EIGHT

HANNAH WOKE TO the sound of voices and laughter. Her parents were up early and had given Elizabeth her breakfast.

"Morning, love. Did you sleep well?"

Hannah kissed him. "Better than expected, actually." She sat next to her daughter. "Well, look at you all dressed and ready."

Her mother had just come into the kitchen. "I hope we haven't upset your routine, Hannah." She looked nervous. "But we let you sleep for a while longer while this young lady chose what to wear."

"Of course not. It's a treat, isn't it, Elizabeth, having Nanny and Granddad here?"

"Yes." Elizabeth beamed at them all.

"Would you like them to take you to nursery today?" Her daughter's smile was answer enough.

THE LAST PERSON Hannah expected to hear from was Richard Lomax. He phoned her early that morning. "I was hoping to catch you, Hannah. I wondered if you'd like to talk to my parents. They're back in London, well staying with me for Christmas, and now to arrange my aunt's funeral."

"Thank you, I would." He gave her his address and telephone number. She didn't have the heart to say that the vicar had given her those details for all choir members. "By the way, Richard, do you think your aunt's allergy was generally known? By people at church?"

"I don't know. I'm not even sure people knew we were related."

"No, I can see that. But she did carry an epi pen with her and I would have thought from a health and safety point of view someone should have known."

"You're right, of course. Perhaps the vicar or the church-wardens? Anyway I'll tell my parents to expect you."

HANNAH WAS READY to leave when her parents arrived back. Her father had bought some newspapers. He held out *The News*.

"I saw a proof last night. They didn't run with it on the early edition so that other papers didn't steal their thunder." Her father nodded. Another scoop she'd been involved in. "I have to interview someone this morning. Sorry to leave you. You have keys so you don't have to stay indoors." The car she'd booked arrived. "Nursery closes tomorrow after their Christmas party so then we can have full-on family time."

WHILE SHE WAS in the car, she rang Peter Savage. "Hello, Hannah, I have the archdeacon with me at the moment."

When was he not there? Hannah wondered "I won't keep you then. But just one question: was it generally known about Ruth Robertson's allergy?"

"Well, I didn't know."

"But from a health and safety perspective, someone should. Maybe the churchwardens?"

"That's just what the archdeacon said." He sounded thoroughly fed up. "I'll call you later."

RICHARD LOMAX LIVED in a terraced house in Peckham very much like the house Jonathan Cartmel had been lodging in. His father opened the door and welcomed her in. "Such a dreadful business," he said, leading her into the sitting room where Hannah almost did a double take, seeing an older version of Ruth sitting waiting for her, dressed totally in black. She stood and shook Hannah's hand. "Would you like some coffee or tea?"

"No thank you, Mrs Lomax."

"I'm Betty and my husband is Kevin." She turned to him. "I'd love a tea." This was obviously his cue to leave the two women alone. Hannah sat opposite her. "Do you mind if I record our conversation?"

"Not at all." She took a deep breath as Hannah switched on her tape recorder. "I was devastated to hear about Jonathan's death and then, of course, Ruth's. It's such a sad story. Kevin and I met a university and stayed in Sheffield after we married. I was pregnant with Richard and didn't even know about Ruth's condition or that she'd subsequently given up the child for adoption. My parents never said a word to me. We moved back to London for Kevin's work and when both my parents died, Ruth stayed on at the house. She was wonderful with Richard and looked after him a lot – along with Jonathan when they were in primary school together."

Hannah nodded. Kevin came in with Betty's tea. He touched her shoulder as he left. "Ruth had studied for her degree in London. I always thought it was curious that she never moved away, and worked from home. But then I didn't know about Jonathan. Apparently, it had been a private arrangement – the adoption – and Ruth knew the Cartmels who were kind and sensitive. My sister only told me all this relatively recently, after Jonathan died. She was a very private woman."

"Did you know about her allergy?"

"No I didn't, but she never discussed personal things. We weren't close, and I think she only told me about Jonathan's death as there was no one else to share it with. Even Richard didn't know."

HANNAH FELT DRAINED and saddened when she returned home. The house felt different. Then she realised it was the smell of food cooking, and smiled. Her mother showed her love in practical ways. They were both in the sitting room reading. Daphne looked up and smiled. "Some flowers arrived for you. I left them in the kitchen."

Two enormous bouquets were waiting for her on the table: one from Leo and the other from Albert Croxton. *Thank goodness I'm not allergic to anything*, she thought irreverently.

THIRTY-NINE

LEAH HAD CONSIDERED cancelling their drinks party but Brian talked her out of that thought. "We're having the party to introduce your family to our friends. There's no reason Adam, Stella and Scott should have the festivities ruined by the death of someone they've never even heard of."

Leah smiled at her husband. "You're right, of course. And I've been so looking forward to having them here."

Brian smiled. "You deserve to have a wonderful time. And so do they." The party went ahead as planned.

HANNAH HAD BOOKED Alesha to babysit and had worried she would back out but she was her usual cheerful self when she arrived, driven over by her father. "Good evening, Mr Weybridge, Mrs Weybridge. How was your journey here?"

"The crossing was awful but we survived." She smiled at Alesha in a way that was unfamiliar to Hannah. "And please call us Daphne and Donald. I know you're like one of the family."

Alesha beamed and winked at Hannah. "Your daughter is an honorary auntie in my family. Oh and before I forget, Hannah, I've brought the book so you can sign it for Dad."

"Of course." She took the book. "I'll sign it upstairs as I've already composed a dedication for him."

Hannah had thought about what to write for Sanjay and had rewritten her words until she felt she had achieved the right tone. She copied her dedication into the book carefully then joined her family in the sitting room.

"Here you are. I've left you some snacks and you know your way around, Alesha. Plus we're only across the road."

THEY DIDN'T BOTHER with coats but there was an icy chill in the air that made them shiver before a radiant Leah, glorious in her role of hostess, opened the door.

"Come in, come in!" She hugged Hannah and whispered, "Thank you." Then, bright-eyed, she welcomed Daphne and Donald.

The house was heaving with guests. Hannah was disorientated until she was suddenly in a bear hug. "Hey, Hannah, so good to see you again, mate." It was Scott, Leah's nephew who had come to London to try to discover more about his father's English family. "Come on, there's someone who can't wait to meet you."

She was led or rather pulled into another room where an older version of Scott stood up. "Hannah! At last we get to meet. You're looking great, girl." He too hugged her tightly. There were tears in his eyes as he stepped back. "I'd like to talk to you but not now. Not here."

He beamed as his wife, Stella, kissed Hannah's cheek. "We're all so grateful."

Hannah hadn't been prepared for the emotional onslaught she felt. The memories of where her investigation into the Child Migration Scheme had led colliding with the recollection of the attempt on her own life. A light-headedness engulfed her, as people seemed to undulate in front of her. She felt someone take her arm and guide her away. Reverend Peter Savage handed her a glass of wine and stood in front of her, allowing her time to collect herself.

She looked up at the man who had led her a not-so-merry dance. "Thank you."

He stared at her for a moment. "I know I owe you some explanations but obviously now isn't the time or place. Please don't think too badly of me in the meantime." He turned as he heard Hannah's name. "And you must be Hannah's parents. She looks so very like you, Mrs Weybridge."

Hannah's mother blushed – something Hannah had never seen happen before. "I have been trying to persuade your daughter to have Elizabeth christened…" He carried on talking as they moved away from her, and Brian appeared at her side as she turned to examine the books displayed in the alcove.

"Thank you for being here with Leah. Terrible business with Ruth…"

Hannah smiled. "That's what friends are for." She sipped her drink. "Is it you or Leah who is the expert on flora?"

Brian looked at her blankly.

Hannah waved her arm. "All these books on flowers …"

His laughter seemed tinged with relief. "Neither of us, I'm afraid. We inherited those from Leah's mother. She can't bear to part with them – for sentimental reasons." He took her arm and guided her away. "Let me introduce you to someone you might like to chat to." He stopped in front of a tall, dark-haired man who wouldn't have looked out of place in a toothpaste ad. "David, this is our neighbour and friend Hannah."

David shook her hand; a look of boredom clouded his features. "Hannah collaborated with the late Joan Ballantyne on her memoir."

He looked at her more keenly. "That was quite a coup. Congratulations." He raised his glass to her.

Hannah wondered if she'd imagined the sense of resentment from the man. "Thank you. It was a mixed blessing."

"David is also an author." Brian seemed proud of his connection.

"Oh, what do you write about?"

"Crime novels." He pointed to a row of books in the other alcove. "Those are all mine."

"Wow, that's quite an oeuvre."

"Keeps me busy."

"How on earth do you find your ideas?"

"From real-life cases. Of course I fictionalise them." He looked stern as though expecting a criticism.

"Does anyone ever complain?"

David's laugh seemed genuine. "By the time I finish with the characters, their own mothers wouldn't recognise them. Or if they do they'd keep schtum in case of repercussions."

She swallowed her distaste. "So how do you know Leah and Brian?"

"I play squash with Brian…"

He said something else which Hannah didn't catch as the sound levels in the room had increased. Then suddenly it was quiet as Brian called for everyone's attention.

"A toast. I'm sure you'll all join me in welcoming back our

nephew Scott and his parents Stella and Adam, Leah's family from Australia." For one awful moment she thought Brian would mention her, but she was saved from that embarrassment as everyone raised a glass to the family reunion.

Scott came across to her. "There's something I'd like to show you, mate," he said before leading her into the kitchen and helping himself to some food…

Hannah smiled at him. "So what do you want to show me?"

"Nothing. You looked like a possum out of its sack. Thought you needed rescuing."

Hannah helped herself to some food. "Thank you."

"There you are, Hannah." Leah was so happy and in her element it was hard to think that only a few days ago she had been distraught when Ruth died. Hannah wanted to ask her if she knew about the allergy or if she'd seen Ruth's handbag, which contained the lifesaving epi pen.

"I just wanted to see if you are okay after yesterday?"

"Yes it was all rather dramatic but ended well."

"Maybe. Now there's someone I'd like you to meet."

Did she really just say "maybe"? Hannah thought as she re-joined the party. Across the room a man and a woman turned towards her: Jonathan and Ruth smiled before they faded away.

EPILOGUE

"IS THERE SOMETHING going on between those two?" Hannah's mother was intrigued by Leo Hawkins sitting close to her daughter, and both looking as though they were discussing some serious topic. She posed the question to Lady Celia Rayman, who looked over at them and smiled.

"No idea, but they seem relaxed together, don't they?" She looked away to the portrait of Liz on the chimneybreast. "My daughter and he used to play together as children. There was a time when I thought…" She changed the subject. "Daphne, we are so grateful that you agreed to share your Christmas day with us." For a moment her expression was unbearably sad. "As you know, it's the first Christmas since…"

Daphne touched her arm. "I'm so sorry. I do understand. When I thought…" she took a breath, "but we were spared your loss."

"We couldn't have borne to have lost Hannah as well." Momentarily Celia's face wore a gossamer veil of grief, quickly replaced by her hostess demeanour.

It was on the tip of Daphne's tongue to make some acerbic comment but she swallowed the words. For once she could be generous and share her daughter. Love wasn't finite, as her husband was always telling her. It made her wonder about Lord Rayman and the loss Celia had suffered all those years ago. Then she caught sight of Donald with Mary, who was keeping Elizabeth entertained with toys. Hannah never spoke about their relationship and always referred to Mary as Celia's companion. Daphne smiled. *Perhaps not such a loss*, she thought.

HANNAH WAS SIPPING a glass of champagne. Seeing Leo had been a shock. "I had no idea you were coming."

"When Celia invited me, I asked her not to mention it to you. Just in case."

The arch look held a hint of humour. "In case?"

"In case you still weren't talking to me."

"And you didn't think to mention it when we were talking?"

He contemplated her in a way that made her wish they were alone. Then Elizabeth arrived with a new toy to show her.

"And Leo, Mama, let Leo have a turn."

SHE FELT CURIOUSLY CALM. Singing at Midnight Mass had been fun – in the end. The choir rehearsal an hour before did not bode well for the service. Hazel and a couple of men were obviously drunk. Craig didn't seem to notice as Marianne manoeuvred Hazel so that she wouldn't be quite so visible to the congregation. During a break, Dinah took her aside and asked if she were okay. "I saw *The News* coverage."

"Oh that wasn't me – only bits of it – the assistant editor and a photographer had been sent. Tipped off by Albert Croxton."

Dinah frowned.

"Sorry, long story. But are you okay?"

"Yes. We should catch up after Christmas. Debrief over a meal?"

"You're on." And then they were processing in for Mass.

After everything that had happened in the church, the magic and mystery of the Christmas story took over – even for Hannah. Peter Savage was in his element and only in the prayers did he refer to the two deaths in church, revealing Ruth and Jonathan had been mother and son united in death. Apparently the Lomax family had asked for this. Dinah had given her a lift home where her parents had sat up waiting for her with champagne to celebrate the day.

She had thought about giving the Christmas morning Mass a miss. But her parents were keen to go and Hannah knew Elizabeth would love it. And they had no Christmas meal to prepare. Elizabeth entered like a princess and even her parents, who seemed a little anxious, once they were in church relaxed at her antics. The service was mercifully short and seriously child-friendly. Brian had accompanied Leah and her family so they all walked home together, declining an invitation for a drink as they had a car booked to take them to Celia and Mary's.

And here they were, surrounded with happiness but tinged with the grief and sadness which would always be a part of their lives. But with the hope of more joy to come. And the scent of freesia was reassuringly powerful.

ACKNOWLEDGMENTS

As I publish the sixth book in my Hannah Weybridge series, I realise how fortunate I am to be doing something I love. Authors often go through periods when they feel like giving up but the thought of a life without writing spurs them on. Writing and creating Hannah Weybridge's world in 1990s London has been a fabulous experience for me especially when characters, who have become my imaginary friends, take me on so many unexpected journeys. And then there are those precious moments when a reader tells you they loved your last book or a friend says how much they are looking forward to reading your next book, and any doubts evaporate – for the time being!

However, publishing *Murder in the Lady Chapel* has been a steep learning curve for me as it is the first book in the Urban Fox Books imprint that hasn't had a previous edition. I am indebted to Kenneth Ansell from Wildcat Design not only for the brilliant cover and formatting but also for the help and support that's just been a telephone call away and to Julia Gibbs for her proofreading skills and sharp eye for repetitions.

My thanks to Dr Geoff Lockwood who continues to offer advice on medical matters – sadly I still haven't convinced him to write medical mysteries with me – and Reverend Rosemary Shaw, who has followed all Hannah's investigations and gave me some prayers for the dying. The Reverend Alistair McCulloch, graciously checked all things priestly and anyone who knows him will imagine the laughs we had. Any mistakes, of course, are all mine!

Another thank you goes to Paddy Herron who runs the Children in Read auction which raises money for BBC's Children in Need. In 2021 and 2022 I offered a copy of *Stage Call* and the opportunity to be a named character. Pete Savage and Craig Fletcher made incredibly generous bids and so they became the vicar and the musical director in this book.

Joining St John's choir has been a life-saver for me. While I concentrate on singing, I can't worry about other things so it's good for my mental and physical wellbeing. I joined as a regular (previously I had sung with them on an intermittent basis) as the pandemic was easing and we were allowed back in church. The musical director, John Webber, welcomed me even though I'm not a "natural singer". My fictional MD is not based on John, but there are a few generic similarities, which I hope will raise a smile… My fellow choristers are not featured in the book probably to their relief but special thanks must go to Roger Nichols who posed for a photo that was used on the cover.

And so to the wonderful fellow authors and reviewers who have read the manuscript and been so supportive. You are all wonderful and greatly appreciated – as are you the reader!

And last but not least, my daughter Olivia who is such a constant support and inspiration in my life.

ABOUT THE AUTHOR

For most of her working life in publishing, Anne has had a foot in both camps as a writer and an editor, moving from book publishing to magazines and then freelancing in both.

Having edited both fiction and narrative non-fiction, Anne has also had short stories published in a variety of magazines including *Bella* and *Candis* and is the author of seven non-fiction books.

Telling stories is Anne's first love and nearly all her short fiction as well as *Dancers in The Wind* and *Death's Silent Judgement* began with a real event followed by a 'what if...'. That is also the case with the two prize-winning 99Fiction.net stories: *Codewords* and *Eternal Love*.

Murder in the Lady Chapel is her sixth thriller starring investigative journalist Hannah Weybridge.

Keep up to date with Anne Coates on:

Twitter: @Anne_Coates1
Facebook: Anne Coates Author
Instagram: anne_coates1
Website: https://www.annecoatesauthor.com

ANNE COATES

Printed in Great Britain
by Amazon